"Cleverly balancing humor, romance, and a healthy dose of thrill, Buchanan delivers a perfect mystery. You won't be able to put it down!"
—MICHELLE COX, author of the *Henrietta and Inspector Howard* series

"Get ready to stay up late because you won't want to put it down."
—ANN GARVIN, *USA Today* best-selling author

"Buchanan has done it again—created an atmospheric thriller with an intriguing cast of characters who gather at the Pines & Quill writer's retreat in the Pacific Northwest. Grab a cup of your favorite beverage and settle in for an immersing read!"
—DEBBIE HERBERT, *USA Today* best-selling author

"Buchanan is a first-rate storyteller who grabs your attention from page one and holds it tight until the end."
—CHRIS NORBURY, author of the *Matt Lanier* novels

"Beautiful prose, vivid descriptions, a cast of fascinating characters, and a gripping story. This thriller has it all. The second book in the Sean McPherson series starts with a bang and never lets up. Bravo, Buchanan. Keep them coming."
—GREGORY LEE RENZ, author of *Beneath the Flames*

"Buchanan builds the tension until you're almost afraid to turn the next page."
—JEFF NANIA, author of the *John Cabrelli Northern Lakes Mysteries*

"It's as good to be back at the Pines & Quill writers retreat and with the familiar cast of characters as it is terrifying to watch events unfold from the point of view of the killer."

—SHEILA LOWE, author of the *Claudia Rose Forensic Handwriting Mysteries*

"Descriptive and captivating, *Iconoclast* serves as a strong follow-up to this excellent series. Looking forward to number three!"

—MARIANNE LILE, author of *Stepmother: A Memoir*

"Buchanan places the reader in the wooded acres, inhaling the scent of pine and sea salt, alternately enveloped in dense fog or surrounded in a cloak of blue sky, treading each careful step with the innocent and the guilty."

—JOY RIBAR, author of the *Deep Lakes Cozy Mystery Series*

"Buchanan is a master of suspense as she pulls us along on this nail-biting journey of delicious deceit, danger, and daring. Who will make it to the end? Who will be unmasked for who they truly are? I'm not telling . . . but I promise you that you won't be able to turn out the light and go to bed until you know the truth!"

—VALERIE BIEL, author of the award-winning *Circle of Nine* series

"Buchanan hits a grand slam home-run with this second book in the Sean McPherson series. First base—a luscious setting, full of imagery that puts the reader in the story. Second—relatable characters, some good, some bad, but all well-drawn. Third—enough edge-of-the-seat tension to keep pages turning. And home plate—a heartfelt tale well-told."

—SARALYN RICHARD, author of *Bad Blood Sisters* and the *Detective Parrott Mystery Series*

"Readers won't be able to put down this suspenseful book that showcases the author's extensive knowledge of guns and police and medical examiners' procedures that make the story alarmingly authentic."

—SHERRILL JOSEPH, author of *The Botanic Hill Detectives Mysteries*

"Read this series and experience mystery and adventure, as well as the comfort of a supportive cast of characters who can pursue criminals and camaraderie at the same time."

—TOWER LOWE, author of the *Molly Donovan Suspense Series*

"Wonderful to be reunited with the main characters from *Indelible,* whom I feel like I know intimately as I anxiously await to be invited to the next three-week writers' retreat. *Iconoclast* adds a new set of writers and riveting suspense. Who is embedded in the local police department, ready to set up and kill for revenge? Are the writers who and what they seem, or are one or more hiding their true identity? Amidst the mystery is sumptuous food cooked by the resident chef, a surprising murder just as the book begins, and a sweet dog who trots along aiding and abetting the romance and suspense throughout this page-turner."

—PAMELA S. WIGHT, author of romantic suspense, memoir, and children's books for all ages

"Once again Buchanan delivers an exciting cast of characters, each with their own unique and compelling needs, who are driven to the writers retreat of Pines & Quill. Romance, friendship, and danger all await the arrival of guests to the remote retreat. I love the setting, the characters, and most of all the suspense that she weaves through this brilliant story."

—SHERRY BRISCOE, author of the *Moon Shadows* series

"Loved renewing my acquaintance with Mick and Emma and pleased to see Pines and Quills is still in the able hands of Niall and Libby. The atmosphere of a writer's retreat, Pines and Quill, is inspired as the background for such horrific crimes that the author has served up! The contrast of descriptive detail of the foodie meals and the depraved acts of malice make this cozy mystery that much more delicious. And, Hemingway continues as the lively character to add levity!"

—MAREN COOPER, author of *A Better Next: A Novel*

"*Iconoclast* jumps right in with the action, setting the stage for everything that transpires throughout the rest of the book. We get to know the main characters we met in book one, *Indelible*, in more detail. If you haven't read it, the author catches you up with what you need to know (or may have forgotten), so you can read this as a standalone as well. From mouthwatering dinners, to psychopathic villains, to unexpected 'family' members, *Iconoclast* keeps you entertained and turning the page for the next twist."

—SHARON DUKETT, author of *No Rules: A Memoir*

ICONOCLAST

ICONOCLAST

A SEAN McPHERSON NOVEL

BOOK TWO

LAURIE BUCHANAN

This book is dedicated to authors,
their creative muses, and the craft of writing.

Published by SparkPress, a BookSparks imprint,
A division of SparkPoint Studio, LLC
Phoenix, Arizona, USA, 85007
www.gosparkpress.com

Published 2022
Printed in the United States of America
Print ISBN: 978-1-68463-125-4
E-ISBN: 978-1-68463-126-1

Library of Congress Control Number: 2021914671

Interior design by Tabitha Lahr

While Bellingham and Fairhaven are
real towns in the state of Washington,
I've added fictitious touches to further the story.

*"May your pens never run out of ink,
your computer never run out of power,
and your brain never run out of brilliant ideas."*
—JESSICA LAVE, *Quiet on the Set: A Novel*

PROLOGUE

> *"For success, the author must make the reader care about the destiny of the principals, and sustain this anxiety, or suspense, for about 100,000 words."*
> —KEN FOLLETT

"Forgive me, Father, for I'm about to sin."

A suppressor muffles the sound of six consecutive rounds fired below the screen through the thin wooden partition separating saint from sinner in the confession booth.

As Father Paddy's body slumps to the floor, the iconoclast slips out a back door.

Rounding the corner, she does a tactical scan to ensure there's no one around. *All clear.*

She looks up to make sure the black sock she put over the security camera is still there. *In place.*

She removes the oversized trench coat and pulls off a short gray wig, mustache, and beard. She rolls them, along with her gun and suppressor, into the coat, and tucks everything into the briefcase. Before getting into the car she borrowed from Vito, she places the briefcase on the floor behind the driver's seat.

As she pulls away from the curb, she smiles. *I entered St. Barnabas as an old man. I left as a woman. Now if that's not a miracle, I don't know what is.*

Thirty minutes later, she drives down a gravel road to the Scrap Heap. On the surface, to an innocent passerby, it's a wrecking yard where vehicles are brought, and their usable parts are salvaged and sold while the unusable metal parts are sold to recycling companies. In reality, it's a place where people and things who've outlived their usefulness pass through.

The tips of Toni's nails, polished in "dagger pink," tap the steering wheel through thin, nitrile gloves. Usually, it's a fifteen-minute drive, but she takes a route devoid of street cams.

Two snarling Dobermans greet her through an eight-foot-high chain link fence topped with triple concertina wire. The result is an extremely effective barrier.

Tapping the fence, Toni muses. *This is the second barrier I've dealt with today—first, the screen in the confessional, now the chain link fence. If I had a shrink, they'd probably conclude that I enjoy keeping barricades between the men I don't like and me. And they'd be right. I can always see them from the outside, where I stay safe and maintain control. They're defenseless and easily manipulated on the inside.*

A huge bald man in oil-stained coveralls steps out of the doorway of a small shack by the gate. "Hey, Toni."

"Hey, Vito. Did you wait as I asked?"

"I did. Just a sec. Let me get these guys."

After shutting the dogs behind the door of the shack, Vito opens the gate.

Toni drives through, opens the back passenger door, and retrieves the briefcase.

Before they head into the central part of the yard, Vito closes and locks the gate.

Toni follows him to a waiting pile of wrecked cars. She hands him the open briefcase, peels off the nitrile gloves and tosses them in, then tucks her hands into her back pockets. *Such a waste. That was a sweet Smith M&P 22 compact and .22LR suppressor.*

After closing the briefcase and giving it a speculative weight check, Vito shrugs his massive shoulders and tosses it through the air into the top car's open trunk. Then he climbs up a ladder into a rig next to the pile of cars and starts the engine. When he pushes a black-knobbed lever, the car crusher begins its descent, closing the top car's trunk as it does.

Toni notices two words spray-painted on the side of the machine: BIG BANG.

She looks up at Vito. His face is red, and his head is glistening with sweat. He wipes the moisture from his forehead with the front of his hairy arm.

He looks down at her and gives her a thumbs-up.

When it's all over, he climbs down. "How about dinner sometime?"

"I'd like that." She mentally applauds herself for not finishing the sentence with *idiota*—Italian for idiot.

Nodding toward the pile of crushed cars, Vito holds out a hand.

Toni looks at his waiting palm. *If his fingers were laced together, his hand would look like a baseball mitt.*

"That'll be five hundred bucks," Vito says. "But when we go out, it's on me."

"It's a deal," she says.

After she pays Vito in cash, he unlocks the gate and opens it.

Toni thanks him again, then gets in her own car and drives away. Looking in the rearview mirror, she sees Vito. *I'd rather die.*

Clutching her glasses in one hand and a crumpled tissue in the other, Carol Stapleton, an elderly penitent, steps into the confession booth. She's crying because she knows she has to tell the priest the hateful thoughts she's entertained about her neighbor. She sits down, closes her eyes, and tries to compose herself as she waits for the priest's usual greeting.

After tucking the tissue in her sleeve, her now-empty hand fingers the string of pearls at her neck. After a few minutes tick by in silence, she retrieves the tissue and blows her nose. Clearing her throat, she says, "Father MacCullough?"

When he doesn't answer, she wipes her lenses with the hem of her cotton dress and puts her glasses on. That's when she notices the splintered wood. *What on earth?*

She presses her wrinkled face to the small ornate screen in the partition that divides them. Red oozes down the wall where the priest should be seated. Her nose wrinkles at the faint coppery smell. Her forehead furrows. *Is that blood?*

Heart pounding, she pushes her ashen face forward a little more to look down. It's hard to see, but it seems like Father MacCullough's crumpled on the floor. Carol crosses herself.

Calling his name again, she steps out of her side of the booth and opens his.

Panic rips her chest, clawing to climb out of her mouth when she sees the bloodied, hole-pocked vestments. The door on the priest's side of the confessional had been blocking the pool of blood Father MacCullough is lying facedown in. Now unblocked, it slowly spreads, inching toward the tip of Carol's black orthopedic shoe.

A primal scream pierces the sanctuary.

CHAPTER 1

"There is only one plot—things are not what they seem."

—JIM THOMPSON

PAM WILLIAMS

With her law practice still under reconstruction, Pam's looking forward to her time at Pines & Quill to finish her manuscript about the pandemic of racism. She's worked hard to prove herself. In doing so, she's made a few enemies. A testimony to that fact, her small building in New Orleans was burned to the ground. It was ruled arson, but authorities haven't caught the culprit yet.

Before closing her laptop and tucking it in her briefcase, she confirms—once again—that the most recent version of her document, *Peaceful Turbulence: The Nonviolent Pursuit of Equality*, is on her hard drive.

While she's at it, she takes another look at her newly revamped website. As a civil rights attorney and activist, her website gets a lot of traffic. Most of it's good—people who are looking for representation. Unfortunately, some of the traffic is bad. Hateful, really. Like the people who burned her building to the ground.

She clicks on the "About" page, looks at her photo, and makes a face. *Well, at least I like my new glasses.*

Her brother, Kyle, steps up behind her, leans over her shoulder, and says, "Those glasses make you look intellectual instead of like the snotty brat you really are."

"And you're a big dork!" she teases back. "Thank you for stopping by to see me off."

"You're welcome. But I didn't do it for you; I did it for me. I'm worried about you and wanted to see for myself that you're okay."

"You don't need to worry about me," Pam assures him.

"You're my little sister, and I love you. It's my job to worry about you. And besides that, your office building was just burned down. If that's not grounds for worry, I don't know what is," Kyle says. "And what do you *really* know about this writers' retreat?"

"I did my research," Pam says. "The reviews are nothing short of incredible, and I also spoke with a few writers who've attended."

Holding up his hands in resignation, Kyle shakes his head and says, "Okay, okay. I give up."

Before hugging her goodbye, he apologizes again for not being able to take her to the airport. "I'm so sorry, but I can't miss this meeting with the mayor. We're going to discuss the potential of bringing a division of Microsoft here. It would mean a huge influx of jobs."

"It's okay, Kyle," she says. "In the event someone decides to add insult to injury and burn my condo to the ground while I'm gone, my car will be safe and sound in long-term parking." She hopes that the added security measures she's taken are enough to deter anyone from trying. As Kyle heads out the front door, she says, "I love you. I'll see you in three weeks."

Pam makes a final walkthrough of her home to ensure that everything's in place. Satisfied, she drapes the strap of her cross-body messenger bag over her shoulder, hefts her suitcases, and enters the garage through the kitchen door.

After stowing her luggage in the trunk of her dark blue Prius, she gets into the driver's seat, puts the key in the ignition, and is about to hit the garage door remote on the visor when the eyes of a ski mask-covered face meet hers in the rearview mirror. Before she can move, honk the horn, or make a sound, a garrote is around her throat.

Pam's eyes and mouth open wide. Her hands scrape and claw at the rope against her throat. She thrashes and flails; her feet kick the pedals. Her arms jerk back against the seat at a sudden tightening of the rope; her body twitches in response. Pam's eyes lock onto the eyes in the mirror. There's no mistake about the intent to kill. She sees it darkening the eyes; it moves there like a living thing, writhing in the dark liquid pools.

TOM GORDON

Militants in southern Afghanistan had already salted the earth with bombs when Sergeant Tom Gordon led his Marines through Sangin. On his final patrol, the ground ruptured under his feet in an explosion of light and blood. The blast tore at his right arm and shattered his feet and legs.

Gordon rained hand grenades on insurgents in Fallujah and braved enemy fire to evacuate two wounded Marines and carry out the body of a third. He was awarded the Navy Cross, second only to the Medal of Honor.

Tom doesn't need to reread the well-worn newspaper article. It's etched in his brain. And if that doesn't serve as a good enough reminder, the prosthetic legs he's packing for his trip to Pines & Quill is a daily memento that he's a double transfemoral amputee—both of his legs were removed mid-femur.

Tom lost more than his limbs. He lost the will to live. In his mind, his legs were what allowed him to power through life. He had planned to open a soccer camp when he got out of the military; it was his lifelong dream. Now his dreams are shattered, and he feels his life isn't worth living.

Tipping his head back to look at the ceiling, he reflects. *Losing the will to live isn't always standing on a ledge. It's not continually being in crisis mode—for me, anyway. It's a dull ache in my chest that weighs me down constantly. I might laugh or appear normal, but that ache to disappear is there, underneath.*

Sometimes I give up on life because everything in my day-to-day is a fight. I'm just too tired, angry, or depressed to fight anymore. Sometimes I don't want to fight anymore for no particular reason other than I'm done. I obsess over that thought constantly. I'm just done.

A devout Catholic, he believes that suicide is a mortal sin. But that's not going to stop him. Before committing suicide, he visits his priest to receive absolution. Father Mark, who was also Tom's roommate at Saint Joseph's University—St. Joe's—says he'll grant him absolution on one condition—that he wait. He says, "In college, you loved writing. I want you to write everything down—the who, what, when, where, and why of it."

That cathartic exercise took on a life of its own and evolved into a manuscript. Tom hopes it will become a published book. That's why he's about to catch a plane to Pines & Quill. *And if I can write a book, then I can open a soccer camp—one for kids who've lost limbs. Then maybe, just maybe, I'll have a reason to live.*

Knowing it'll be easier to get through airport security in Philly and Seattle if he uses his wheelchair, he packs his legs. After seeing examples of prosthetics from days gone by in his doctor's waiting room, Tom appreciates today's technological advancements.

He's had a lot of luck with his prosthetic care, first trying several different systems until arriving at the current "final" one: from liner with pin to liner with vacuum lips to full-contact vacuum Milwaukee shaft with BoaSystem. *I'm grateful I was allowed to test different knees during this time to see what suits me best before making the final decision.* Of course, he's spent a lot of time with a technician and a physical therapist. *Sometimes the socket can be too big, sometimes too narrow. Sometimes a part breaks here, and sometimes I just need a second opinion. On the whole, however, I'm satisfied with the way things have gone so far.*

After Tom zips the bag with his prosthetics shut, he rolls his wheelchair over to the door and places the prosthetics bag next to his laptop bag and guitar case. He remembers the first time he stood with his prosthetic legs. *During physical therapy and gait training, I'd watched YouTube videos on how to run, jump, play football, and do other things with artificial limbs. Suddenly, I was teetering on prosthetics. That's when it became clear that this wasn't going to be a walk in the park and would demand a lot of sweat, blood, and mental strength. This journey is far from over.*

LINDA WASHINGTON

Linda glances in the mirror a final time before heading to the airport. Her expressive hazel eyes convey a mischievous twinkle. Angling the medicine cabinet mirror for a better view, she turns her body first to one side, then the other. She doesn't mind that her ash-brown hair hasn't fully grown back from cochlear implant surgery. *I know that many deaf people are okay with remaining deaf; it's not a foregone conclusion that we all want to become hearing, but it was the right choice for me.*

When Linda was three years old, she lost all hearing in her left ear and eighty percent of the hearing in her right ear after suffering through measles and high fevers. She was declared legally deaf. Hearing aids weren't an option for her situation. And at that time, cochlear implant surgery wasn't only cost-prohibitive, there were more cons than pros involved.

Linda's parents were afraid of the cons—the risks—that include meningitis, an infection of the lining of the surface of the brain, and cerebrospinal fluid leakage, a leak from a hole created in the inner ear from a hole in the covering of the brain as a result of the surgical procedure.

Linda's greatest fear was a potential injury to the facial nerve, the one that goes through the middle ear to give movement to the muscles of the face. It lies close to where the surgeon needs to place the implant, and it can be injured during surgery. An injury can cause a temporary or permanent weakening or full paralysis on the same side of the face as the implant.

Linda's parents were committed to letting her live as normal a life as possible. Against the advice of doctors, they resisted sending her away to a special school for the deaf. Instead, they enrolled her in local programs with support services for children with hearing loss. They also encouraged her early interest in the arts.

She attended the Center on Deafness (now the International Center for Deafness and the Arts), where deaf and hearing kids join together for recreational activities. It's here that she caught the photography bug. It's here that she got the idea of taking such excellent photographs that you can "hear" them even though there's no sound. She lives up to that dream. Her work has been featured at some of the best photography galleries in Chicago—the Museum of Contemporary Photography, the Chicago Cultural Center, the Mary

& Leigh Block Museum of Art, and the Museum of Contemporary Art.

Linda's most recent work was included in the "Nature in View" exhibit hosted by the Garden Photographic Society at the Chicago Botanic Garden.

After swiping her top and bottom lips with her favorite shade of lipstick, "Heat Wave," and capping the tube, Linda signs to herself in the mirror. *You've got this!* Then she says it out loud. Before sashaying out the bathroom door, she laughs with delight because she can hear herself.

At the front door, Linda picks up three bags—her suitcase that she'll check through to Seattle, her purse, and a laptop tote that doubles as a camera case that she'll carry on the plane with her.

She smiles when she hears the sound of the cabbie's horn. It won't be long until she's at O'Hare, where she'll catch her nonstop flight to Seattle. She plans to give as much effort to her book while she's at Pines & Quill as she does everything else—her all.

MEGAN DUPREY

Megan bites her lower lip as she looks around the confines of her office, a small enclosed space just off the kitchen of her French restaurant, La Mandarine Bleue. *Inutile de s'inquiéter— there's no need to worry*—she mentally chides herself.

With great care, she checks and double-checks her bag to make sure she has her competition-would-kill-for recipes and wine pairing notes. *Check.*

She tucks her Kindle into her purse. *Even though the flight from Boise to Seattle is only an hour and a half, I want to enjoy every minute of it.*

Luggage in hand, she steps through her office door into a large kitchen. It swings behind her with a hushed flapping sound.

Fastidious as always, Simon—the maître d'—steps up to Megan.

"*Merci.* I appreciate everything you've done and will do on my behalf," Megan says.

"Meg—"

Holding up a hand to stop him from saying anything further, she continues. "I've never left the restaurant for more than a day or two before. I'm excited, and I'm scared, but if I don't do this now, I never will."

Simon removes the luggage from her white-knuckled grip and sets it on the pristine tile floor. "I'll carry that to the car when your Uber driver arrives," he says.

"Thank you," Megan says. "I have a few things on my mind." She wrings her hands and resumes. "I want a deposit made every single day. Double-check the doors to make sure they're secure every night when you close. Make sure the reservations stay on schedule. And make certain that the meat and produce are fresh daily."

Simon nods his assurance and says, "There's no need to worry."

Megan looks into his heart-melting brown eyes. "I'm not worried," she says. "What makes you think I'm worried?"

He blinks, a long, slow flutter of dark eyelashes against his clean-shaven cheeks.

A woman—or a man in Simon's case—could happily drown in those liquid pools, Megan thinks.

"For starters," Simon answers, "your shoulders are practically up to your ears, you're biting your lip, and your eye is twitching."

"My eye is *not* twitching," Megan says.

"I made that one up. But the other two are dead giveaways."

Megan swipes at him. "Be serious," she says, trying not to smile.

Always soothed by her pleasing French accent, Simon counts out his responsibilities on his long, slender fingers and assures Megan: "I'll make the deposits every day. I'll make certain the doors are secure when we close each evening. I'll ensure that we keep the reservations on schedule. And I'll make certain that the meat and produce are fresh daily. Most importantly, I'll do my best to fill your shoes while you're gone."

As he looks at the uncertainty in her face, he continues. "You're not going to get anything accomplished or enjoy yourself if you're worrying about La Mandarine Bleue." Walking over to a magnetic tool strip that holds knives and kitchen utensils of every shape and size on the wall between a massive commercial stove and a stainless steel, industrial-size refrigerator, Simon grabs a pair of kitchen shears. "Here," he says, handing them to Megan.

Her eyebrows raise. "What am I supposed to do with these?" she asks.

"I want you to pretend that there's an umbilical cord attached from you to the restaurant."

"Okay," she says with a note of hesitation in her voice.

"And then I want you to cut the umbilical cord. Megan, we're viable. I promise that we can function for a month without you." Seeing the hurt look in her eyes, Simon continues. "It'll be hard without your guidance, but we can do this. You've trained us well. From the wait staff to the sommelier, and everyone in-between, you're the one who taught us what it takes to reach and maintain the premier status that La Mandarine Bleue has achieved under your management. And we'll maintain the momentum while you're at the writers' retreat finishing your cookbook."

Fiona, the sommelier, pops her head around the swinging traffic door that separates the dining area from the kitchen. "Your Uber's here," she says to Megan.

"Thank you, Fiona. I'll be right out."

Simon follows Megan to her ride and puts her luggage in the already-open trunk.

Megan places a hand on each of his shoulders and leans in. She places a soft kiss on each of his cheeks. "*Au revoir. I'll* be back before you know it."

THE PERPETRATOR

The perpetrator watches panic carve into Pam's face and applies ever-increasing pressure. She waits as Pam's pupils constrict, and continues to apply pressure. The killer is heaving now with excitement, exertion, and power.

The body goes slack. In the rearview mirror, the killer sees that the black centers of the victim's pupils have widened into fixed dilation. The deed is done.

The perpetrator steps out of the door behind the driver's seat. She pulls off the ski mask and continues with the tasks at hand, calmly stating the twelve steps she memorized:

1. Keep my nitrile gloves on.
2. Remove Pam's clothes from her body.
3. Put on the nonprescription, look-alike glasses from my shirt pocket.
4. Remove my clothes and put Pam's clothes on.
5. Take the suitcases from the trunk and put them in the back seat.
6. Put Pam into the trunk of the car along with my clothes and the garrote. Damn, it's a good thing I work out. They don't call it "dead weight" for nothing.
7. Check the code I received for Pam's phone to make sure I can get to the boarding pass.
8. Back out of the garage slowly.
9. Check to make sure that nothing has fallen onto the garage floor.
10. Close the garage door.
11. Drive to Swamp Adventures where Sam—one of our inside guys—will take the body for alligator bait. My

handler, "Smith," said, "This isn't Sam's first rodeo. You'd be surprised to learn who all have been disposed of this way."

12. Take a deep breath, Shelly, and slip into your new persona, your *nom de guerre*. From now on, you're Pamela Williams, a civil rights attorney and activist.

My handler made it clear that it isn't my skill set that landed me this hit or the one to follow. It's my uncanny resemblance to Pam Williams. He told me, "It's been said that everyone has a doppelgänger—a visual double. You could pass as her twin. Don't screw up."

CHAPTER 2

"When I sit down to write a book, I do not say to myself, 'I am going to produce a work of art.' I write it because there is some lie that I want to expose, some fact to which I want to draw attention, and my initial concern is to get a hearing."

—GEORGE ORWELL

Mick dreads the monthly trek to SEATAC—the Seattle-Tacoma International Airport—to pick up the writers in residence. He dreads it because every overpass he drives under opens old wounds and cuts fresh ones, triggering a grim reminder of what lies coiled inside him, ready to spring if disturbed.

It doesn't matter that five years have passed. When Sean McPherson—Mick—closes his eyes, the memory is as fresh as if it had happened today.

A bullet explodes between his partner's eyes. The amount of blood that hits Mick is small compared to what covers the back of the cruiser. The sharp taste of copper fills his mouth.

Mick watches Sam slump forward; the shoulder belt prevents his weight from hitting the steering wheel, but not from gunning the accelerator. The car surges onto the right shoulder, and Mick braces himself for the inevitable impact of metal against the concrete abutment.

The snap of shattering glass mixed with the high-pitched scrape of steel fills his ears. He chokes on the scream lodged in his throat as the cruiser collides with the bridge's unforgiving underpinning.

It hurts to open his eyes. Mick is aware that the underpass is lit by flickering red and blue lights shimmering on cement. He hears people shouting.

"This one's alive, the other one's dead. We're going to have to cut him out. Get the Jaws of Life," one of them yells. "Hurry—I smell fuel!"

Suspended by the seatbelt system, Mick hovers over Sam. He sees his eyes wide open and vacant, his mouth parted. Mick swallows the bitter taste of bile that hits the back of his throat. Sam is more than a partner; he's Mick's best friend.

Months after the accident, Mick's sister, Libby, and brother-in-law, Niall, pick him up at the hospital and take him to Pines & Quill, their writing retreat in Fairhaven, Washington, to finish recovering in one of their four writers-in-residence cottages—Austen, the wheelchair-friendly one.

Swallowed by the unending tasks of groundskeeper and all-around handyman, Mick soon discovers that the Zen-like energy of the wooded acres works on him like a soothing balm, breathing life back into his weary soul.

As he pulls into the airport parking lot, Mick shakes his head to clear the memory. *Before Emma came into my life, my daily mantra was "Just make it through today."* He smiles at the change. *My toes are on the edge of whatever's next. I'm excited and scared.*

After hooking his sunglasses over the visor, Mick looks in the rearview mirror, thumps the steering wheel, and says, "Don't do anything to mess this up."

Grabbing the nameboards from the passenger seat, Mick steps out of the van, takes a deep breath of the sweet June air, and fobs it locked before heading to the luggage carousels in the arrivals terminal. *Today I'm focusing on two things: pick up our guests, and return to Pines & Quill as quickly as possible.*

The arrivals and departures board indicates that the plane for the first guest, Tom Gordon, arrives soon from Philadelphia. The flights for the other three guests are staggered to arrive over the next hour. *Please don't let them be late.*

Mick enjoys getting to know the guests who carve out three weeks from their schedules to write in near seclusion. Each one has a unique process for transferring ideas from their head to the page. They arrive on the first day of each month and depart on the twenty-first. Three weeks offers them a significant amount of protected time to work on their manuscripts. *I wish I were as dedicated to working on mine.*

The fourth week of each month—guest free—provides Niall, Libby, and Mick with time to relax and prepare for the next group of writers. It also allows the siblings to take turns visiting their parents in San Francisco, a two-hour nonstop flight from Seattle.

Each month when Libby hands Mick the guest nameboards for meeting their guest authors at the airport, she shares a brief commentary of what she imagines their personalities to be like based on the phone conversation or email correspondence she has with them. Mick enjoys indulging his sister because her predictions are darned close, if not dead-on.

"Let's see now," she says, tapping her right index finger on her chin. "Tom Gordon is coming from Philadelphia. He's single. My guess is that he's in his mid-thirties. He strikes me as smart, kind, and good, like someone who strives to make things better. He plays guitar for Resilient—a band of wounded warriors who are healing through music. He lost both of his legs while serving in Afghanistan. He's our wheelchair guest this month."

"How long has he been in a wheelchair?" Mick asks.

"He didn't say, but I get the feeling that it hasn't been long. He mentioned that he's in the early stages of using prosthetic legs."

"Okay," Mick says, nodding. "How about the next guest?"

"Linda Washington is flying in from Chicago. She lost her hearing when she was a toddler and just had cochlear implant surgery."

Mick raises his eyebrows and cocks his head. "What's that?"

"I did a little research," Libby says. "A cochlear implant is a surgically implanted neuroprosthetic device that provides a sense of sound to a person with moderate to profound hearing loss. Cochlear implants bypass the normal acoustic hearing process, instead replacing it with electric hearing. The sound sensation comes from sound converted to electric signals, which directly stimulates the auditory nerve. The brain adapts to the new mode of hearing and interprets the electric signals as sound and speech."

"That's impressive," Mick says.

Libby nods in agreement. "Linda told me that while she's getting used to hearing herself and others, she still reads lips. I laughed when she told me, 'I'm good. Not only can I read lips from across a room, I can practically read them around a corner.'"

Mick laughs. "It sounds like she has a great sense of humor. That's two of our guests. What about number three?"

"Megan Duprey is arriving from Boise. I think she's about my age—"

"You mean ancient?" Mick teases.

"Watch yourself, little brother. I can still beat the tar out of you."

Mick holds up his hands and pretends to duck.

Libby gives him a playful warning look, then continues. "I enjoyed listening to her French accent on the phone. She strikes me as being an extremely focused businesswoman, but with a sense of whimsy. She owns a French restaurant, La Mandarine Bleue. Translated that means—"

"The Blue Tangerine," Mick finishes her sentence.

"I'm impressed," Libby says. "I didn't know you speak French."

"When I was in the hospital those months recovering, I was bored out of my mind, so I took a Rosetta Stone language course." Raising his right hand, he holds his thumb and index finger close together. "I know just enough to keep myself out of trouble," he says. "What about the fourth person?"

"Pam Williams is flying in from New Orleans. When we spoke on the phone, she pronounced it 'Nawlins.' She's a civil rights attorney and activist. She was a pleasure to speak with. She strikes me as a fiercely energetic forward thinker, a problem solver, and an excellent communicator with a strong sense of justice." Libby pauses to think for a moment, then continues. "She's someone I'd want to have in my corner."

Amid a busy hub of travel activity, Mick's thoughts return to his surroundings. His gaze sweeps the space, taking everything in like a dry sponge soaks up water. At the onset of his police training, he learned, "It's all in the details."

Ever vigilant, Mick watches the baggage area as it disgorges travelers young and old. He mentally notes hair color, facial expressions, body language, tattoos, jewelry, clothing, footwear, and baggage details.

He returns to the task at hand, raising the nameboard for "T. Gordon" to be visible from a distance. Mick scans the crowd and spots Tom first. He has a thick shock of black hair with premature strands of silver at the temples. His jaw is sharply cut, and his blue eyes are alert and penetrating.

He's wearing an olive green T-shirt over broad shoulders that narrow down to a thin waist, a physique carved from military training. A laptop bag rests across his thighs. His khaki shorts have empty leg holes.

Mick's impressed that he's using an arm-powered, manual wheelchair. *Just like Emma,* he thinks.

Tom rolls to a stop in front of Mick and holds out a hand. "I'm Tom Gordon," he says.

As he reaches for Tom's hand, Mick notices that Tom has retained his military bearing in the ramrod-straight posture. "It's nice to meet you. I'm Sean McPherson, but please call me Mick, everyone else does."

Their hands meet in a firm handshake.

"Let's go get your bags from the carousel," Mick says.

As he leads the way to the ever-circling conveyor belt, Mick feels a wave of guilt. *You should be ashamed of yourself at the amount of self-pity you nearly drown in because you've got a limp. Get over yourself, buddy. Tom's lost both of his legs. Be grateful you still have yours.*

"When will the others arrive?" Tom asks.

"We're waiting for three more within the hour," Mick replies. "Libby MacCullough is my sister. She tells me that you play bass in a band." Jutting his jaw toward Tom's left hand, he continues. "I'd have known you play some type of string instrument from the callouses on your fingertips."

"You've got a good eye," Tom says, impressed.

"I was a cop. We're trained to notice details."

"Was?" Tom asks, eyebrows raised.

"Yeah, it's a long story. I'd like to hear yours sometime."

"Maybe we can swap stories one evening," Tom says. "There's one of my bags now." He points to a large suitcase tumbling onto the conveyor belt. "It's got my legs."

"Well, we sure don't want to leave those behind," Mick says, grabbing it. After collecting a hard-shell guitar case and another suitcase, Mick puts them on the baggage trolley and checks his watch. "The next guest is about to land."

———

As passengers from the Chicago flight pour into the baggage area, Mick holds up a nameboard with "L. Washington" printed on it.

A slender woman in her early-to-mid-thirties with shoulder-length ash-brown hair makes eye contact with Mick. Her hazel eyes crinkle at the edges when she smiles.

As she walks toward Mick and Tom, her movement causes the handkerchief hem of her casual pink skirt to swing just above her knees. The classic tank-style top shows off lovely shoulders. Neither is lost on Tom.

"I'm Linda Washington," she says, the sound of her voice throaty. Her pleasant smile, white against her fair complexion, creases her eyes as she reaches out a hand to shake his outstretched one.

"I'm Sean McPherson. Please call me Mick."

Turning to Tom, Mick says, "I'd like to introduce you to another writer in residence, Tom Gordon. He arrived just ahead of you from Philadelphia."

"It's a pleasure to meet you," Linda says, shaking his hand. "I'll go collect my luggage," she says.

"We'll help," Mick says. When she turns and heads toward the baggage carousel, Mick sees shorn hair and cochlear implants behind and above each of her ears. *That's so darned cool. It blows me away that cochlear implant surgery can create hearing.*

———

Mick checks his watch then looks at the arrival board. Tapping his fingers on his thigh, he thinks, *I need to finish clearing space for Emma's potter's wheel in the workshop before her brothers arrive.*

Fifteen minutes late, the Boise flight carrying Megan Duprey lands just ahead of Pam's flight from New Orleans. Megan's wearing a trendy teal jumpsuit featuring a V-neck, a cinched-waist cord, flowy wide legs, slant pockets, and turned-back short sleeves. Mick guesses she's about five foot six, and he wonders if her quick stride signals anything about her personality.

Megan possesses an easy smile, as though whatever she's doing brings her great joy. Shaking Mick's hand, she says, "*J'ai apporté du chocolat pour tout le monde*—I brought *chocolat* for everyone."

"The word 'chocolate' stood out for me,'" Mick says.

Eyes twinkling with merriment, Megan reaches into her large tote and lifts out a pale pink bakery box with a clear window on top.

Tom rolls up. "Hi, I'm Tom Gordon, and I like you already."

Mick grins. "I second the motion."

Linda steps forward and joins in. "Hi, Megan. I'm Linda Washington. You had me with your beautiful French accent." Peering through the cellophane window, she continues. "They look delicious. What are they?"

"*Mort par le Chocolat*." Megan gives them a mischievous wink. "Death by *Chocolat*."

"What a way to go," Mick says.

"What's in them?" Linda asks, still looking wide-eyed through the cellophane window.

"These *pâtisseries* are made with *fleur de sel*, caramel ganache, dark *chocolat* sabayon, all on top of a dark *chocolat* cookie."

Tom pats his stomach. "I gained a pound just listening to the ingredients."

Keeping an eye on the time and the arrival board, Mick sees that the flight from New Orleans just landed. He holds up a nameboard that reads, "P. Williams."

Within minutes, a tall, slender woman joins the group. She has high, defined cheekbones, toned muscles, and collarbones that overshadow her chest. Her dress has a tie at the hip and a high-low hemline that enhances her willowy silhouette. Embroidery on the bodice adds an eye-catching touch. The color—chambray blue—is the perfect foil for her short, curly, black hair. Her glasses serve to enhance licorice-colored eyes rimmed with thick black lashes.

Holding out his hand, Mick says, "Welcome. I'm Sean McPherson—Mick."

Taking his hand in a firm shake, Pam says, "Thank you. I'm Pam Williams."

Mick turns and introduces her to the other three writers in residence. Indicating each person in turn, he says, "This is Tom Gordon from Philadelphia. This is Linda Washington from Chicago. And this is Megan Duprey from Boise."

"It's nice to meet you," Pam says. Nodding at the pastry box, she looks up at Megan and smiles. "Especially you."

Mick and Linda walk to baggage carousel number three. As Linda points out her suitcases, Mick lifts them off the conveyor belt with ease, and then they walk back to the group. Mick deposits her things on the luggage trolley with the others and turns to Pam. "Ready to point out your luggage?" he asks. "The marquee over carousel number four indicates that's where luggage from the New Orleans flight will offload."

"Let's do this," Pam says, falling into step beside Mick.

As they approach, they see that a crowd at the black and silver conveyor system is three deep. The snippets of conversation around them sound ominous: "It's not moving." "Something's wrong." "Where's our luggage?" "Well, shit! I told you we shouldn't check our bags."

Mick glances at the heavyset man next to him, whose face swells with anger, and the vein running down his forehead begins to bulge. "God damn it! Where's my luggage?" he bellows.

The blast of hostility is like invisible shrapnel.

Arms at his sides, when Mick looks down, he sees that his hands are balled fists. Taking a deep breath, he relaxes them on the exhale.

Just then, a sweaty head with a tonsure of gray hair pops out from where luggage would normally disgorge. "Hello, folks," the maintenance man says. "As you can see, we've encountered a small snag. We're working on it right now and should have it fixed in a jiffy."

"Define 'jiffy,'" the angry man barks.

"I can't say for certain, but we've located the source of the problem, so it shouldn't take long." Before disappearing back into the bowels of the conveyor system, the man smiles and says, "Thank you for your patience."

Relax, Mick says to himself. Nodding a silent "thank you" to the angry man who made an ass of himself, he thinks, *There's no need to get worked up, Mick. There'll be plenty of time to clear the rest of the space in the workshop for Emma's potter's wheel.*

He turns to Pam. "Let's walk back to the others and explain what's going on."

Without exception, they agree to use the unexpected gift of time for a bathroom break.

True to the maintenance man's word, in less than fifteen minutes, conveyor belt number four begins to regurgitate luggage from the New Orleans flight.

After collecting Pam's bags, the small group heads en masse to the parking area.

Pam brings up the rear. She feels a wave of inflated purpose remembering the orders she received and why she's here: *Kill Mick's fiancée, Emma, before she tells anyone that Toni's a dirty cop. Toni said that when Alex Berndt held Emma hostage, he told her where he stashed the ten million dollars of heroin they stole from the SFPD lockup. Find out the location before killing her.* Pam smiles when she thinks about the final directive she received. *"If you have to kill Sean McPherson—or anyone else who gets in your way—do it."*

Eyeing the group in front of her, Pam takes mental stock, assessing anything that might hinder her job. *This group consists of a handsome man in a wheelchair. No threat. A young woman whose build speaks of grace. No problem. And an older woman. No issue.*

Pam turns her attention to Mick, in front, pulling the baggage trolley. *He's fit, strong, and moves quickly despite a limp.* Focused on his gait, she watches Mick twist his left hip forward slightly before propelling his right foot in front. *Not an obstacle I can't go through*, Pam muses, with a self-satisfied smirk.

CHAPTER 3

*"Here's the truth you have to wrestle with: the
reason that art (writing, engaging, leading, all of
it) is valuable is precisely why I can't tell you how
to do it. If there were a map, there'd be no art,
because art is the act of navigating without a map.
Don't you hate that? I love that there's no map."*

—SETH GODIN

In the big kitchen of the main house, apron-clad Niall
MacCullough, hands on his hips, turns toward the
mudroom where his four-legged companion, Hemingway, is
watching. The Irish wolfhound's bearded chin rests on the
bottom half of the closed Dutch door. The bustling, five-
year-old, rough-coated Hemingway tips the scales at just
under one hundred and fifty pounds. Well-muscled, lean,
and strong, his appearance is commanding. An ancient breed,
wolfhounds were bred to hunt with their masters, fight beside
them in battle, and guard their castles. Hemingway possesses
the ability of a fierce warrior, but he's gentle with family and
guests, a magnificent combination of power and grace.

After snagging a dog treat, Niall walks toward the mudroom. A cross between a utility room and a spacious walk-in closet, a Dutch door separates it from the large, well-appointed kitchen. The door—divided horizontally into two half doors—allows either half to be left open or closed. The mudroom is where the MacCulloughs stow outerwear, boots, and anything else they might need when venturing outside, including Hemingway. It also houses his food, water bowls, leash, and bed.

Most people prefer not to have a curious, tail-wagging, pony-sized dog in their midst while eating, so they close the bottom of the Dutch door, leaving the top portion open during meals. This allows Hemingway to pop his head over—with his awning eyebrows and mop-like beard—and still be part of the gatherings without being directly in their midst.

"Hey, big fella. I need to pick up a few things in town," Niall says to Hemingway while opening the door. "Would you like to come along?"

With thrashing tail, Hemingway all but knocks Niall over in his excitement about a ride in the car.

"Okay, you're on. I'll just grab my list. We've got a couple of—"

Before Niall finishes his sentence, his beautiful wife, Libby, walks through the open doorway of the mudroom. Tall and slender, her shoulder-length brown hair windblown, her sapphire-blue eyes light up when she sees Niall and Hemingway.

"Well, hello, gorgeous," Niall growls appreciatively.

As she sets down a basket of fresh-cut flowers, Libby smiles. "What are you two boys up to?" Holding up a hand, she says, "Wait, don't tell me. You're up to no good. Am I right?"

Niall laughs. "You caught us red-handed. We're heading into town to pick up a few last-minute items for this evening's menu." Waggling his eyebrows suggestively, he continues. "Would you care to join us?"

"Unlike some"—she pauses for effect, looking pointedly at Niall—"others have work to do." With feigned drama, she holds the back of her hand to her brow and continues. "I have to put the finishing touches on the guest cottages." Not skipping a beat, she sways her hips in a sultry fashion and walks toward Niall. "But thank you for the kind offer, sir. Maybe we can muss our sheets up later." She flutters her eyelashes and kisses him on his slack-jawed mouth.

———

Much like a brilliant, multifaceted gem nestled on the ragged hemline of the northern Pacific coast, Pines & Quill, a wooded retreat for writers, sits Zen-like on twenty forested acres overlooking Bellingham Bay in Fairhaven, Washington. It provides respite from the distractions of everyday life so that writers can focus on what they do best—write.

An environment that offers peace, quiet, and inspiration, Pines & Quill boasts four secluded cottages: Dickens, Brontë, Austen, and Thoreau, each handcrafted by a long-dead Amish man whose skill and devotion to his trade is still evident in his work. When the structures were modernized, meticulous care was taken to reflect the same excellence in craftsmanship.

The awe-inspiring mango-colored sunrises and blood-orange sunsets at Pines & Quill compete in their breathtaking showiness, each vying for the rapt attention of would-be onlookers. One heralds the beginning of the day, the other bids adieu, sending it off into the ink-black night sky.

Libby enjoys free rein expressing her natural flair for style and interior design in the main house, her brother's cabin, and the four writer's cottages. And while the original Amish builder saw that each cottage is similar in size and design, surrounded by its own type of tree, she ensures that they each have unique personalities: color scheme, furnishings, and hand-selected artwork created by local artisans.

In addition to electricity and internet access, each cottage has air-conditioning, a woodburning stove, and a bathroom with a shower. They're also equipped with an efficiency kitchen that includes a mini fridge, microwave, toaster oven, coffeemaker, and a fat-bellied tea kettle, ideal for a long day of writing.

On each desk is a phone. Retro, they're bulky and square, from an era before cell phones, even before cordless. Their sole purpose is to connect with the main house. A guest needs only to lift the receiver and dial zero to ring through to the MacCullough's kitchen.

The main house, large and rugged, is inviting in a down-home sort of way. Built for comfort, not grandeur, it sits at the center of Pines & Quill. And while each writer has the option to have breakfast and lunch delivered from the main house to their cottage door, they gather for dinner each evening at the enormous pine table Libby acquired at an auction in Seattle. Said to have seated a dozen threshers at mealtime in the early 1900s, it now serves the writers who've come to escape the distractions of life—come to this nurturing place for the sole purpose of writing.

Even though his brother, Paddy, is a priest, Niall's not much of a brick-and-mortar churchgoer. He believes that anything done with care and joy is an act of worship. That's why he strives to be a kind presence in people's lives; that's why the cookery and garden at Pines & Quill are his cathedrals. The casual atmosphere of sharing a meal in the spacious kitchen of the main house is conducive to *esprit de corps*—camaraderie.

Every scratch and divot, a history of purpose and bustling activity, reads like braille in the wide, buttery pine boards of the floor in his sanctuary.

With each group of writers in residence, Libby and Niall nod to each other under copper-bottomed pots that hang from the rustic beams in the kitchen ceiling. In over thirty years of marriage, they've built an extensive repertoire of facial expressions that only they're privy to the meaning of.

Each month they settle back like satisfied cats washing their whiskers as they watch a small community form, bonds deepening through conversation. Their guests share stories, histories, breakthroughs, and roadblocks, offering advice and feedback, challenging each other to take risks. The group of writers this month should prove no different.

With its bevy of comfortable, overstuffed chairs, the living room is the after-dinner gathering place for guests to continue visiting over dessert while enjoying drinks from the small but well-stocked main house bar, the Ink Well. The floor-to-ceiling bookshelves and massive fieldstone fireplace serve as an ideal focal point, with the large mirror above the mantel gathering the entire room in its reflection.

The retreat's journal resides in this community space, a journal where guests are encouraged to make notations during their stay. Some of the script is small and tight; some is fiercely slanted. Other handwriting is long and loopy, while some is printed with precision, each letter like a soldier marching across the page.

With entries dating from its inception in 1980, the Pines & Quill journal is a living legacy, a tangible way for writers to connect with those who came before and those who'll come after. And on more than one occasion, it's served as a guide, yielding clues that helped solve mysterious occurrences that have taken place at this writer's haven over the years.

Just last month, there was a macabre entry that led to the resolution of a cold case. *Look in the mirror and what do you see? An eerie reflection that looks like me.*

Between nonfiction and fiction, every possible genre is penned at Pines & Quill. From biography to self-help and everything in-between: romance, business, humor, science fiction, children and young adult, political, crime, screenplays, essay, poetry, fantasy, history, and mystery.

Dedicated writers come to Pines & Quill to gift themselves with time and space, let go and connect with nature's muse, find their creative rhythm, and write about the many intersections of human activity both real and imagined.

Seated on the periphery of the historic Fairhaven district of Bellingham, Pines & Quill is made of fog-kissed bluffs, great horned owls and red-tailed hawks, winding paths, solitude, and the blissful absence of noise, demands, and chores—an ideal place for contemplating many things.

And though Niall would never say it himself, Libby often says, "Niall's a maven when it comes to preparing food."

In addition to Niall's gourmet cooking, another popular feature at Pines & Quill is Libby's movement meditation sessions—tai chi. Many guests avail themselves of this misty morning offering as a beautiful way to warm up for a productive day of writing.

Libby takes the all-terrain vehicle to put fresh linen in each of the cottages. With its rugged stance, canopied top, and knobby tires, their ATV is invaluable for getting around the property, regardless of the weather.

She smiles when she thinks about the humorous description she heard the meteorologist on KGMI use for the weather in this part of the Pacific Northwest. "There are only three types of weather in Bellingham," he said. "It's about to rain. It's raining. It just finished raining."

That's why Niall calls meteorologists "weather guessers," Libby thinks. *They're not always right.* She lifts her face skyward to feel the warmth of the sun before heading north to Dickens cottage. She smiles when she sees a weathered Adirondack chair on the covered front porch. A writer herself, she knows full well the value of not being confined, of being able to move around, and that nature's breath, fresh air, is an encouraging muse.

With this in mind, during the planning phase, she ensured that the porch of each cottage—Dickens, Brontë, Austen, and Thoreau—has ample space for quiet reflection. A handcrafted, bent-willow chair with a deep seat, the graceful lines of its arms open in welcome, and plump pillows are ready to receive a weary back at the end of a productive day of writing. After making the beds with crisp, clean linens and setting out fresh towels and washcloths in each cottage's bath and kitchen area, Libby leaves a cheerful monogrammed note-card with P&Q, the retreat's initials, on each kitchen counter. Inside is printed:

Pines & Quill offers writers a peaceful, inspiring, wooded setting to pursue the work they love. We aim to encourage artistic exploration, nurture creative thought, and forge bonds between diverse thinkers. Our vision is for you to find inspiration and make progress in your work.

Located between the main house and the garden is a common area that includes laundry facilities and supplies, a printer and paper, and assorted office supplies should you need them. There are also bicycles with covered saddle baskets if you feel adventurous and would like to explore the surrounding area or pick up sundries in town. Each basket contains a map of the town, a brisk twenty-minute walk or a five-minute bicycle ride from Pines & Quill.

Satisfied that everything's in place for their guests' arrival, Libby returns to the main house under a saturated blue sky dotted with white cushions of clouds.

CHAPTER 4

"The difference between the right word and the almost right word is the difference between lightning and a lightning bug."

—Mark Twain

Through the tinted lenses of her sunglasses, Pam watches as Mick pulls a silver van curbside. She's aware that the shades make her less approachable. *I don't want to get drawn into a bunch of chitchat.*

Silently, both side panels of the van slide open for the waiting guests.

"I call shotgun," Linda says, opening the front passenger door.

"I'll take the seat behind Mick," Tom counters.

Pam observes Mick transfer the mountain of baggage from the trolley into the back of the van while everyone gets into their seats. *He makes it look effortless.*

Jabbing her sunglasses into her hair, Pam bends her willowy frame and eases herself onto the bench seat in the far back. *From this vantage point, I can observe the others without being scrutinized myself.*

Megan uses the grip bar and enters the van. She takes the smooth, gray leather bucket seat behind Linda.

The toned muscles of Tom's arms and shoulders make it look easy as he transfers himself into the van.

Don't underestimate this one, Pam thinks.

Situated behind the driver's seat, Tom collapses his wheelchair and stows it in the space to his right.

Pam's eyes meet Mick's in the rearview mirror. She returns his smile. *It's best they think me sweet and harmless, a smiler—maybe even a shy person who smiles a lot—because it's in my favor. "She couldn't kill anyone; she's so sweet."*

"Buckle your seatbelts," Mick says to everyone. "We've got a hundred-mile drive ahead of us. It could take a little more than two hours, depending on traffic. At about the midway point, Marysville, we'll stop for a few minutes so everyone can stretch, get a breath of fresh air, and use the restroom. Once we arrive at Pines & Quill, dinner will be served within an hour."

Looking out the side window, Pam surreptitiously slips the sunglasses back over her eyes and settles into the comfortable leather seat.

Tom asks, "I'm curious to know why you have your guests fly into Sea-Tac in Seattle instead of Bellingham International Airport. Wouldn't it be a much shorter drive for you to pick us up there?"

Curiosity piqued, Pam leans forward a bit. *I wondered that, myself.*

Mick nods. "It sure would. But—" He holds up a finger for dramatic effect. "Experientially, we learned that it's *the drive* that cements the initial bond among our writers in residence." He looks at everyone in the rearview mirror before continuing. "As a captive audience, you get to know each other even before you arrive at the retreat. And in this case,"

Mick says, catching Megan's eyes in the rearview mirror, "we get to enjoy 'Death by Chocolate.' Added to that, you benefit from enjoying the beautiful scenery while I share a little bit about the surrounding area."

Satisfied, Pam leans back again.

When Mick eases the van out from under the enormous cement overhead, they're greeted by the sky's June cape—blue and clear.

"Take a good look at that gorgeous sky," Mick says. "It's *not* raining. With an average of thirty-eight inches of precipitation a year, it's no wonder Washingtonians refer to rain as *liquid sunshine*."

Megan turns around in her seat and hands the bakery box to Pam. "You're first," she says. "Take one and pass it forward."

"Thank you. I don't mind if I do."

When the box reaches Tom, Pam thinks, *The grin on his face makes him look like a kid in a candy store.*

Pam watches as Tom extracts one of the delicacies and takes a bite. She sees him roll his eyes in mock ecstasy. Then to everyone's delight, he places his fingers on his lips, and with a kiss and flip of his wrist, offers an enthusiastic, "*Magnifique.*"

"*Très bien*—very good," Megan says.

"Hey, save some for the rest of us," Mick teases.

"What's it worth to you?" Tom banters back.

The mood in the van is jovial. Tom, Linda, and Megan talk like strangers do, sharing snippets and brief histories, putting the best light on things.

From her position in the back seat, Pam listens to the burbling tones of conversation. She pitches in with her two cents' worth every once in a while. As a person who thrives on schadenfreude, she's more interested in listening for any weak links, noting hesitations and evasions, storing them for future consideration—ammunition. *Though I doubt their backgrounds are anywhere near as fabricated as mine.*

When there's a lull in the conversation, Mick, with a decided knack for storytelling, shares the most recent information about Sasquatch sightings and the five volcanoes that Washington is home to—Mount Baker, Glacier Peak, Mount Rainier, Mount St. Helens, and Mount Adams.

Pam watches the captive audience. They're spellbound and request more. *I have to admit Mick plays the part of host well. I'm interested, too.*

Mick accommodates by sharing the backstory of why Seattle is called the Emerald City. "The city of Seattle lies between two bodies of water, Puget Sound on the west and Lake Washington on the east. In the mid-1980s, the city was given the nickname *Emerald City* by tourism officials promoting Seattle for its lush, green forests and more than six thousand acres of parks within the city limits."

Then changing the timbre of his voice to husky, low, and sinister, he tells them the local lore about the ghosts who reside in Fairhaven.

As the silver van catapults north on Interstate 5, Pam absorbs the conversation, noting how often Tom secretively glances at Linda. At one point, she sees Linda's eyes make contact with Tom's, and then her mouth blossoms into a sweet smile. Although Pam can only see his face in profile, she knows that Tom's grinning like a fool.

After a brief stop in Marysville, the conversation turns to the Indigenous tribes of Washington. "The Lhaq'temish, the Lummi Nation, are the original inhabitants of Washington's northernmost coast and southern British Columbia," Mick tells them. "For centuries they've worked, struggled, and celebrated life on the shores and waters of Puget Sound. They're a self-governing nation within the United States. The third-largest tribe in Washington State, they manage thirteen thousand acres of tidelands on the Lummi Reservation."

At long last, they round a bend and stop at a massive wrought-iron entry gate, its overhead sign silhouetted against a softly caressing sun beckons, WELCOME TO PINES & QUILL.

Pam sits up straight in her seat and pushes her sunglasses to the top of her head.

"We've arrived," Mick announces. "If you wear a watch, you won't need it. The pace of life at Pines & Quill is much slower."

Mick presses a button on the remote attached to the visor over the driver's seat. The huge gate swings open, and the vehicle sensor buzzes in the main house, notifying the occupants that their guests have arrived.

"I've traveled all around the globe," Mick says, "but this is my favorite place on Earth. I think you're going to like it, too."

Pam notices the van's occupants are wide-eyed with an appreciation of their forested surroundings. *Usually, I'd hate it here*, Pam thinks, *but I have to admit, there are plenty of places to dispose of a body.*

Mick uses the automatic controls to lower their windows and takes the main house's lengthy drive slowly so they can drink in the surrounding beauty.

They see towering stands of pine and western hemlock jostle for space on the shoulder of the road.

Their nostrils meet with pine and a slight brackish scent.

As he drives, Mick explains, "Beyond the main house, cottages, and trees is a bluff. Below that, the surf of Bellingham Bay is rolling in."

Tom says, "I don't know why, but the smell reminds me of Sunday morning pancakes."

Pam watches as Linda turns in her seat and shoots him a curious look.

Mick laughs. "It's actually not that odd. Once you're settled, and out on the property, stick your nose into the bark on a Ponderosa pine and take a big sniff. To some people, it smells like butterscotch or vanilla. To others, it smells more like cinnamon, or coconut. We've even had guests who say it smells like baking cookies."

"I'm going to try that," Megan says.

"We're lucky to have so many Ponderosa pine this far west. They're more prevalent in the Columbia Basin. My sister, Libby, loves them because they're host to butterflies."

The van continues to glide around curves.

Through the open window, Pam notices that the trees open into a natural space, and then the main house comes into view. The two-story home sits on a gentle rise, accentuated by a large circular drive surrounding low, well-maintained shrubs and bushes.

Pam's gaze sweeps the area, taking everything in. As Mick eases the van into the roundabout, she makes a mental note of the side road off the circle leading to a large garage and what appears to be a workshop. Pam also notices the nearby two-car parking space with plantings that integrate it into the landscape.

The van stops, and Pam slips on a mental cloak. *Like a chameleon, I can adapt to any situation—blend in. My first goal is to project what others want to see because, as my handler says, "When people see what they expect, they don't notice or remember."*

Pam smiles. *It's show time.*

CHAPTER 5

"Just write every day of your life. Read intensely.
Then see what happens. Most of my friends who
are put on that diet have very pleasant careers."

—RAY BRADBURY

Dressed in latte-colored linen slacks, flat-soled sandals, and a white blouse open at the neck, Libby watches the silver van as Mick pulls it to a stop. When the sliding doors glide open, she, Niall, and Hemingway step forward to greet the new arrivals.

From the passenger side of the van, Megan stretches out her hand and wiggles her fingers.

Hemingway knows an invitation when he sees one. He shifts into a happy, full-body wag and steps to the open van door, plunging his whiskered muzzle into Megan's hand.

She tosses her head back; the sound of her laughter coats the sky.

Libby steps forward and takes hold of Hemingway's collar with one hand while extending the other. "Welcome to

Pines & Quill. I'm Libby MacCullough." She nods toward Niall and continues. "And this is my husband, Niall."

Megan shakes Libby's hand, then Niall's. "I'm Megan Duprey. *C'est un plaisir de vous rencontrer*—it's a pleasure to meet you."

"Let me introduce you properly to this big lummox," Libby says. She turns to Hemingway, taps his rump, and says, "Sit." When Hemingway does—his wiry tail dusting the ground behind him—Libby continues. "Good boy. Now give Megan your paw."

Hemingway lifts his massive paw, and Megan takes it in her hand.

"Megan, this is Hemingway," Libby says. "He's bold as a thistle. If he becomes a nuisance, just point to the main house and tell him 'go home.' If you're lucky, he'll leave."

Looking at Hemingway, Megan says, "*Tu es comme un petit cheval*—you're like a little horse."

She scratches him behind one of his wiry ears, the only unassuming thing about him. Within moments, one of Hemingway's back legs starts twitching like a rabbit's.

Libby laughs. "You've found his spot."

Under awning-sized eyebrows, the now-delirious Hemingway's eyes roll back, and his long, pink tongue lolls out the side of his mouth.

"You've got a friend for life now," Libby says.

Linda and Pam step out of the van. "Holy Toledo," Linda says, appreciating the Irish wolfhound's massive size.

"I second the motion," Pam says. Looking at Hemingway's long legs, she whistles. "I bet that big fella can outrun just about anything."

"He's fast," Libby agrees. "Unless, of course, he's sleeping off a meal. Then he's four legs sideways in a food coma, still as a stone." Libby regards Pam thoughtfully. Her intuitive radar kicks into a low hum. *There goes that feeling in the pit of my stomach,* she thinks. *I know the sensation well. Some people call it a "sixth sense." I don't know about that, but I've learned to trust my gut. And right now, it's sending warning signals.*

Pam lifts her head from admiring Hemingway and looks at Libby.

Licorice-colored eyes meet sapphire blue.

Libby sees the dark flints in Pam's black eyes flash. Her expression sends a brisk chill over Libby's body, lifting the hairs on her arms. During the long moment that stretches between them, Libby's mind scrambles for traction. *She's nothing in person like she was on the phone.*

Libby senses an intricate puzzle of warring emotions. The way the late afternoon sun's rays caress Pam's face creates shadows beneath her high cheekbones, turning her back into a riddle before Libby can fit the pieces.

Libby watches as Pam turns to face the van.

"Is there anything I can do to help?" Pam asks Tom.

"Thanks," he says. "I've got it." He rolls up to the small group and holds out his hand, first to Libby, then to Niall. "I'm Tom Gordon," he says. "It's nice to put faces with names finally."

"How was your flight from Philly?" Libby asks, shaking his hand.

"You know what pilots say," Tom says. "Any landing you can walk away from is a *good* one, but if you can use the plane again, it's a *great* one."

Libby's and Niall's laugh causes a robin to flush from under a tree skirt.

"It's a pleasure to meet you," Niall says, taking Tom's extended hand.

Not wanting to be left out, Hemingway nudges Tom's hand with his wet nose for attention.

"You must be Hemingway," Tom says. "I read about you on the Pines & Quill website. You're even more impressive in person."

Looking pleased with himself, Hemingway wags his tail. His happy expression makes him look like he's grinning at Tom. "I can see we're going to get along just fine."

Turning to Tom first, Libby says, "Tom, you're in Austen cottage." Then to each of the women, she continues. "Megan, you're in Thoreau. Linda, you're in Brontë. And Pam, you're in Dickens."

Libby looks at the group and nods with satisfaction. She sees that everyone's wearing expressions of delight except for Pam. Libby observes her nose crinkle in what looks like disdain as Pam watches Hemingway lick Tom's hand.

The uneasy feeling in Libby's stomach stirs again. *I've trusted my gut since I was a kid. I know that if I try to ignore it, it'll grow until I do something about it. Now all I have to do is figure out what that is.*

During the introductions, Mick shifts the luggage from the van to the back of the ATV. Joining the group, he says, "I'm ready to take you to your cottages."

Libby extends her hand. "Mick, here are the tags for Tom's luggage."

"If you don't mind, I've got my own set of wheels," Tom says, patting his chair. "I'd like to get the lay of the land. Just point me in the right direction."

Mick points him in the direction of Austen cottage, and says, "If I get there before you do, I'll set your luggage inside your door."

Just then, Emma rolls up in her wheelchair. "I'll show you the way to Austen cottage," she says to Tom.

Hemingway shifts his allegiance at the sight of Emma, one of his favorite humans. He steps behind her and nuzzles her shoulder with his bearded chin.

"Hey, handsome," Emma says, raising her hand to stroke his whiskered face.

Mick's heart swells in his chest. He beams and says, "Everyone, this is Emma Benton, my fiancée."

Then pointing to each guest, in turn, Mick introduces Emma to the new arrivals.

———

A tingle of excitement travels up Pam's spine when Emma joins the group.

She's my hit.

Pam smiles at the newcomer and listens as Emma offers to show Tom to his cottage.

———

"It's a pleasure to meet you," Emma says, her gaze taking them all in. "I look forward to hearing about the books—"

A muffled scream stops Emma midsentence.

All heads turn to see Megan Duprey bending over an open suitcase that fell off the ATV.

"*Mon Dieu,*" Megan cries. "I remembered a small gift in my bag that I wanted to give Niall, and I accidentally toppled the whole thing." Megan's blue eyes swim in pools of tears that stream down her face in muddy streaks of makeup.

Emma sees what everyone else's eyes are fastened on, causing them momentary immobility. A silver cremation urn. Rolling into action, Emma's the first one to arrive and offer help. She hands Megan a tissue from a pocket in her wheelchair.

Megan looks at the group. "I'm so embarrassed," she says.

"There's nothing to be embarrassed about," Emma says.

"It's just that I bring Adrien's ashes with me wherever I go."

"Who was Adrien?" Emma asks gently.

"Adrien was my husband," Megan sniffles. "One of my girlfriends who's also a widow told me that carrying your husband's ashes is a 'widow's prerogative.'" Rummaging through the bag, Megan finds what she's searching for.

Like the sun coming out from behind a cloud, Emma watches Megan's face transform from grief to triumph as she extracts a beautifully wrapped package.

"I brought a small gift for you," she says, handing the parcel to Niall.

"Oh, my goodness," Niall says, accepting the package. "What's this?"

"It's a little something from one chef to another. Go on, *ouvre-le*—open it," she says.

Emma watches Niall tear the wrapping from the gift and stuff it in the front pocket of his apron. He reads the label on the glass jar out loud. "Fleur de sel." Then beaming like a proud father, he holds it up like a newborn baby for everyone to see.

Curiosity piqued, Emma asks, "What's Fleur de sel?"

"It's a salt that forms as a thin, delicate crust on the surface of seawater as it evaporates," Niall says.

"That's right," Megan says, nodding. "It's a finishing salt to garnish food. The name comes from the flower-like patterns of crystals in the salt crust."

Pam steps forward. "Did you know that mixing salt and water and pouring it directly onto a cut or wound can help stop the bleeding?" she asks.

"No, I didn't," Niall says. "But working in the kitchen with sharp knives the way I do, that's good information. Thank you."

Emma watches perplexity cross Libby's features as she takes in the exchange between her husband and Pam.

Turning back to Megan, Niall continues. "Thank you so much. I can hardly wait to use it."

"Tom," Emma says. "I was about to show you the way to Austen cottage. You're going to love it. I know that I sure did."

Hemingway steps around Emma and looks at her with soulful eyes.

"Do you mind if Hemingway joins us?" she asks Tom.

"Not at all."

Before the group breaks up, Niall glances at his watch. "While you folks are settling into your new digs, I'll put the finishing touches on dinner. We'll see you back here at six o'clock. That gives you just about an hour to catch your second wind."

———

A short, low-pitched caw rakes the air.

A raven glides graceful and steady on a wind current. Its black feathers stroke the sky now and again.

Libby remembers the uneasy feeling she had about Pam just minutes ago. Shaking her head, she mentally dismisses the myth that ravens are harbingers of bad luck and death and turns to the lingering group.

"Mick will give you a lift in the ATV while he takes your luggage to the cottages," Libby says. "Or, you can walk with me on the pathways. It's up to you."

"I'd like a ride," Megan says.

Turning to Linda and Pam, Mick asks, "How about you two?"

"I'm a bit travel-weary," Linda says. "I'd enjoy a ride."

"I've been sitting all day. I'd like to walk," Pam says. "Just point me in the right direction, and I'll find my way."

Libby points Pam in the direction of Dickens cottage, and says, "If Mick gets there before you do, he'll set your luggage inside the door."

Pam heads toward her cottage, and Libby turns back to face the others. After a few moments, Libby's gut instinct prickles.

She glances over her shoulder and sees Pam watching her—her dark brows, eyes, and hair add a threatening intensity to her stony expression.

<hr />

On the way to the west side of the property toward Austen cottage, Tom tells Emma, "I knew that as a wheelchair-friendly facility Pines & Quill would have smooth surfaces, but this is exceptional."

"I thought the same thing the first time I rolled my wheelchair on the pathways here," Emma says. "Nothing juts out; everything's even."

"I never gave it any thought before I was in a wheelchair," Tom says. "My dream is to open a soccer camp for kids who've lost limbs. I'm going to use Pines & Quill as a model."

"Just wait until you get inside Austen cottage," Emma says. "There's not a bit of cork or carpet flooring anywhere."

They both laugh, having experienced navigating those surfaces in a wheelchair.

"They slow you down, that's for sure," Tom says.

"Like a herd of turtles in a jar of peanut butter," Emma replies.

Tom slaps what remains of his thigh. "Now, *that's* funny."

For a moment, they stop to admire the surroundings in the tranquility of the dappled sun. The faint tinkling of wind chimes and the rustling of leaves from the breeze through the copse of trees surround them.

Tom reaches out his hand toward Hemingway.

The big dog moves his wiry head under Tom's strong fingers so he can more easily scratch behind his ears.

"You're a good boy," Tom says.

Hemingway moves even closer and leans against his wheelchair.

A northern flicker rattles in a nearby tree.

Tom draws in a swift breath, winces, and ducks his head between his shoulders as the bird makes a loud, rolling rattle with a piercing tone that rises and falls in volume several times.

"Are you okay?" Emma asks, her voice laced with concern.

"Yes," Tom says. "I'm sorry." He shakes his head. "Ever since I was in Afghanistan, I startle at loud noises. My doctor says it's because I have PTSD—post-traumatic stress disorder."

Looking down at the empty leg holes of his shorts, he continues. "From my experience over there."

"That must be hard," Emma says. "Just so you're prepared, their song lasts seven or eight seconds. It happens regularly at this time of year because pairs are forming, and they're establishing their territories."

"Thank you. That's good to know," Tom says. "Let's keep going."

"You're going to love Austen cottage," Emma says. "Mick's sister, Libby, and brother-in-law, Niall, learned so much when Mick was in a wheelchair. When we get there, you'll see that they put everything they learned into practice."

Tom looks at Emma in surprise. "Mick was in a wheelchair?"

"Yes, but that's his story to share, not mine," she says.

Tom tips his head back and inhales the earthy fragrance wafting from the forest surrounding them. "That scent could make an angel sing," he says.

Emma smiles in agreement. "I like it, too."

As they continue toward Austen cottage, Hemingway in tow, Tom admires the subtle walk lights along the path.

Emma explains, "All of the pathways at Pines & Quill have solar-powered walk lights that come on at dusk and go off when their batteries deplete. That time differs from day-to-day, depending on the amount of sunlight. Niall and Libby want their guests to feel as comfortable in the evening as they do during the day. Here we are."

Nestled in a glade of blue elderberry, Austen cottage

features womb-like seclusion. The cottage's front window reflects some of the nearby tree branches, making it look almost like a painting.

Emma gives a hand signal to Hemingway that conveys, "Sit and stay." After he drops to his bottom, she activates a button on the outside wall, and the door swings open. "There's a matching button on the inside," Emma says, "but it works manually, too."

Tom watches Emma roll up the ramp with ease, continuing right through the extra-wide doorframe.

He follows suit.

Spinning slowly in his wheelchair, he takes in the cottage with evident appreciation. "This is nice," he says.

Fading pools of late afternoon sun puddle on the hardwood floor, while slanting shadows smudge the sage and lavender walls. The effect is at once intimate yet mysterious.

"I'll leave you to explore," Emma says. "I think you'll find everything to your satisfaction." And with that, she rolls out. Before closing the door, she adds, "See you at the main house at six o'clock."

I wish I hadn't mentioned the soccer camp to Emma, Tom thinks. Rubbing the stumps of his legs, he worries. *What if I can't make it happen? What if I'm not the one who was supposed to live?*

Pam's glad for the opportunity to find Dickens cottage on her own. She sets off down the pathway, thinking about the package she's supposed to retrieve in the wooded area between here and town. Her handler's going to give her explicit instructions on where to find it. *I wish they'd hurry up. Then again, there's no harm looking on my own.* She knows what it contains. *A Ruger GP100. My favorite weapon of choice.*

Pam gives in to a gnawing impulse to turn and look at the group.

Her eyes lock with Libby's.

You shouldn't have turned around, she mentally chides herself. *You never were one to look back at the wreckage in your wake.*

CHAPTER 6

*"I do not over-intellectualize the production process.
I try to keep it simple: Tell the damned story."*
—Tom Clancy

Tom's had some practice walking on his prosthetic legs outside of physical therapy. His initial preparation consisted of putting his full weight on his prostheses as he stood between and held onto parallel bars.

His physical therapist, Jack, said, "Stand with your weight equally on both legs, then shift your weight to your prostheses. Good. That's good. Now do it again, but this time hold on with only one hand. And remember, grab the bars if you feel unstable."

Now, sitting on the bed in Austen cottage, Tom unzips his suitcase and removes his prosthetic legs and trekking poles. He looks at them warily, the glint of challenge in his eyes. *I don't want to make a fool of myself in front of anyone. Especially Linda.*

He remembers when his prosthetist, Susan, helped him to choose the best artificial limbs based on his needs. Unlike Jack, her job was to measure, have manufactured, and fit his trans-femoral prosthetics, designed to replace his sockets, knees, shins, and feet.

When they arrived, Susan introduced him to his new legs, explaining the different parts. "There's the prosthetic limb itself," she said, "then the socket. It's the connection or 'interface' between the prosthetic limb and your body." Pointing, she continued. "And this is the attachment mechanism."

Now, Tom focuses on his left side first, placing the contoured shape of the remaining bone and muscles into the suction socket. It's designed to accommodate sensitive nerve areas and improve the residual limb's overall health.

Once secure, he repeats the process on his right side, then wrestles both legs into a pair of lightweight, khaki pants.

Tom grips the trekking poles, leans back, then thrusts himself up, using the poles to keep from toppling forward onto the ground. His balance is a bit dicey at first, but Tom wins this round. "Damn straight," he says. "Let's do this!"

Maintaining his stance, he walks to the front door. With the rubber tip of one of the poles, he presses the wall-mounted button and opens it.

Tom sets his jaw, then begins making his way to the main house for dinner.

When Pam arrives at Dickens cottage, it's like slipping into an old photograph of warm sepia tones—chocolate and ecru. The colors of unbleached silk and linen fabrics throughout the small space are welcoming and pleasing to the senses.

She stands still in the center of the room and takes a deep breath. *Something smells good.* Following her nose to the kitchen, Pam finds a glass fragrance diffuser with a handwritten note:

Designed to comfort, the top notes are fresh pine sprigs and mandarin orange. The middle notes are pomegranate and cinnamon. And the base notes are roasted chestnuts and Madagascar vanilla. Enjoy!

The tension in her shoulders melts, and an unexpected smile perches on her lips. *I've got three weeks to make the hit. I was going to do it sooner,* she thinks, *but I might just take a little vacation on the boss's dime. Emma will be just as dead if I kill her later.*

Fading light catches her reflection in the glass of the window. Walking toward it, Pam's hand glides over the smooth surface of a walnut desk.

Gazing out the window into the woods, she sees that the shadows have grown more profound. The spatters of red and gold give way to the blues and purples of the depleting sun. *The better to hide you with, my dear.* She chuckles at her twist on the children's story, "Little Red Riding Hood."

Through the window, Pam notices a spiderweb splayed from the rain gutter attached to the cottage's side. Its silver strands catch the fading light at certain angles. A bug had flown into the sticky threads, its wings fluttering uselessly against the trap. *It's strange how that works. A spider can lie in wait, knowing that a fly will eventually ensnare itself.*

After changing her clothes, Pam ventures out, but instead of heading straight to the main house for dinner, she takes a circuitous route to investigate the other cottages. She discovers that a copse of trees surrounds each one. Her cottage, Dickens, is encompassed by big-leaf maple trees. Douglas firs circle Brontë. Blue elderberry trees enclose Austen. And Thoreau is surrounded by western red cedar trees.

Other than on the pathways, lush maidenhair ferns cover the forest floor. *The wooded area is supposed to provide the writers in residence with privacy, but it's the perfect camouflage for me.*

After noting the windows, doors, and each cottage's unique surroundings, she brushes bits of fern from the short-sleeved, teal dress she found in one of the suitcases tucked next to a book about winning law arguments. *I wouldn't have chosen either one, but then there's no accounting for taste.*

At five minutes till six, Pam arrives at the main house.

A minute after she uses the polished brass knocker, Niall meets her at the front door and extends his hand. "Please come in; dinner will be ready soon. I'm headed back to the kitchen," he says over his shoulder. "Follow me. What can I get you to drink?"

"Thank you," Pam says, "but I'll wait till the others arrive."

"I could listen to your accent all day," Niall says. "I know it's not a Southern drawl, but I'm not certain what it's called."

"In *Nawlins,* we call it *yat,*" Pam says. "It comes from the phrase 'Where ya'at?' If you follow the New Orleans Saints, it may sound familiar, considering the famous cheer, 'Who dat? Who dat? Who dat say dey gonna beat dem Saints?'" she finishes, laughing.

Niall's laugh joins Pam's. "It almost sounds like you're from the Big Apple, not the Big Easy. Why is it that two cities thirteen hundred miles apart have such similar sounds?"

"You've got a good ear," Pam says. "*Nawlins* and New York were both large port cities in the mid-to-late 1800s, with settlers emigrating from the same countries: France, Italy, Germany, Ireland, to name a few. The gumbo of immigrants in both cities created similar dialects.

"But you were right, Niall. The Southern tongue does exist in *Loo-see-ann-a.* And so does Cajun. Generally speaking, these dialects are divided into different regions throughout the state. We take pride in our respective regions because there are several identities, traditions, and voices specific to the certain areas in the state."

Niall whips butter in a small bowl until it's fluffy. "Like any good attorney, your facts are at the ready," he says.

Pam nods. "They are, indeed." She watches Niall grate a teaspoon of lemon rind and squeeze a tablespoon of lemon juice into the butter, then whip it until it's well blended.

"I love citrus," Pam says. "And if I'm not mistaken, that's lemon butter. What's it for?"

"I'm going to drizzle it on steamed asparagus," Niall says.

"It's clear I came to the right place to work on my book," Pam says, patting her stomach.

Hemingway, observing their exchange from behind the Dutch door in the kitchen, thumps his tail against the washing machine.

Noticing the large clear jar of dog biscuits, Pam asks, "May I give him a treat?"

"Yes, but in the interest of full disclosure," Niall warns, "he'll be your friend for life."

That's precisely what I'm after—his trust.

Linda's photographer's eye instinctively frames up potential images on the way to the main house for dinner. She looks up as a pair of Canada geese glide across the expanse, their bodies silhouetted against the pre-dusk sky. *I wish I'd brought my camera. That would have been a perfect shot.*

She smooths a hand on her upper arm as a gentle breeze caresses her shoulder. *I didn't see a wedding ring on Tom's left hand. I wonder if he has a girlfriend?*

A noise interrupts her mental reverie. Stopping to listen, she speculates on what type of bird it might be and touches one of her cochlear implants, marveling at its miracle. *I can hear birds sing!*

Linda startles as a full-cheeked squirrel darts in front of her, another on its heels chattering away. *I didn't hear them coming.* Caught off guard like that, she scolds herself. *You can't hear everything. Pay closer attention.*

Continuing along the pathway, her mind shifts gears. *Mick put a guitar case with the rest of Tom's luggage. I'd love to hear him play.*

Before heading to the main house, Megan changes her clothes and then settles herself in a chair facing the glass wall. *Stop stressing about La Mandarine Bleue, Megan. Do the calming meditation you learned in yoga class. You know you'll feel better if you do.*

Inhaling through her nostrils, Megan closes her eyes and thinks, *Peace within.*

Exhaling through her mouth, she mentally says, *Peace in the world.*

She inhales again through her nostrils and this time thinks, *Peace in me.*

Then on the exhalation, she mentally says, *Peace in the world.*

After three rounds, Megan lets go of the desire to call Simon to find out how the restaurant is doing.

Prior to leaving, she turns to the silver urn she'd set on the desk earlier. *I'll be back in a little while, mon chéri.*

CHAPTER 7

*"Long patience and application saturated with your
heart's blood—you will either write or you will
not—and the only way to find out whether you
will or not is to try."*

—J<small>IM</small> T<small>ULLY</small>

L inda and Megan arrive at the circular drive in front of the
main house simultaneously. Both women have changed
from their travel clothes—Megan into coral slacks and a white
blouse, Linda into an indigo sundress.

"You look lovely, Megan," Linda says.

"*Merci*. And that deep shade of blue compliments your
hazel eyes," Megan says.

They climb the broad stone steps to the rustic, paneled
oak door.

Turning to Megan, Linda says, "I don't know why, but
I'm a little bit scared."

Megan's eyes widen. "What is there to be scared of?"

"I'm just nervous, I guess. People will be talking at the same time, and I'm not sure that I'll catch everything."

"Let's sit together," Megan suggests. "If you miss anything, nudge me, and I'll fill you in."

"Oh, that would be wonderful," Linda says. "Thank you."

Lifting the heavy brass knocker, Linda strikes the plate.

Within moments, Libby opens the big door. "Welcome to our home."

Stepping back into the gracious foyer, Libby invites them into the casual elegance of the main house. "Dinner's almost ready. Let's head back to the kitchen. Pam's already there."

The aroma of grilled shrimp mingled with mysterious spices tease Linda's nostrils as they walk along gleaming hardwood floors, passing rooms on either side that feature wide windows boasting beautiful views.

A west-facing terrace leads to a garden of native plants where subtle uplighting exposes a handful of colorful birdhouses crafted by local artisans. Linda pauses to watch the sun cast deep purple shadows amid vivid wildflowers before it begins its decent.

When they arrive at the massive eat-in kitchen, Linda and Megan express their appreciation of the cathedral ceiling and large picture window with a southern exposure.

Bowing at the waist with a flourish, an apron-clad Niall says, "Welcome to my domain."

"This is where all of the culinary mystery and magic occurs," Libby says.

On their way to the main house, Mick and Emma see Tom making his way, slowly but surely, along the well-lit pathway.

They pause and wait as he closes the gap between them.

Emma pats the arm of her wheelchair. "I'm grateful for my wheels tonight. Physical therapy was brutal today.

But"—she holds up her hand—"I'm not complaining. It's a great problem to have. I'm glad I'm walking again, even if it's only baby steps right now."

As Tom draws closer, Mick looks up. "You look like you've got the hang of it," he says.

"I'm getting there," Tom says. "I appreciate the seamless pathway. I'd shake your hand, but trust me, if I let go of this pole"—he raises one slightly—"I'll tip over. And that wouldn't be good because I'm hungry. I read online about Niall's gourmet cooking, and I'm ready to tuck in."

The three of them continue toward the main house.

"I'm looking forwa—" Tom starts, but his sentence cuts off when he stumbles.

Mick leaps forward and stops his fall. "Easy does it."

"Thank you," Tom says. A flush creeps across his cheeks. "That was embarrassing."

Mick shakes his head. "Don't be. I can't begin to tell you the number of times I fell when I was learning to walk again."

"I'd like to talk with you about that sometime," Tom says.

"I'd like that, too," Mick says. "Now, we better get going before all the food's gone."

Mick leads Emma to the country kitchen where polished cutlery flanks sangria-red plates. Her artistic eye notices the hand-painted serving pieces. Swirls of sage and ochre in the gleaming stemware complement the glazed dinnerware. *Old-world style*, Emma thinks. *I love it.*

Hemingway's tail shifts into propeller mode, letting God and everyone know that Emma's arrival hasn't gone unnoticed by him.

Mick watches Emma roll her wheelchair over to give Hemingway a scratch under his bearded chin. "Hello, handsome," she says.

Hemingway stretches his neck further over the lower half of the Dutch door. "May I give him a biscuit?" she asks Niall, eyeing the clear container set out of Hemingway's reach.

"I just gave him one," Pam says.

A big softie, Niall says, "I don't suppose one more will hurt."

Mick sees Linda, and then Megan, settle into chairs next to Tom. Satisfied that he's in good hands, he turns to his fiancée and gently kisses the top of her head before they pull up to the table.

With a symphony of voices around the dining room table, some loud and enthusiastic, others muted and reserved, Pam takes the opportunity to study the siblings, Libby and Mick.

Libby's shoulder-length hair, a captivating shade of sable with a few silver strands, is tucked behind ears adorned with hammered-silver and lapis earrings. *Give a wide berth to this wise woman*, she tells herself. *If I've learned anything, it's that wisdom trumps street smarts every time. I may be a pro when it comes to surface details, but Libby's someone who understands what's going on at the heart of matters, and I'm at least smart enough to know what I don't know.*

Pam turns her head to observe Mick speaking with the newly seated Linda and Megan, next to Tom. She takes in Mick's arresting green eyes. *This is the most dangerous of all creatures*, Pam thinks. *He's a man with nothing and everything to lose.*

Although the resemblance between brother and sister is strong, Pam also notes that there are striking differences.

Unlike Libby's straight, delicate nose and flawless facial features, Mick's nose is crooked. *It must have been broken at some point.*

A thin scar creases his forehead at an angle, from his hairline down through his left eyebrow.

Both imperfections complement his square jaw and chiseled features.

Glass in hand, Pam draws closer to the others with studied casualness, her ears alert for information that she can use to her advantage later.

Behind the lower portion of the Dutch door, Hemingway watches with unveiled interest.

"Dinner's ready," Niall announces. "Please help yourselves."

Pam glances at Emma. *If she knew this was going to be her last meal, I wonder if she'd want something else. I remember reading about Hitler's last meal. One of his biographers said that the German dictator's last meal on April 30, 1945, was the day he finally realized he'd lost the war. Holed up in his bunker, Hitler ate spaghetti with "light sauce," although some biographers say he had lasagna. Hitler wanted a simple meal without any mention of Berlin's fall, so the conversation consisted of dog breeding methods and "how lipstick was made from sewer grease." Shortly after the meal, Hitler and Eva Braun, whom he had married less than forty hours earlier, went into a private room and took their own lives.*

––––––––

An adept hostess, Libby keeps the conversation pump flowing while Niall serves the meal. An author herself, she knows that part of a writer's job is reading.

Turning to Megan, she asks, "What book are you reading?" Then she sits back in catlike satisfaction as each person, in turn, shares their current book.

Niall pairs a vivid and citrusy chardonnay with dinner. After a toast to "inspiration and the flow of creativity," the group begins its meal.

Between the *oohs* and *aahs* of enthusiastic appreciation for the grilled shrimp on a bed of fat, homemade pasta noodles, steamed asparagus drizzled with lemon butter, garden-fresh organic salad, and aromatic garlic bread—homemade this morning—Libby orchestrates the conversation with ease.

"If you were stranded on a desert island," Libby asks, "and can only have *one* book with you, what would it be?"

She leans back against her chair, satisfied with the resulting avalanche of animated conversation as Pam starts them off.

"Even though it's considered an oldie, it's a goodie because it's still relevant in today's courtroom and society. It's titled, *How to Argue and Win Every Time: At Home, At Work, In Court, Everywhere, Every Day*, by Gerry Spence."

"Give us a one-sentence logline," Libby encourages.

"*How to Argue and Win Every Time* is the 'bible,'" Pam says, making air quotes with her hands, "on the laws of arguing. It reminds lawyers that we're capable of making the winning argument in any situation." She slaps the table. "I rest my case."

"I realize this is off-topic," Megan interjects, "but I have to ask. Niall, did you make the dressing? It's delicious."

"Yes," Niall says. "It's barrel-aged balsamic vinegar blended with pomegranate-infused olive oil. I'm glad you enjoy it."

Turning to Libby, Megan continues. "And I wanted to thank you for the beautiful scent you put in Thoreau cottage. I love it. Did you blend it yourself?"

Before Libby can answer, Linda and Pam chime in, thanking her for the fragrance in their cottages, too.

"I might as well admit that I like mine, too," Tom says, embarrassment painting his face.

"I'm glad you enjoy them," Libby says. "I found the infusers at a local shop that carries a variety of handblown glass. And yes, I dabble a bit with essential oils. I couldn't resist."

Linda asks, "Do we all have the same scent, or are they different?"

"I try to create a unique blend for each writer in residence based on our email or phone conversations," Libby says, shifting her gaze to Pam.

"Getting back to our original topic," Pam says, I'm interested in what the rest of you are reading. Emma, what's on your nightstand?"

"I just finished reading *Dinner with Anna Karenina*," Emma says. "I loved it!"

"And the one-sentence logline?" Libby prompts.

"Six diverse women in a book club are bonded by their love of literature."

The conversation around the table continues. With strains of Mannheim Steamroller playing softly in the background, the formalities begin to slip away. The conversation expands and contracts, voices rise and fall, and faces flush with the exhilaration of the discussion and the wine.

Libby glances at Pam, her mind nagging at the unsolved puzzle the attorney presents. *The book that Pam's currently reading sounds like the type of material the law-savvy person I spoke with on the phone when she booked her reservation at Pines & Quill would read. But in person, she's a contradiction— like two completely different people. This person's voice sounds a bit rough, gravelly, like a smoker. The person on the phone was smooth and clear. And her accent is different than when I spoke with her on the phone.*

Shaking herself from her thoughts, Libby says, "Okay, everyone, it's time to adjourn to the Ink Well. Niall and I will join you soon."

"Thank you for the exquisite meal. I'm stuffed," Tom says, patting his stomach for emphasis.

"Yes, thank you," the others chime in.

As Libby watches the writers head toward the Ink Well, she thinks, *I haven't had a chance to share my thoughts about Pam with Niall. He'll probably say that I'm overreacting, reading into things. But my gut keeps nudging me. I can't quite put my finger on it, but there's something off about Pam. She doesn't at all seem to be the same person I spoke with on the phone. But how can that possibly be?*

CHAPTER 8

"The best time for planning a book is while you're doing the dishes."

—AGATHA CHRISTIE

The living room, with floor-to-ceiling bookshelves on either side of the massive fieldstone fireplace, serves as the after-dinner gathering place for guests to continue visiting over dessert while enjoying drinks from the MacCullough's small but well-stocked bar.

With his appetite satisfied, Tom surveys the large, cozy room, enjoying its welcoming ambiance. In doing so, he notices rosy pink toenails peeking out of Linda's sandals and that her indigo sundress is a perfect foil for her shoulder-length ash brown hair.

To avoid staring at Linda, Tom picks up the trekking poles from next to his chair and makes his way over to an oak pedestal with an open book on top.

Turning to Libby, he asks, "Is this the journal I read about online?"

"Yes, it is," she says.

As Tom looks at the pages, he sees several entries; some are small and tight, while others are long and loopy.

Libby says, "We encourage guests to make entries during their stay. We have entries dating from 1980 when Pines & Quill opened its doors. This journal has become a living legacy—a way for writers to connect with those who've come before, and with those who'll come after."

"And if memory serves me correctly," Tom says, "didn't it also say that this journal has provided clues that have helped solve mysteries that occurred here?"

"That's right. And Hemingway, too," Libby says. "He's our resident Sherlock Holmes. Just last month, the journal, Hemingway, and Emma played an integral role in solving a crime."

Tom turns to Emma. "You helped to solve a crime, too?"

Emma tucks deeper into her wheelchair.

Tom notices a pink flush sweep her cheeks.

"We'll share those stories another evening," Emma says. "Right now, I'm curious to know what each of you is working on. What is your book about, Tom?"

Tom walks back to his chair and sits down, returning the trekking poles to the floor beside him. He places his palms on the khaki material where his natural and artificial limbs meet and remembers the scarring it covers.

His mind wanders back to his final patrol in Afghanistan. *The ground ruptured under my feet in an explosion of light and blood. The blast tore at my right arm and shattered my feet and legs.*

Tom swallows the swelling in his throat. "So much of life is merely grinding through. So many moments exist just to deliver us to the ones that follow. But this moment," he says, patting his legs, "was a destination in itself.

"I'll never forget what my therapist said. 'You can't fix everything. Not even close. But you can look for reasons to be grateful. More than that, you can work to create them.' That was the impetus for the book I'm writing. The working title is, *War-Torn: A Casualty's Manifesto for Peace.*"

The silence in the Ink Well all but vibrates.

As if on cue, Niall enters with a large, dessert-filled tray. "Can I interest anyone in a piece of bourbon-pecan tart with chocolate drizzle?"

Grateful for the interruption, Tom takes a dessert plate from Niall's proffered tray and jokes, "Clearly, I'm going to have to go jogging in the morning."

The group in the room chuckles. Tom has accomplished his goal; he put them at ease.

"You offer tai chi classes, right?" Linda asks Libby as she, too, accepts a calorie-laden dessert.

Megan moans as she lifts a dessert plate from the tray. "*Seigneur, aide-moi*—Lord, help me," she says.

As Emma and Mick each accept a plate from Niall, Emma turns to Megan and asks, "What's your manuscript about?

"Well, as you know," Megan says around a bite, "I'm a chef and I own La Mandarine Bleue, a French restaurant in Boise. I'm writing my first cookbook. It's titled, *One Heaping Teaspoon: Simple, Fresh, and Tasty Meals for a Busy Lifestyle.*"

"I need all the help I can get in the kitchen," Emma says. "When it hits the shelves, I'm going to snap it up."

Megan turns to Niall. "I hope you don't mind if I pick your brain while I'm here. This"—she pauses to take another bite—"is delicious."

"Maybe we could test some of your recipes," Niall says. "I love trying new creations."

"I'd like that," Megan says.

"What are you working on?" Tom asks Linda.

Linda stands and turns around so the whole group can see the back of her head. "You might have noticed that I recently had surgery." She points to the cochlear implants behind and slightly above each ear. "My book is titled *Life after Deaf: Piercing the Sound of Silence with Cochlear Implants.*"

"*Life after Deaf.* That's a *great* title," Libby says.

"Thank you." Sitting back down, Linda continues. "I'm still getting used to the implants. Even the sound of my own voice is new to me. It's still atypical. It's a bit"—she considers the right word—"*throaty,*" she explains.

Tom looks around the room. *Everyone is able—everyone except me.*

His gaze stops on Linda. *I'd love to spend time with her, but I doubt that she'd be interested in me. There's only one way to find out.*

Megan's voice cuts across his thoughts. "Linda, I think you're doing great."

"Me, too," Tom agrees.

"Thank you," Linda says, a pleased blush creeping up her cheeks. "I have a slight advantage. I'm post-lingually deaf."

At the perplexed looks on their faces, she explains. "I wasn't born deaf. I lost my hearing when I was three—after I was already speaking. That gives me a bit of a leg up."

Linda turns to Pam. "I'd love to hear what you're writing about."

"Well, you know from our conversation on the drive from the airport," Pam says, "that I'm a civil rights attorney and activist. My book's in keeping with that. It's titled, *Peaceful Turbulence: The Nonviolent Pursuit of Equality.*"

Just then, Mick's cell phone rings. As he reads the display, Tom notices his eyebrows draw together.

"Will you excuse me for a moment, please?" Mick says as he leaves the room.

As Mick steps into the kitchen, he answers. "McPherson."

"Mick, it's Joe. Toni and I are about a minute out."

"What's up, buddy?"

"I'm sorry to say that I have bad news," Joe says.

The vehicle sensor buzzes in the kitchen, notifying Mick that the cruiser's at the main gate. Mick pushes a button on the wall to give them entry.

"What bad news?" Mick asks, his forehead wrinkling.

"It's about Niall's brother, Patrick. I don't know how to tell you this," he says. "He's been killed."

The knuckles on Mick's hand protrude as he grabs onto the back of a chair. His heart accelerates as he lowers his voice. "What do you mean Patrick's been killed? When? How?"

Headlight beams wash across the kitchen walls as the patrol car pulls into the curved drive in front of the main house.

"Mick, someone has to tell Niall," Joe says. "I'd do it, but it would be better coming from someone who loves him and who loved Patrick. It would be better coming from you."

Hemingway, who's familiar with Mick's emotions, whines over the closed portion of the Dutch door.

"Actually, Mick," Joe continues, "Patrick was murdered."

Hearing the vehicle sensor, and curious as to what's keeping Mick, Niall and Libby emerge from the Ink Well doorway behind Mick. He doesn't see them.

"Why would anyone murder Paddy?" Mick asks in horrified disbelief.

"What?" Niall gasps.

Mick spins around at the anguished sound of his brother-in-law's voice.

Niall clutches his chest and cries, "Oh God, no! It can't be Paddy."

Libby envelops her husband in her arms.

Mick steps forward, his strong arms enclose them both. "I'm so very sorry."

Niall raises his head from Libby's shoulder to look at Mick.

Mick sees that the blood has drained from his brother-in-law's face, leaving a white mask. He watches as varying emotions play across Niall's face until one settles. A look of determination.

Breaking their embrace, Niall bolts for the front door.

"Paddy can't be dead," he chokes. "I just spoke with him on the phone this morning. I'm going to tell the police they've made a horrible mistake."

Hemingway peers into the room then lies down behind the lower portion of the Dutch door. His ears droop as he rests his head on top of his paws, sensing sadness in the air.

The brass knocker's strike on the door of the main house reverberates, announcing the arrival of Joe Bingham and Toni Bianco.

The sound of Niall's heart-wrenching sobs and the arrival of police bring the occupants of the Ink Well into the dining area.

Sacré bleu! Megan's hand flies to her throat at the stricken tableau in front of her.

With incredulous stares, the writers cluster around the large pine table as Niall leads two police officers into the heart of his home.

Mick addresses the group.

"The phone call I received was news that Niall's brother, Father Patrick MacCullough, has been killed. These are officers Joe Bingham and Toni Bianco."

———

Joe stands on the threshold of the room and takes in the gathering.

When he turns to Niall to offer his sympathy, he sees skin bunched around his eyes and the pained stare of disbelief. Tears shine his cheeks. "I'm so very sorry for your loss."

"I don't understand what happened," Niall says. "Paddy can't be dead. I told you, I just talked with him this morning."

"Father MacCullough was found in the confessional by one of the parishioners," Joe says. "He'd been shot six times."

Hope flashes across Niall's face. "St. Barnabas has security cameras! Did you check them?"

"Yes, we did," Joe says. "They were covered."

"Oh, my God," Niall cries. "Why would anyone want to kill Paddy?" His eyes plead for an answer.

"We don't know yet, but because the cameras were covered, we know it was planned; it was done by someone who knows what they're doing. We think it may be related to one of your guests last month, Jason Hughes. We now know that was an alias, that his real name was Alex Berndt."

Niall sinks onto a chair.

Libby lowers herself onto the floor beside Niall and takes him in her arms, rocking him back and forth as if he were a little boy.

"But he's a priest," Niall cries.

"That right," Joe says. "And your brother was on chaplaincy duty at St. Joseph's Hospital when Berndt was admitted. Father MacCullough sat with him in the ICU after he got out of emergency surgery, and he was the last person to see Hughes before he died."

Joe's partner, Toni, turns and coughs into her elbow, looking at Pam as she does.

Emma holds Mick's arm for support and stands up from her wheelchair. "I was also one of the last people to see Jason Hughes."

At seeing the shocked looks on the faces of the writers in residence, Emma looks down at her legs, then back up again. "It's a long story, but I'm just learning to walk again."

The writers gather in a cluster by the now-open Dutch door. Hemingway slips between them and goes to Niall. He offers comfort by laying his head on his lap.

———

Mick looks at his brother-in-law, and his heart breaks as he watches the play of emotions on Niall's face, emotions that Mick's all too familiar with. *I felt the same way when my partner, Sam, died. Brokenhearted, bewildered, and lost.*

———

Linda hadn't missed Toni's cough and Pam's response—an almost imperceptible nod. *I wonder what that was about?*

She continues her observation and watches Pam step over to Officer Bianco. *They don't know that I can read lips.* And though she can't see what Pam says because her back is to Linda, she sees the officer's response.

Leaning forward, Officer Bianco mouths, "Don't let that wheelchair fool you. You'd be surprised at just how capable Emma is."

As Toni straightens, she surveys the room and looks straight into Linda's hazel eyes before continuing to pan the room.

"About being one of the last people to see Father Mac-Cullough," Toni says to Emma. "We thought the same thing. Do you mind if Joe and I ask you a few more questions?"

"Not at all," Emma says.

"Before you start," Libby interjects, "will you need Niall or me anymore this evening?"

Toni looks over at Joe, her eyebrows raised in question.

"Not tonight. But Niall, as Father MacCullough's closest living relative, we need you to come to the morgue tomorrow and make a formal identification."

Mick's head snaps upright. He shoots Joe a questioning glance. "I can do that," he says.

Joe holds up his hands. "You were on the force, Mick. You know it's—"

"I *want* to do it," Niall interrupts. "I want to see my brother one last time."

Megan pulls Libby to the side. "It looks like this might take a while. Would you like me to make coffee for everyone? I don't want to make any assumptions, nor do I want to intrude."

"That's so thoughtful," Libby says gratefully. "Yes, thank you. Please make yourself at home in the kitchen."

"I know Niall has to identify his brother in the morning. I'm so sorry."

"Thank you," Libby says.

"Please let me take care of breakfast. It's the least I can do."

"Thank you. You're a godsend," Libby says, agreeing to Megan's kind offer.

Before heading upstairs with her grief-stricken husband, Libby turns to address the group. "I'm sure that under the circumstances, you'll understand there won't be any tai chi in the morning. We're reeling from the shock of this devastating news. Megan has offered to take care of breakfast. We're fortunate to have a gourmet chef in our presence. Please be here at—" She looks at Megan to fill in the time.

"Nine o'clock," Megan says.

Tom makes his way over to Officer Bingham.

"If you don't need the rest of us tonight, perhaps we should head back to our cottages."

"Yes, that would be helpful," Joe says.

Tom turns to the other writers. "Let's call it an evening and give them some space."

"I'm leaving in just a few minutes," Megan says. "But first, I'm going to make some coffee." She glances toward the two officers, then Mick and Emma.

The officers nod gratefully.

Tom pulls the front door shut behind himself, Linda, and Pam, and says, "Poor Niall. I can't believe what happened to his brother. Murdered." He shakes his head in disbelief.

"That's awful," Pam says. "Who'd kill a priest? And why? I'm heading to my cottage. I'll see you back here at nine o'clock in the morning."

With a slight wave, Pam steps off the porch and heads down the pathway.

If my heart beats any louder, Linda thinks, *Tom's going to hear it.*

Tom looks at Linda. "Normally, I'd offer to walk a woman to her door."

He motions toward his legs and continues. "But could I be bold enough to ask you to walk me to mine? I'm new at using these prosthetic legs and nearly fell on my way to dinner this evening. And I would have, too, if Mick hadn't caught me."

Linda looks into Tom's blue eyes. *Here's a man who's overcome one of the largest hurdles that life can throw at a person—the loss of limbs. I wonder how Niall's going to deal with the loss of his brother? Another enormous hurdle.*

"I'd be delighted to walk you to your door," she says.

All thoughts of telling Tom what Officer Bianco said to Pam ("Don't let that wheelchair fool you. You'd be surprised at just how capable Emma is.") fly out of Linda's mind as her heart blooms with joy.

―――――

Pam strikes out in the direction of Dickens cottage. When she's sufficiently far enough away from the main house, she turns around. In the distance, she pins Linda and Tom with her sharp gaze, their silhouettes uplit by the solar-powered walk lights along the pathway.

Intentionally veering off course, she vanishes like a shadow in the dark of night. *Who'd have thought that a dead priest would be the diversion that gives me the perfect opportunity to slip away to pick up my gun?*

Pam flashes a cold smile. *Death. Once again, you've proven to be my ally.*

CHAPTER 9

*"Ultimately, you have to sit down and start to write.
. . . It is a matter of discipline."*
—MADELEINE L'ENGLE

With Libby and Niall upstairs in their room, Tom, Linda, and Pam back at their cottages, Megan—the only writer in residence left at the main house—is busy making coffee for the small remaining group. The beguiling scent of herbs and spices from the evening's meal is a pleasant accompaniment to its smooth, rich fragrance, but it does little to assuage the intense feeling of loss in the room.

As Megan waits for the coffee to finish perking, she glances at the remaining cluster around the kitchen table: Officers Bianco and Bingham, Emma, Mick, and Hemingway under the table where he lies, head on his paws.

———

The two officers, Toni and Joe, sit next to each other across the table from Emma and Mick.

Toni notices that other than a lingering veil of fatigue, Emma's on the mend from the gunshot wound she received last month when Alex Berndt, who'd been posing as Jason Hughes, shot her in the back.

Berndt was given a single task, Toni thinks. *And now I have to clean up his mess before anyone discovers that I was the cop inside the SFPD lockup who arranged the theft of over $10 million of heroin.*

Toni looks at Emma. "Would you like to go outside for some fresh air?" Her invitation doesn't include anyone else.

"Yes," Emma says. "That would be nice. But let me grab a cup of coffee first."

"I'll get it for you," Mick says. "Do you mind if Hemingway and I tag along?"

"I'd love that," Emma says.

Damn it, Toni thinks. *I was hoping to have caused an unfortunate "accident." A fatal one.*

———

Emma wheels through the main room, out the sliding glass doors, and pulls up next to a wrought-iron patio table with chairs.

Malibu lights are evenly spaced around the patio's terra-cotta tiles and strategically placed throughout the garden.

Twilight becomes night. In the distance, she hears the ocean sough gently over now-dark sand.

Surrounded by Libby's garden, Emma knows that if it were daytime, she'd see terra-cotta pots bursting with color— scarlet geraniums in every nook and cranny, butter-yellow daffodils, narcissi in profusion with their pale outer petals and their dark orange trumpets, and multicolored million bells.

Emma watches the unmistakable shape of Hemingway circle, then settle himself near her feet.

She takes a deep calming breath, then another. *It smells so good,* she thinks, though the fragrant blend is so complex that her nose can't identify the individual scents.

———

Toni lifts a butane lighter from next to the large hurricane lamp on the table and lights the three-wick candle before extracting a pen and small notebook from her jacket pocket.

She leans forward, feigning sympathy. "You've been through so much already, and now Niall's lost his brother. I hope you don't mind revisiting your recent ordeal with Jason Hughes. It's just that the last time we spoke, you shared that your doctor believes some of your memories from being held hostage in the cave are currently suppressed and will surface at some point."

While waiting for her answer, Toni studies Emma's face in the semidarkness. Her eyes are luminescent and haunting in the firelight. Toni searches for any sign that Jason ratted her out—told Emma that she's a dirty cop.

"What would you like to know?" Emma asks.

"Please start at the beginning and tell me *everything* Mr. Hughes—who we now know was, in reality, Alexander Berndt—did and said."

Emma watches the flames on the triple-wicked candle dance in the gentle breeze; they seem to snicker at her.

Under the night sky with the scent of flowers strong and sweet—and Mick and Hemingway by her side—she swallows a sip of coffee to ease the tightness in her throat before she begins recounting her night of terror.

Megan deposits a fresh pot of coffee and the plate of remaining bourbon-pecan tarts on the pine table.

"How did you become interested in cooking?" Joe asks.

"When I was in business school in the states, I met Adrien Duprey. He'd just returned from a gap-year of backpacking around Europe. While there, he fell in love with the food and wine. Pairing wine, specifically, became an obsession with him.

When he told his parents he planned to become a sommelier instead of going to college, they almost flipped."

"I can imagine," Joe says.

"They negotiated, telling him that he'd go much further if he at least got a bachelor's degree in business. They argued, 'It doesn't matter how much you know about wine. If you don't know the business side of things, you won't succeed.' That got his attention. When he graduated, his parents gave him enough money to go back to Europe. Mine sent me a return ticket home to France. Through Adrien's eyes, I, too, fell in love with the food and wine. With me, it was more the food; with Adrien, it was always the wine. After we got married, we returned to the States so I could attend Le Cordon Bleu College of Culinary Arts in Atlanta. And the rest is history."

"So you and Adrien now own a French restaurant?" Joe asks.

"I do," Megan says. "Adrien was killed in a car accident two years ago."

"I'm so sorry," Joe says.

"Are you married, Officer Bingham?" Megan asks.

"I am indeed. To the love of my life. I don't know what I'd do if I lost Marci."

Megan takes a seat across the table from Joe. "It's a terrible thing that's happened to Niall's brother," she says.

"Yes," Joe agrees. "This family's already had enough heartache."

"What do you mean?" Megan asks.

"Five years ago, when Mick was on the force, his partner and best friend was killed. He was like a brother to Mick. For that matter, he was like another younger brother to Libby."

"So, Mick's no longer on the force?" Megan asks.

"Unfortunately, he was severely hurt in the accident and was put on indefinite medical leave. But in my opinion, he shouldn't have been. Just last month, he was instrumental in working with the police department and the FBI to save Emma."

Megan scrunches her forehead. "*Mon Dieu!* Why was the FBI involved?"

Joe leans forward. "Because the perpetrator was a serial killer who'd crossed multiple state lines."

"It sounds like you're well acquainted with the family," Megan says.

"I am," Joe says, without elaborating. "While we're waiting for Officer Bianco, Emma, and Mick to return, tell me a little bit more about yourself. I got to know last month's writers in residence pretty well."

"Do you get to know each month's writers?" Megan asks.

"No. Last month was an exception," Joe says. "I can't divulge anything that hasn't already been printed in the paper. Suffice it to say, one of the guests took Emma hostage, and he's no longer alive."

Megan takes a sharp breath. Wide-eyed, she covers her mouth with her hand. "*Sommes-nous en danger*—Are we in danger?" she asks.

CHAPTER 10

"Style means the right word. The rest matters little."
—Jules Renard

On the garden patio under the night sky, with Mick and
Hemingway by her side, Emma relays to Toni what
Jason had said and done during the time he'd held her hostage.

"It all started when Mick got a call from Libby saying
that Hemingway had just turned up and was hurt really bad."

Hemingway's tail thumps at the mention of his name.

"I told Mick to run, that I'd catch up. We'd been making tea."

———

Oh, for fuck's sake, Toni thinks. *Tea? At this rate, it'll take
all night.*

Her face masked by a courteous expression, Toni interjects. "I don't mean to interrupt your train of thought, but
what does making tea have to do with the incident?"

———

"While Mick was out looking for Cynthia," Emma says, "I remembered that the burner under the teakettle was still on, so I went back to Austen cottage to turn it off. That's when Jason"—*His name feels like glass in my mouth*, she thinks—"took me. He was on the back patio, watching me through the sliding glass door."

Emma shudders involuntarily.

"He told me that if I made a sound, he'd slit my throat. He was behind my wheelchair, pushing. I knew he was hurt because he held an arm to his chest. I didn't know where we were going, but I thought that if I left a short trail by dropping my earrings along the way . . ." Emma takes a deep breath to steady herself before continuing. "When we were on the incline, he lost control and let go of my wheelchair.

"I think I must have passed out for a moment. When I came to, Jason said, 'You happened to have landed almost on my doorstep. I'm taking your wheelchair in with me. If you want to use it again, you'll have to earn it back. Since you're only a gimp from the waist down, you can use your arms and crawl on your belly. And don't try anything clever, I'll be watching you from inside.'"

Toni bends to retrieve the pen she dropped. Candlelight flickers across exposed skin where her shirt untucks at the small of her back.

Is that a tattoo? Emma wonders. It's hard to tell in the low light. She can make out the word "First" beneath another word or symbol that's mostly covered by the hem of her shirt.

Toni straightens back up.

Emma takes another sip of her coffee and continues to retell her story. "Using his good arm, he picked up my damaged wheelchair and disappeared through an opening in the mountainside.

"I remembered playing with my brothers. They'd—"

Emma watches Toni lean back in her chair. She sees what looks like resignation on her face.

"Is something wrong?" Emma asks

"I don't understand how playing with your brothers when you were kids has anything to do with this," Toni says.

Emma sits up even straighter in her chair. She feels Mick bristle at her side. "It has everything to do with how I got inside the cave," she says. "If you want me to fast forward to the end, I can. But you asked me to start at the beginning and tell you *everything*."

"Yes, I'm sorry," Toni says apologetically. "Please continue."

Emma nods her assent. "I remembered my brothers crawling on their bellies up and down the hallway mimicking the GI Joe character on television. That's how I got into the cave.

"The blackness was smothering—like being buried alive, only above ground. I heard dripping noises, and what I thought at first was mice, but it turned out to be bats."

Emma rubs her arms with her hands and looks at Mick. He squeezes her hand to encourage her.

Emma wrinkles her nose. "I smelled Jason before my eyes grew accustomed to the dark. He'd been drinking. He had whiskey stashed in a backpack. He also had a gun and a flashlight. He held the flashlight under his chin, turned it on, and said, 'Welcome to Devil's Canyon.' That's when the bats flew out of the cave."

Reaching a hand up to her cheek, Emma says, "Every time I said something he didn't like, he hit me." The sobs come even before the tears—ugly, panting, desperate heaves that rip through her, tearing the delicate fibers that hold her together.

Mick circles Emma in his arms and holds her until her tears subside.

"Thank you, I'm okay now," Emma says into Mick's shoulder before he sits back in his chair.

Emma turns to Toni. "I'm sorry. I don't know where that came from. I thought I had it all together, but I guess not. I'm ready to continue if you are."

In her peripheral vision, Emma sees Mick clench and unclench his fists. *It makes him feel angry and helpless when something—or someone—hurts me. If Jason Hughes were still alive, Mick would kill him for what he did to me.*

"What happened next?" Toni asks.

"Jason said, 'It doesn't matter what you know because I'm going to kill you, and you'll carry my secrets with you to the grave. You're the ideal bait because I've seen how Lover Boy looks at you.'"

Emma looks at Mick, then continues. "'Once he realizes that you're gone, he's going to come looking for you, and I'm going to derive a great deal of pleasure watching him crumple as I slit your throat. You'll be the second person he cares for that I kill.'

"I asked him, 'Who was the first?'

"He said, 'His name was Sam. Poor, unfortunate bastard. He was McPherson's partner.'

"I told him that I didn't understand.

"He sneered at me and said, 'A little slow on the uptake, aren't you? Five years ago, my brother and I helped orchestrate a heist involving well over ten million dollars in heroin. The problem was, the goods were in the SFPD evidence lockup. But we had someone on the inside helping us—a dirty cop.'"

Even though it's dark, Emma thinks she sees Toni stiffen.

"Did he tell you who it was?" Toni asks.

"No, but he winked at me and said, 'Stay wary, for treachery walks among you.'"

With Mick in the lead, Emma, Toni, and Hemingway return to the kitchen where there's a lively conversation between Joe and Megan.

Mick sees Joe turn to Toni and raise his eyebrows.

She shakes her head and mouths, "Nothing new."

"If you're done for the evening," Mick says, "I think everyone will agree that it's been a long day."

Turning to Megan, Mick continues. "Thank you for everything. I hope you sleep well. If you need anything, pick up the phone on your writing desk. It'll ring straight through to the main house."

***

Tom and Linda make their way to Austen cottage slowly and carefully, both of them grateful for the smooth, well-lit pathway.

Outside the front door, Tom says, "Thank you for escorting me home."

"You're welcome," Linda says. She leans in and kisses his cheek. "The pleasure was mine." And with that, she turns and heads down the pathway, tossing over her shoulder, "Sleep well."

Dazed, Tom absently releases a trekking pole to reach up to touch the spot where a moment earlier, Linda's soft, warm, lips had been. This moment of forgetfulness lands him on his butt on the front porch.

During physical therapy and after, this is the only fall that's left him with a face-splitting grin.

For him, that little kiss turns what had only been hopes and wishes until then into something that brims with promise.

After righting himself, Tom enters the cottage. His eyes drink in the welcoming, soft hues of sage and lavender.

Having just fallen, he especially appreciates the wheelchair-friendly design with interior elements spaced for a smooth transition.

The wooden floor reflects the same warm, honeyed tones of a massive beam that runs the structure's length, parallel with the pitch of the vaulted ceiling.

He grabs a tube from his Dopp kit, takes off his prosthetic legs, gets into his wheelchair, and rolls back out onto the front porch to think, to replay this evening's events.

He draws in a deep, refreshing breath. The stillness is peaceful, a far cry from the hustle and bustle of Philadelphia. In the quiet, he hears the distant hum of a boat. He knows that Austen cottage is near Bellingham Bay, a large inlet somewhat protected by Lummi Island to the west.

Tom's mind wanders. He thinks about what his therapist said. "Every night before you go to bed, think of things that you're grateful for."

I'm grateful for my knack of connecting with people. Within minutes of meeting someone new, I can usually discover a passion of theirs. Let's see now, he muses.

Megan enjoys long bicycle rides, especially on the auto-free greenbelt that runs parallel to the Boise River.

I thoroughly enjoyed a discussion with Pam about civil rights, particularly related to the Americans with Disabilities Act—a civil rights statute that prohibits discrimination against people who have disabilities.

And with Linda, he reaches up to touch his cheek, *I discovered a shared love of old movies. After a round of verbal fisticuffs,* he laughs out loud at her tenacity, *we finally agreed that* The African Queen, The Bridge on the River Kwai, *and* Rebel Without a Cause *belong in the top ten.* "But they must be watched with popcorn," she'd insisted, getting in the last word.

After squeezing thick, white prescription cream out of the tube into his hands, Tom massages his aching stumps.

Sadness and anger wash over him when he remembers the look of devastation on Niall's face after learning that his brother is dead. Murdered.

Suddenly alert, Tom freezes. *Did a twig just snap?*

The hairs rise on his arms when he feels the gut sensation of "danger-close."

He had the same feeling in Afghanistan when he and his men made their way down a narrow footpath single file on a primary mission to interdict a "high-value" target when they were ambushed.

Tom shakes his head. *I overdid it today. Tomorrow it's the wheelchair for me.*

Linda wills her feet to slow down once she's out of Tom's sight. But her heart doesn't receive the same message.

I can't believe I kissed Tom!

The cool palms of her hands touch her burning cheeks. *But I'm glad I did.*

An eerie stillness crawls across her skin like shivers every time she pauses.

The only noise she hears is the whisper of her sandals on the pathway and the gentle whoosh of her breath.

As she approaches the front porch of Brontë, Linda remembers, *I meant to tell Tom what I saw Officer Bianco mouth to Pam*—"Don't let that wheelchair fool you. You'd be surprised at just how capable Emma is."

Everyone was oblivious to the covert looks and silent communication that Officer Bianco and Pam exchanged throughout the evening.

Everyone except me—a woman who's studied faces and read lips since I was three years old.

Located on the south end of the property, one must know where they're looking to glimpse Thoreau cottage. Even in the daytime, Megan learned that a double-take is in order because, by all appearances, it seems to have sprouted among the western red cedar woods surrounding it.

Megan remembers the summer she and Aiden visited the replica of Henry David Thoreau's cabin on Walden Pond, in Concord, Massachusetts. It was the epitome of minimalism—simple, yet full—in natural surroundings. Her cottage at Pines & Quill isn't much bigger than its namesake's cabin.

By the time Megan reaches the front porch, the day has caught up with her, and she's exhausted. *I thought that talking about Adrien would make me sad, but it felt good. And I love Niall's kitchen—it's so organized. I'd do well to take a page from his book.*

Megan falls asleep thinking about what Niall had pre-planned for breakfast in the morning.

———

God damn it! Where the hell's that fucking package?

Pam stealthily makes her way back to Dickens cottage. The lush maidenhair ferns, tree trunks, lichen, and moss collaborate to create a perfect camouflage.

From what Toni conveyed, the hit's still on. A bit more difficult without the gun, but I've got my hands. And how in the hell am I supposed to be at the main house by nine o'clock for breakfast? My evening's only begun.

CHAPTER 11

*"Put a group of characters (perhaps a pair; perhaps
even just one) in some sort of predicament and then
watch them try to work themselves free."*
—STEPHEN KING

The kitchen in the main house fills with the gentle bouquet of fresh berries as Megan preps for breakfast. She stops for a moment to breathe in the morning quiet.

A noise catches her attention. She turns to see Libby and Hemingway descend the stairs. *Libby's heading for the coffee pot as if it's a beacon, drawing her in. And what's that Hemingway's got in his mouth?* As they get closer, Megan nods her understanding. *It's a teddy bear with stuffing bleeding out of its seams. Like a child, the dog is probably comforted by it.*

"Good morning," Megan says.

Libby reaches up and touches her elflocks. "I must look a fright." As she turns to the fresh pot of coffee, she inhales deeply. "I thought I smelled heaven. May I please adopt you?"

"It might be a bit awkward," Megan says. "I think we're about the same age."

Libby looks at the clock. "It's only seven. You're here awfully early. Didn't you sleep well?"

"I slept just fine," Megan assures her. "The fresh air at Pines & Quill agrees with me. But I want to get the lay of the land. When I was snooping"—she turns, making an all-encompassing gesture to the kitchen area—"I found Niall's menu plans for this week tacked to a cork board inside the pantry door. I'm envious of his meticulously organized cabinets."

"It's not snooping when you're invited to make yourself at home," Libby says. "I'm glad you're here; thank you. And you're right, Niall dots his i's and crosses his t's in the kitchen. It's his sanctuary. He's not happy when things are unsettled; order is what makes him happy."

As she notices the dark half-circles under Libby's eyes, Megan asks, "How is Niall?" Then laying her hand on Libby's forearm, she adds, "And how are *you?*"

"I'm doing much better than he is," Libby says. "I've never seen Niall like this, not even when his parents died. Understandably, he's grieving the loss of his brother. Neither of us can wrap our heads around his death—that he was *murdered.*" Libby visibly shudders. "I think that Niall's in denial," Libby says. "But when he identifies Paddy's body this morning, I'm afraid it will become all too real. He's a gentle man, a sensitive man. This is going to rip his heart out."

"Do you think it might help give him closure?" Megan asks.

"Closure?" Libby asks. "I don't think Niall's emotional wound will ever fully heal. But if the police can find the missing piece of the puzzle—*the why*—it'll go a long way toward healing."

Megan watches Libby wipe tears away with the back of her hand. "Yes," she agrees, nodding. "That and the passage of time. When my husband died, I learned that grief isn't something we move on from; it's something we move forward with. But only after we've sat with it for a considerable amount of time."

After Libby and Hemingway go back upstairs, Megan thinks, *I know how painful it is to lose someone and how hurtful it is for the others affected by it, too. I never met Father MacCullough, but as a guest at Pines & Quill, it's heartbreaking to watch the family experience his loss. The tangible thing I can do to help ease their burden is the cooking.*

Megan looks up when she hears footsteps. "*Il est neuf heures sur le point*—it's nine o'clock on the dot," she says as Tom rolls into the kitchen with Linda and Pam. "I appreciate your punctuality."

"Before heading to our separate cottages last night," Tom says, "we agreed to meet in the circular drive at eight fifty-five in the hopes of making things easier in a difficult situation."

Pam steps closer and takes a deep whiff. "Whatever you're making, it sure smells good," she says, rubbing her hands together.

"It's Niall's recipe for berries and cream-stuffed French toast casserole." Trying to lighten the atmosphere, she holds a finger to her lips, and continues, "Shh, don't tell anyone, but I'm going to steal his recipe."

Pam winks. "Your secret's safe with me." She nods toward the half-closed Dutch door and adds, "I bet it's safe with Hemingway, too, for the price of a biscuit."

"I'm willing to wager that you're right," Megan says.

Mick and Emma arrive. "Good morning," they greet the group.

Megan sees exhaustion etched in both of their faces. *I'm sure they didn't get much sleep last night.*

"What can I help with?" Mick asks Megan.

I know from experience the importance of keeping busy, Megan thinks. "Would you pour the coffee, please?"

As Mick walks around the table, a pot of coffee in one hand, a pitcher of orange juice in the other, Megan places the piping-hot casserole on a trivet in the center.

Everyone leans in closer to admire the slices of French bread stuffed with fresh berries and cream cheese filling, covered in a custard mixture and baked until fluffy and slightly crispy on top.

"Oh. My. Blessed. *Word!*" Linda signs as she says each word with emphasis.

"I second the motion," Emma grins.

"Uh oh," Tom says to Megan. "I recognize that warning look. It's the same one my mom's given me a million times."

"Niall's notation on the recipe says, 'Because this casserole is made with tons of eggs, it has to sit for fifteen minutes to let the eggs calm down and come back together. Otherwise, it'll be sloppy when you cut into it.'"

Tom holds up his hands in feign resignation. "I assure you that my mom did a good job. I can mind my p's and q's when I *have* to," he says.

Megan doesn't miss the grin playing at the corners of Tom's mouth. *I think he's a person who smiles to cover an awkward or stressful situation. It's more common than people realize.*

"What types of berries are in it?" Linda asks.

"Let's see now," Megan says. Ticking them off her fingers, she continues. "There's blackberries, blueberries, and raspberries. Oh, and to top it off, we have lingonberry syrup."

"What's lingonberry?" Pam asks, a perplexed look on her face.

"Lingonberries are native to Scandinavia," Megan says. "In fact, they're a staple in their cuisine. The Swedes use it on *everything.* From herring to creams and sauces, to meatballs and potato pancakes. In the States, you can buy lingonberry preserves and syrups at any IKEA store."

"I love that store," Linda says.

"I do, too," Pam says.

"Shopping." Tom makes a face and rolls his eyes. "Not to change the subject, but what does lingonberry *taste* like? Not that I'm hinting about digging in or anything."

"You'll get to find out shortly," Megan says. "But if I had to make a comparison, I'd say it comes close to cranberries."

"I love cranberries," Tom says.

"Me, too," says everyone else at the table.

Megan wipes her hands on her apron and looks at the faces around the table. She's pleased that she's able to contribute. Her mouth slacks a bit. *No one helped me when I lost Adrien.*

Mick remembers how hollow he felt when he lost his partner and best friend, Sam. He thinks about his sister and how he might help her. *Libby's all about hospitality, about connection. She always makes people feel at home. If she were downstairs right now, what would she—*

A lightbulb comes on. "I know how to use the fifteen minutes the casserole needs to rest," Mick says. "I'll be right back."

Mick goes into the Ink Well and returns a moment later with a small box and book. Holding it up so that everyone can see it, he says, "This is called the Observation Deck. It's a great tool for writers; it helps to prime the writing pump. If Libby were down here, she'd have each of you draw a card."

Mick walks over to Linda, opens the box, and says, "Will you please start? The idea is that you draw a card from the deck and get a short assignment that helps jumpstart inspiration, writing, and storytelling."

Linda's hand hovers over the deck for a moment before removing a card.

"What does it say?" Mick asks.

"It says, 'Raise the Stakes.'"

Mick hands her the book. "Use the table of contents to find 'Raise the Stakes,' and then read what it means."

Next, Mick walks to Megan with the deck. "It's your turn to draw a card."

After making her choice, Megan reads the card out loud. "'Create a Sacred Space.'"

"Okay, once Linda finds her assignment," Mick says, "you can discover yours."

As Mick walks to Pam, he says, "Now, it's your turn to draw a card."

Without hesitation, Pam draws a card and reads it out loud. "'Explore the Underside.'" Before Mick can comment, she continues, "I know, I know. Look through the book and find my assignment."

Tom is the last one to draw a card. After making his selection, he reads it out loud to the group. "It says, 'Get Specific.'"

When Pam's done with the book, Tom finds the supporting page for his card and reads a brief rally against the vague and superficial, then finishes by reading an example. "'If you write that there are elephants flying in the sky, readers aren't going to believe you. But if you write that there are four hundred and twenty-five elephants in the sky, readers will sit up and take notice. They believe you.'"

Mick surveys the group around the kitchen table, cards in hand. He knows Libby would be pleased that their guests are still on task for a day of writing.

The kitchen timer's ding—the signal that the casserole's ready to eat—interrupts Pam's train of thought. *The card I drew says, "Explore the Underside."*

She hides a smirk. *If they only knew.*

CHAPTER 12

"You don't start out writing good stuff. You start out writing crap and thinking it's good stuff, and then gradually you get better at it. That's why I say one of the most valuable traits is persistence."
—OCTAVIA E. BUTLER

The main house sits on a gently sloping hill. From the upstairs master bedroom, the panoramic view of the surrounding forest usually makes Libby feel like she's in the Swiss Family Robinson treehouse. But this morning, her heart feels like it's in a vice. One side presses with sorrow for the loss of her brother-in-law; the other side seethes with anger at how it came about—murder.

Libby stands at the window, barely seeing the branches sway in the breeze through her tears. Then she walks over to Niall and touches his hand.

"I know you don't want anyone else along. But let me at least text Mick to tell him we're leaving for the medical examiner's office. I don't want him to worry."

Her hands move to his shoulders, where she gently kneads them. "He'll understand that you don't want to visit with anyone this morning. I'll let him know we're going out the back way."

"I'm sorry, Libby. I just can't face our guests right now."

"I understand," Libby says.

She sends a text to Mick's cell phone. *I'm taking Niall to identify Paddy. We're heading out the back way because he can't face company right now.*

Mick responds. *I'll come with you if it makes things easier.*

Thank you for offering. Niall just wants it to be the two of us. But will you please help me with the funeral arrangements this afternoon? I can't bear to do it by myself.

Absolutely. Just let me know when you're ready. Mick presses the "send" button, and the text leaves with a whoosh.

Thank you, Libby replies, then tucks the phone into her purse.

When she turns back to Niall, she sees tears streaming down his face. Libby grabs tissues from a box on the dressing table and hands them to him.

"Thank you," Niall chokes. He wipes his face dry, then steps into her arms where they comfort each other.

When they're ready, they head down the back stairs. Libby hears the muffled inflection of voices—rising and falling—drifting from the kitchen. Her eyes glisten. *I wish more than anything that Paddy was still alive and that we were all in the kitchen enjoying Niall's cooking while getting to know our guests.*

Linda's first bite of the breakfast casserole is heaven. Besides berries and cream cheese, hints of brown sugar, butter, and cinnamon meld in her mouth, sparking pleasant associations with childhood treats and holidays and happiness.

She looks at the others and suddenly feels ashamed to feel joy amid such sorrow.

Pam takes guarded glances around the kitchen table while listening to snippets of conversation between the *oohing* and *aahing* over the fruit and cream-stuffed French toast casserole.

In an attempt to lighten the emotional atmosphere, Tom engages Emma in a playful game of one-upmanship, comparing notes about their wheelchairs.

"The titanium in mine," Tom says, patting his chair, "was developed by NASA. It has razor-thin inverted wheels like the paraplegic basketball players use."

"Yes," Emma says, pointing down, "but look at this footplate."

"I'll grant you it's a beauty, but get a load of these push rims," Tom counters.

"They're nice," Emma says. "But look at how trim and compact mine is. It's super easy to propel and maneuver."

"I'll grant you that, but can yours do this?" Tom backs up from the table and does a little spin.

Emma joins him, popping a wheelie.

Tom's glad when the others join in by clapping their appreciation.

"We must have had the same physical therapist," Tom says. "Mine was like a drill sergeant."

"Then we *definitely* had the same one," Emma agrees. "When I asked my PT *why* I needed to know all this stuff, she told me, 'Because you need to know how to control your wheels.' 'But *why*?' I pushed. 'Because you need to know how to manage all kinds of terrain.'"

"Like when you encounter steps," Tom says. "Or potholes, or a curb. Hey, what did you get when you 'graduated'?" Tom makes air quotes around the word.

"I got a pat on the back," Emma says. "Why? What did you get?"

"I got a T-shirt that reads, 'That's how I roll.'" And the group joins their laughter.

I feel like I helped relieve the tension and lighten the emotional load, Tom thinks. *I know how heavy it can be. Soul-crushing.*

———

As Emma and Tom continue their conversation about turning and rotating in place, Pam thinks, *I can't take any more of this gimp glee club crap.*

She directs her attention to Linda and Megan instead.

"That's right; you've got it," Linda says to Megan, who's mimicking sign language symbols for the alphabet.

"So anyone who learns sign language speaks a universal language, right?" Megan asks.

"No," Linda shakes her head. "Each spoken language has its own sign language. I'm showing you, ASL—American Sign Language."

I didn't know that, Pam thinks. *I thought all sign language was the same.* She continues listening to their conversation.

"And here I thought I'd travel the globe being fluent wherever I go," Megan says.

Linda shakes her head. "And just to make it more complicated, within ASL and any other sign language system, there are dialects and 'accents.'"

"What do you mean?" Megan asks.

"For instance, you and I might sign, 'Hello everyone,'" Linda says. Then turning to Pam, she says, "While someone in the South might sign, 'Hey ya'll.'"

Pam presses her hands together. "Who knew?" she says, pretending interest.

"I know, right?" Linda says.

"Well, I'm still game to learn more if you're willing to teach me," Megan says.

"I'll make you a deal," Linda says. "I'll teach you ASL if you teach me to cook."

"You're on," Megan says.

I have carte blanche, Pam thinks. *The freedom to act as I think best as long as I take out the target.* She looks at Emma. *But the rest of this group could use a bit of thinning, too.* Her fingers lightly thrum the table as she turns to look at each of the other faces in turn: Megan, Mick, Tom, and Linda.

———

Pam notices a movement in her peripheral vision and turns her attention back to Mick. *His face looks pale and haggard. I bet it's from a sleepless night over the good padre's death.* She watches him take his cell out of his pocket, read the screen, press a few keys, then put the cell back in his pocket.

Mick's eyes meet Pam's. "How are you doing this morning?" he asks.

"I'm well, thank you," Pam says. "Breakfast was delicious. Now that I'm fueled up, I'm ready to dig into my manuscript. How about you?"

"I enjoyed breakfast, too," Mick says. He nods toward Megan. "She's a wonderful cook, as evidenced by the empty casserole dish and the fact that we all licked our plates clean."

Pam nods. Then, letting just the right amount of sadness seep into her voice, she says, "I'm sorry about what happened to your brother-in-law's brother."

"Me, too. Thank you," Mick says. Pushing away from the table, he stands up and heads toward Hemingway. "Right now, I'm going to take this big lummox for a walk."

Get in as much exercise as you can, Pam thinks. *Who knows? You might be in for a long dirt nap.*

———

Pam turns back to the faces around the table and thinks about last night's reconnoitering efforts.

Tom had been sitting in his wheelchair on the front porch of Austen cottage. In the dark, it took her a minute to figure out that he was massaging the stumps where his legs had been amputated. Pam had thought, *This is someone intimately familiar with how awful life can be, someone who carries on anyway.* Shaking her head, she thinks, *I'd off myself—punch my own ticket. He should do the same. But then, that's not my decision . . . or is it?*

Pam turns her attention to Megan. She watches the way her smile comes and goes without disrupting the laugh lines near her eyes. *She was sound asleep when I slipped into Dickens cottage last night.* Pam shakes her head slightly in disapproval. *She's much too trusting. She should know better than to leave her door unlocked.*

Pam looks at Linda. When she arrived at Brontë cottage last night, Pam peeked in the window and did a double take. Music was playing, and Linda was dancing—by herself. *Linda looked like an idiot swirling and twirling in the middle of the room.* Then Pam brings herself up short as she remembers the laser-focused way Linda interacts with others. *Nothing much gets past her.*

Pam shudders as she remembers her evening encounter with Hemingway. *It could have been bad if it hadn't been for the piece of bourbon-pecan tart that Megan wrapped and gave each of us before we left last night. Thankfully, I baby-talked that hairy mongrel into believing I'm a friend. Note to self—always carry dog treats. Better still, eliminate the threat.*

Pam turns to Emma, who's telling a story. *She's the reason I'm here. She's my target, my next hit.* Curling a lip in disdain, Pam thinks about Toni's part in this. *She's the one who dropped the ball, and I'm here to pick it up. Toni shouldn't have only killed Alex—Jason Hughes to everyone here—she should have eliminated Emma, too, while she was still in the hospital.*

I have to admit it was brilliant how Toni did it, making it look like Alex suffered a massive heart attack after surgery. And who knew that priest was going to visit him in the ICU? Maybe the good father was there to pray for Alex's soul, but I can vouch that he didn't have one.

Toni said that Alex looked into her eyes when he was dying and admitted that he told the priest about her being a dirty cop, and that when he held Emma hostage in the cave, he told her, too. That's why Emma has to be eliminated.

Pam absently rubs her palms together as she thinks. *Alex probably told the priest and Emma both where his twin brother stashed the ten million dollars' worth of heroin they stole from the SFPD evidence lockup. Alex said his brother was killed in prison before telling him the location, but I wonder if he knew all along—if he planned to keep it for himself?*

Come to think of it, Alex and Toni were tight. Maybe Toni knows more than she's letting on.

Pam pushes her plate forward and rests her arms on the kitchen table. *Right now, I'm the one tagged with disposing of Emma. The boss—Giorgio "The Bull" Gambino—can't risk Toni with the job. As "Officer Bianco," she has to stay above suspicion because he needs a mole on the inside of this "sleepy little precinct."*

Sleepy, my ass—if the FBI only knew what was about to hit this part of the Pacific Northwest. With Seattle to the south, the Canadian border a stone's throw to the north, and Bellingham Bay—a gateway to multiple islands, channels, and straits that lead to the Pacific Ocean—immediately to the west, it's the ideal location for the Gambino crime family to traffic drugs, weapons, and humans.

Pam has never met the boss personally. She's much too far down the ranks. But she was told he said, "I don't deal in crime. I deal in power. If sometimes it takes crime to achieve that, then so be it."

If I can help him achieve that, Pam thinks, *then I'll be rewarded. I've worked my way up through the ranks. I've shown myself to be capable, trustworthy, and loyal.*

Lacing her fingers together, she flexes the digits and continues her train of thought. *I'm also aware that they only chose me—this time—because of my uncanny resemblance to Pamela Williams. But I'm going to prove myself. I'm going to kill Emma and find that multimillion-dollar cache of heroin. Then I'll get noticed. And while no one is indispensable, I'm going to come as damn close to it as I possibly can.*

CHAPTER 13

"One thing that helps is to give myself permission to write badly. I tell myself that I'm going to do my five or ten pages no matter what, and that I can always tear them up the following morning if I want. I'll have lost nothing—writing and tearing up five pages would leave me no further behind than if I took the day off."

—LAWRENCE BLOCK

Joe meets Niall and Libby in the foyer of the Whatcom County Morgue on North State Street in Bellingham. *It's obvious that neither one of them slept last night*, Joe thinks.

He shows his badge at the front desk and signs them in.

The current chief medical examiner (CME), Dr. Jill Graham, conducts investigations of violent, sudden, unexpected, and suspicious deaths occurring within Whatcom County or any death where there's no doctor in attendance. The office works hand in hand with local law enforcement and functions as a repository for records, documents, and photographs generated during death investigations.

Joe shakes Libby and Niall's hands. "Thank you for coming. I'll make this as quick as I possibly can."

Niall nods.

Libby mouths, "Thank you."

Joe looks at Niall. "Before we continue, I want you to know that you can confirm your brother's identity via photographs."

"Thank you. Mick told me that would be an option. But I want to see Paddy in person one last time." Tears fill Niall's eyes. While twisting his hands, he clears his throat and continues. "To tell you the truth, I'm afraid I'm going to forget my brother's face. I want to remember it. I want to file away every detail."

Libby hands Niall a tissue, and he wipes his eyes and blows his nose.

As Joe leads the way, his shoes' rubber soles cling briefly to the floor with each step, a rhythmic whisper against the seamless, industrial flooring. After passing through two sets of heavy double doors, they turn left down a hallway and stop in front of another door; its brass plate indicates they've arrived at the autopsy suite.

Joe turns to Niall and Libby. "If you would wait here just a moment, I'll let them know we're here."

———

Joe's eyes sweep the room when he enters, taking in the tile, stainless steel, and porcelain. He shifts his focus to the corpse of a naked woman on a stainless steel postmortem table. There's an inky bloom of bruises around her neck, telling Joe that her death was personal. *It takes a long time to strangle someone— four to six minutes, at least, of staring someone in the eye while you kill them. Someone had to hate her to do that.*

He falls back on his training to distance himself from it. *Compartmentalization is the most useful skill I've ever learned.*

Joe sees Dr. Jill Graham and her assistant, Dr. William Hargrove, each in blue scrubs, shoe covers, latex gloves, and clear protective masks. Like bookends, they lean over the body between them. A surgical saw lies on an adjacent table. Dr. Graham places something covered in blood in a stainless steel organ dish on her side of the table.

Though he's been here hundreds of times, Joe's impressed with the space. Designed for the task at hand, it's completely functional. There are only two colors in the room, white and chrome. Everything is polished and smooth. Easy to clean.

Joe clears his throat to gain the medical examiners' attention.

The small woman with a professional demeanor turns. "Officer Bingham," she says, nodding. "You're right on time."

"Niall and Libby MacCullough are waiting outside the door," Joe says.

"Give me just a moment," Dr. Graham says. Turning back, she drapes the body, pulls off her gloves, drops them into a bio-hazard container, and removes her mask in one deft motion. Then she walks to a hook on the wall, removes a thigh-length white lab coat, and puts it on, covering her blood-spattered scrubs.

Dr. Hargrove does the same.

———

Niall's nostrils meet a cloying scent of blood and a faint sting of bleach. Smell—the most primitive of senses.

A feeling of dread plumes within Niall. Panic creeps up from the bottom of his lungs so that he can only breathe into the top of them, as if concrete blocks sit on his chest.

Refrigerated air gusts from ceiling vents, helping to keep his nausea at bay.

Niall focuses on a wall of floor-to-ceiling squares, each bearing a label identifying its contents.

His mouth dries. A flutter pulse starts up at the base of his throat. In the thickness of shock, Niall can't absorb his loss. Instead, his mind takes him to a fond memory and clings to it. *Christmas morning when I was seven and Paddy was ten. We had to act surprised when we opened our presents because we didn't want our parents to know that we'd snuck down after they'd gone to bed and carefully unwrapped them, discovering fishing poles and all of the gear! We had a devil of a time rewrapping them so they wouldn't catch us. Every Christmas since then, we retell the story, emphasizing the fact that we didn't have to "act" too much because we were giddy with delight!*

A gentle squeeze on his hand captures his attention. When he turns and looks into Libby's eyes, he comes back from where his mind had taken him.

His hand moves to his stomach. *I feel sick.*

Joe introduces the MacCulloughs to Dr. Jill Graham. He sees her penetrating green eyes convey genuine sympathy.

Turning to the man beside her, Jill introduces her assistant, Dr. William Hargrove, DCME—deputy chief medical examiner. Both are licensed physicians certified by the American Board of Pathology in forensic pathology.

"I'm sorry to meet you under these circumstances," Dr. Graham says to Niall and Libby. "Officer Bingham said you were coming. I have the body ready for identification."

Joe nods his silent thanks to Jill for her kindness for removing the emotional agony of pulling Patrick MacCullough's body from a refrigerated drawer. *I hate that Niall and Libby are going through this. Heaven help the son of a bitch who did this to them.*

Joe steps behind Niall and Libby as Dr. Graham walks them to a waist-high table. On it, there's a white cloth covering; the outlines indicate there's a body underneath.

The steady thrum of the ventilation system shuts off; silence engulfs the space.

Joe watches the doctor's hands lightly grasp the top edge of the sheet.

Niall shrinks away from the table. A beat of pure fear, of racing adrenalin, courses through him. He shuts his eyes tight, knowing that after today, his life will never be the same.

Niall opens his eyes when he realizes that Dr. Graham is speaking to him.

"In a moment, I'm going to expose his face," she tells him. Her voice is soft. "Please let me know when you're ready."

She takes a small step back, honoring Niall's evident emotional pain.

Niall can smell his own body, sweaty and terrified.

Bracing himself, he says, "I'm ready."

Dr. Graham pulls back the covering to just below the clavicle bones to avoid revealing the bullet-ravaged torso.

Niall gasps then sways. He feels Libby's arm tighten around him.

He nods in affirmation, tears glistening his cheeks. *Oh, my God! Paddy's shrunken and gray. His face is settled with the awful stillness of stone.*

"Yes, this is my brother," he chokes. "This is Patrick MacCullough."

"Thank you, Mr. MacCullough," Dr. Graham says. Before she can replace the sheet over Paddy's face, Niall leans over and embraces him, rocking to and fro, his shoulders heaving.

The sound of Niall's keening shatters the silence.

After a few minutes, Joe touches Niall's shoulder. "Thank you for coming to identify your brother. I know how painful this is. I'll walk you back out to the front."

"I know you're busy here, Joe," Libby says. "We'll find our way back out."

Before they leave, Niall turns to Joe and cries, "I don't understand why anyone would kill Paddy."

Joe shakes his head. "Neither do I, but we're going to find out."

Niall takes one last look. His brother lies shrunken in

death, hollowed out, deflated. An involuntary shiver slides over him.

He turns to Dr. Graham. "This isn't how it's supposed to be," Niall says. "Paddy was a good man. He should have lived a long life, followed by a peaceful death."

The doctor nods at Niall and then covers Paddy's face.

———

After the door closes behind the MacCulloughs, Dr. Graham walks to an examining table with a body her assistant is working on. Her day has only just begun.

Dr. Hargrove's closing the rib cage in preparation to sew up the long Y-shaped incision on the sternum.

Joe listens as Dr. Graham shares her findings with Dr. Hargrove, who was on vacation last week.

"I'll begin with the obvious," she says, walking the length of the body. "The victim is a female in her late twenties or early thirties. The most conspicuous identifying mark is a tattoo on the small of her back. It says 'Family First.'" She interrupts herself and turns to Joe. "This is the second one of these tattoos we've seen. I don't know, but it's possible it might have something to do with a crime family; maybe it's gang or even mafia related. Look at the table over there." She directs Joe to a stainless steel table with three sealed bags on it. "One has her clothing, one has her shoes, and one has her small personal effects."

"I don't see a purse," Joe says.

"There wasn't one. But look closely at her personal effects. Tell me if you see something odd."

Joe picks up the clear bag. Through it he sees a half-empty pack of menthol cigarettes, a Bic lighter, a stick of Dentyne gum, a tube of lipstick, and what at first glance looks like a folded brochure. He turns the bag over. "Well, I'll be damned. It's a bulletin from St. Barnabas—Father Patrick MacCullough's church."

"I thought you might find that connection interesting."
Dr. Graham continues her report. "The time of death: approximately 1700h. The cause: blunt force trauma to the back of the head, leaving a triangular laceration deep enough to mark the skull."

"Instant?" Hargrove asks.

"Not long after," Graham responds. "As I said, the laceration is deep, right against the skull. There are twenty-two more lacerations on her body. Each of them is approximately two inches long and one inch deep, ten antemortem and ten postmortem.

"There's also evidence that she was raped. The body yielded a wealth of samples: semen, saliva, and two strands of blond hair. The DNA's being processed right now. If he's in the system, we'll know who did this."

Turning to Joe, she says, "And once we know who did this, you can nail the son of a bitch." She's angry, and she doesn't care who knows it. "By the way," she says, her tone returning to normal, "Patrick MacCullough's postmortem's in the morning, about nine. Do you want to be here?"

"Yes, I do. And I have two questions: Do you mind if I take this?" He holds up the bag of personal effects. "And do you mind if I bring someone with me to the postmortem?"

"You can check out the bag at the front desk," Dr. Graham says. Then furrowing her brows. she asks, "Is this person pertinent to the case?"

"He is." Joe nods.

Turning back to the body on the table, she says over her shoulder, "Then bring him."

CHAPTER 14

"Start writing, no matter what. The water does not flow until the faucet is turned on."

—Louis L'Amour

After checking out the bag of personal effects, Joe exits the building. He takes a deep breath of fresh air, then presses a speed-dial button on his cell and lifts it to his ear. After two rings, he hears, "McPherson."

Without preamble, Joe asks, "Do you want to be present at Patrick's postmortem?

"Yes," Mick says.

"Meet me at the morgue tomorrow morning at nine."

―――――

Deep in thought, Niall is silent on the drive home. *The rest of my life will be measured in before and after. Before, when Paddy was still alive. And after, when I'll somehow have to learn to live without the person I was supposed to get a lifetime with.*

As Libby pulls into the circular drive that widens at the front door of the main house, she turns to face Niall.

He turns away and locks her out of the suffering that he wants all to himself.

After shutting off the ignition, Libby reaches for Niall, but he opens the passenger door and bolts, racing through the trees and kicking up dirt in his wake.

Grief and regret hang like weights around his heart; he seeks out pain—he wants to feel its sharp edges. Niall wants to live and breathe his loss.

———

Choking back tears, Libby stares at a thick wisteria vine that's wound its way up the drainpipe and under the eaves. Its showy, pendant clusters of pale blue-violet flowers, long since spent, leave only lush, dark-green foliage.

She remembers Mick telling her about his love-hate relationship with wisteria. He loves the thousands of blossoms hanging from the vines in spring. He hates all the work it takes to keep the behemoth from ripping the roof off the house. The tendrils can grow up to twenty-five feet in one season, and they have an affinity for snaking under and ripping off shingles and rain gutters.

Startled, Libby jumps when she hears a knock on the driver's window. When she turns, she sees Mick and lowers the window. "I was just thinking about you."

Mick's brows are wrinkled. "Where's Niall?" he asks.

"He headed through there," Libby says, pointing to a path that leads through the woods to the bluff. "But I'm worried about him being out there alone. Someone murdered Paddy. What if they want to kill his brother, too?"

"I think Paddy was killed because he was one of the last people to see Berndt alive. Someone thinks he told Paddy something he shouldn't have—a dying man's confession. I don't believe it has anything to do with Niall." Mick squeezes his sister's shoulder reassuringly through the open window.

"Niall just said goodbye to Paddy, and he needs some time alone. His heart's broken at the loss of his brother."

Libby shudders involuntarily. *I can't begin to imagine losing my brother.* "This is going to be hard, Mick. Much harder than when Niall's parents died. You expect your parents to die. You don't expect your sibling to die. You especially don't expect him to be murdered."

————

Mick takes a deep breath and looks up. He sees contrails crisscross the vast topaz-blue sky like a tic-tac-toe game.

After collecting himself, he opens the driver's door. "You head into the house. I'll put the car away and join you shortly. I promised to help you with the funeral arrangements."

"Where are our guests?" Libby asks. "I'd prefer not to run into anyone just now."

"After breakfast, they went back to their cottages to write. Megan wanted to clean the kitchen, but I hogtied her. She's feisty. She reminds me of you. I sent her—kicking and screaming—to Thoreau cottage to work on her cookbook. Emma and I took care of the cleanup."

"Thank you, Mick. Give me a few minutes to catch my breath."

Unfolding from the car, Libby takes a deep breath of fresh air. Mick watches as she tosses back her hair and straightens her shoulders. *She's bracing herself for what comes next*, he thinks.

She walks across the drive, up the steps, and into the main house. Mick knows her well. Already this morning, they'd both given the killer's motivation a lot of mental airtime mulling over the variables.

He knows, too, that the only conclusion that makes any sense leads back to Paddy sitting with Alex Berndt in the ICU, with Paddy being one of the last people to see Berndt—aka Jason Hughes—alive.

A restless energy rolls off Mick after he parks the car in the garage, so he heads over to his workshop. The familiar smell of wood shavings soothes him when he steps through the door.

After the accident, when his partner and best friend, Sam, was killed and Mick was recovering, the only parts of him that worked for a while were his arms and hands. His surgeon suggested that he take up whittling as a way to work through his frustration and anger.

Mick pats the outline of his pants pocket, where he always carries his Deejo wood knife in the event he has time on his hands.

He remembers the first time that Emma saw his whale fluke pendant and admired it, saying, "The craftsmanship is beautiful." That's when he'd told her about his whittling hobby.

"This goes way beyond whittling," Emma had said. "This is a gorgeous piece of jewelry. You're an artist. You could open a shop and sell these."

"Actually," he'd admitted, "there's a store in town that carries my pendants. They carry my walking sticks, too. It's called Hyde and Seek."

"Walking sticks? You mean like the ones with gnarly faces at the top?" she'd asked.

"Yes, that's the kind. Wood spirits, sorcerers, hobbits, and elves. That type of thing."

Thinking about Emma lifts Mick's spirits. *My soul breathes her in like air.* He's pleased with the ample space he cleared for her potter's wheel and other supplies that two of Emma's three brothers, Eric and Ellery, are driving up from her studio in San Diego. They'd texted last night when they reached the halfway point. He couldn't turn them around, not when they'd come that far.

Mick looks around the cleared space. *I never dreamed I'd fall in love again. I never dreamed I'd be with a woman who seizes the day with the same level of competence and gusto she had before transverse myelitis put her life on hold.*

He mentally amends that thought and laughs. *Emma's life isn't on hold. In fact, life is running just to keep up with her!*

In Austen cottage, Tom admires the battered, square oak desk with ample clearance space for his wheelchair. It faces sliding glass doors that reveal a smooth-tiled patio of faded terra-cotta. Outside the doors, a wild profusion of potted flowers greets him. *Even with this gorgeous view, I can't think of anything to write. My mind keeps going back to Niall's brother—a priest—being murdered. Why?*

He leans against the wheelchair's back and shifts his gaze to the vaulted ceiling's honeyed tones. *Come on, buddy, you can do this.*

His eyes roam the room, appreciating the muted hues of the sage and lavender color palette surrounding him. *This is the perfect place to complete my manuscript. And if I can do that, then maybe I can fulfill my lifelong dream of opening a soccer camp.* Looking down at the empty leg holes in his shorts, he mentally adds, *Only this soccer camp will be for kids who've lost limbs. Then maybe, just maybe, I'll have a purpose—a reason to live.*

Tom rolls over to his guitar case. He grabs it up and wheels out the front door. His guitar never fails to inspire, so he sits on the front porch and fingers the strings. His voice, low and mellow, carries softly in the breeze. He knows he should be working on his manuscript, *War-Torn: A Casualty's Manifesto for Peace,* but he's well aware that inspiration through music is his best first step.

He cocks his head. At first, he hears a bit of common chirping like that of sparrows and such. Then they're joined by an accompaniment of warbles and peeping that becomes a symphony of music, a supporting choir sounding from the bushes and trees. He can't help but smile.

———

Before starting on her manuscript, Megan sits and soaks up the joy she feels after cooking for everyone this morning.

Surrounded by Thoreau's minimalist beauty, Megan looks through the south-facing wall of glass and drinks in the Bellingham Bay National Park and Reserve's breathtaking view, home to *El Cañón del Diablo*—the Devil's Canyon, so named because of the boulder field at the bottom of a hundred-foot rock wall.

Next, Megan takes in her surroundings. Before coming here, she'd read online that Libby commissioned the furniture pieces from a local woodworker. Each creation is polished to accentuate its natural character and beauty. The Pines & Quill website said that when Libby envisioned Thoreau's interior, she wanted to convey the idea that "less is more." It described the space as: "Elegant in its simplicity; inessentials are trimmed away, leaving functionality."

Megan exhales deeply. *I'm glad I was able to assist Niall and Libby during this tragedy. I hope they'll let me help in the kitchen again.* Satisfied that she's done her best, she pulls out her laptop and brings up her manuscript, *One Heaping Teaspoon: Simple, Fresh, and Tasty Meals for a Busy Lifestyle.*

———

When Linda arrives at Brontë cottage after breakfast, her eyes feast on the gem-toned palette in the beautiful space. She gravitates toward a cozy window seat with a thick, inviting cushion and matching throw pillows of emerald, ruby, and sapphire.

She shakes her head. Instead of indulging herself in the cozy space right now, she turns and climbs the wrought-iron spiral staircase to the sleeping loft—a haven that strikes the ideal balance between Parisian chic and relaxed bohemian romance.

Linda changes from a casual dress into cropped pants and a short-sleeved tee, much better for bicycling. And that's precisely what she intends to do. Not only to burn calories—*my gosh, that breakfast was delicious*—but fresh air always has a way of opening her mind and clearing the cobwebs.

She takes her camera from its bag and loops the strap around her neck. Looking through the lens, she thinks, *And this never fails to unleash my creative muse.*

The notecard on the kitchen counter says that town is just a few minutes' bike ride from Pines & Quill. As she walks to the bicycle corral between the main house and the garden, a squirrel crosses the path in front of her. He glances her way with jet-black eyes before scurrying into the foliage.

Linda stops. She perceives music at the edge of her hearing. It's whisper faint, but she hears it dotting the otherwise landscape of quiet. *Is that singing?* She shakes her head; *there must be something wrong with my cochlear implants.* She reaches her hands up to the area above and behind each ear. *I still hear it.*

Forgetting the bicycle corral, she follows the sound on a sun-dappled path that heads west—a path that leads directly to Austen cottage—to Tom Gordon.

When Pam arrives at Dickens cottage, she bypasses the overstuffed brown leather chair and ottoman with nailhead trim and heads straight to the large, smooth, walnut desk placed beneath a north-facing window. The Pines & Quill website described it as, "An invitation to survey the cool, quiet woods—Mother Nature's Sanctuary." *What a crock!*

Pam hunkers down to study *Peaceful Turbulence: The Nonviolent Pursuit of Equality.* Arching her back, she thinks, *Not that I believe any of this bullshit, but because I need to speak about it with ease when I sit with those wannabe writers to discuss our works in progress after dinner.*

Her eyes wander up toward the sleeping loft. Her thoughts drift. *My life has expanded from penny-ante, to significant, to someone to contend with—to fear.* She smiles a genuine smile, her first in a long while.

The scent of mandarin oranges, pomegranates, and cinnamon vie for her attention. *Designed for comfort*, she remembers Libby saying. *The only people who are going to need comfort are those who love Emma.*

Scrolling to the next page of the manuscript, she notes the title at the top. "Peaceful Turbulence." She barks out a laugh. *There's no such thing.*

Leaning back in her chair, Pam remembers a court-ordered therapy session from long before the first time she changed her identity. She'd followed the therapist home. After killing him, Pam riffled through his briefcase. Opening her file, she read his barely legible scrawl.

A psychopath is a human predator who wears a mask of sanity, an aggressor who preys on others merely for the pleasure of it. I wonder if there's a normal person lurking inside her? The two sides of a person's character are often in conflict—good and evil. And evil often wins.

She left his home thinking, *Often wins? Not on my watch. I'm better than that. I always win.*

CHAPTER 15

"I had learned already never to empty the well of my writing, but always to stop when there was still something there in the deep part of the well, and let it refill at night from the springs that fed it."
—ERNEST HEMINGWAY

Mick does his best thinking outside in nature. On his way to the main house—his mind jumbled with thoughts about Paddy's murder like a knotted skein of yarn—he pauses to look up at the sky. A gull cruises overhead, brilliant white against the blue expanse.

Mick takes a deep breath. He's determined to unravel his thoughts methodically, one knot at a time. Sitting on a boulder under a tall pine, he starts to make a mental list. *You know the drill, Mick. Get back to basics, and take it one step at a time. Walk yourself through motive, means, and opportunity.*

The reason someone commits a crime is the motive. The most pressing motives for killing include revenge, greed, envy, fear, sex/lust, and power. Who had a reason for killing Paddy?

As the chaplain on duty at St. Joseph Hospital, he was one of the last people to see Alex Berndt alive. Maybe someone's afraid that Berndt confessed something to Paddy before he died.

The ability of someone to commit a crime is the means. Someone shot Paddy six times, so we know the means was a gun. But the weapon hasn't been found yet. And someone put socks over the security cameras, so we know the murder was premeditated.

The chance or availability of resources for the crime to be committed is the opportunity. The killing took place inside the confessional booth. Who had access to the scene? The entire congregation had opportunity, yet there aren't any witnesses. Mick shakes his head.

Whoever planned this was clever, like a mother rabbit hiding her babies in plain sight. It usually works, but not this time. I'm going to keep investigating until I find Paddy's killer.

———————

Libby finds the view from the second-story window of the master bedroom to be like a soothing balm. The ping of her cell phone draws her attention away from the hypnotic branches swaying gently in the soft breeze. Retrieving the phone from her purse, she reads a text from Megan.

I don't mean to intrude, but I'm wondering if I could please use the kitchen in the main house to test one of my recipes. This morning I noticed that you have almost all the ingredients. I'd love to try this dish on the other guests for dinner this evening.

Libby knows that this is Megan's way of helping them to carry their emotional burden. She responds, *Yes, please. That would be lovely. Thank you.* She presses "send" and hears the whooshing sound of the text take flight.

Moments later, Megan responds. *I'm going to make a quick run into town on a bicycle for a few remaining ingredients. I'll drop them off on my way back and then come to the main house at three o'clock to begin preparations.*

Libby answers. *Mick can easily drive you into town.*
That won't be necessary, Megan responds. *But thank you.*
I'm looking forward to the fresh air and the ride. See you at three.
Libby's surprised when her phone pings again. The text
is from Mick. *I'm in the kitchen, ready to start when you are.*
Take your time.

Libby holds the heel of her palm against her chest. *I dread*
the thought of making funeral arrangements, but Niall's too emo-
tionally raw right now. With Mick's help, I can get through this.

———————

In the kitchen of the main house, sunshine slants in through
the blinds and the overhead fans whir. Mick turns on the
burner under the water kettle and sets out the makings for two
pour-overs. Snagging a biscuit from the jar by the Dutch door,
he lets a tail-wagging Hemingway join him in the kitchen. The
dog's large wet nose nuzzles Mick's hand. His soulful eyes
seem to ask, "What's wrong? Is everything okay?"

Mick scratches behind Hemingway's ears. He doesn't
answer Hemingway's unspoken questions, but revisits two of
his own. *Who wanted Paddy dead? Equally important, why?*
I don't have the answers, but I intend to find out.

Mick knows that time is of the essence with premeditated
homicides. What's learned—or not learned—within the first
forty-eight hours is crucial to the outcome of catching the
killer—or not.

Mick thrums his fingers on the counter. *In premeditated*
murder cases, the killer is driven by a motive. A purpose exists
behind Paddy's murder. If I find that reason, that motivation,
I'll be more than halfway to an arrest—if only I were still on
the force. The misery of that knowledge swells inside him like
a black balloon.

When the kettle whistles, Mick pours the water over the
ground coffee in a slow, swirling motion. The grounds bloom

in a puff; then, the water drips through the filters into each mug. He takes a seat at the enormous pine table to wait for Libby.

Hemingway settles under the table at his feet.

When Mick realizes that he's rubbing his leg, he takes a deep breath and slowly lets it out. He remembers what his therapist said. "You can use this habit as a 'tell' that you're worried, stressing, or possibly even getting angry. Leverage it to your advantage. Don't sidestep the issue; use it to tackle the problem head on."

In his mind's eye, Mick sees his partner, Sam, slumped over their cruiser's steering wheel with a bullet hole between unseeing eyes. *If the day's coin flip had come up tails, I would have been the driver. Not Sam. I'd be dead. Not Sam.*

Guilt chokes him. He's all too familiar with the knowledge that guilt can corrode a life right down to the bones.

Mick's mind wanders back in time. He doesn't remember being life-flighted to the hospital. They told him afterward that he almost died during transport. The surgery that saved his life is a total blank. It left him with a limp, survivor's guilt, and the shame of not attending his best friend's funeral because Mick was in the ICU.

The bitter yet invitingly warm aroma of coffee fills the atmosphere and pierces Mick's thoughts. He looks up to see Libby pull out a chair across from him.

Under the table, Hemingway raises an ear and an eyebrow simultaneously, then settles back down when he realizes that no more treats are forthcoming.

Libby sets paper, pens, and the thick sangria-red coffee mugs that Mick had started on the table in front of each of them.

Lifting the warm cup to his mouth, Mick takes a sip. He closes his eyes and savors the taste. This blend has a crisp, bright flavor, with subtle hints of citrus and rich chocolates. It reminds him of his weekly visit with Paddy at Magdalena's Creperie. Paddy always ordered the same thing: *affogato al caffe*—vanilla ice cream "drowned" in espresso. "The only thing that could make it any better," he'd say, "is a wee bit o' whiskey."

Libby blows across the surface of her drink, then takes a tentative sip. "You make a good cup of coffee," she says.

Mick sees a faint mist of steam on Libby's nose. "Thanks," he says. "But, I don't know much about making funeral arrangements. It might be easier if we divide and conquer."

Libby nods in agreement.

Mick pulls his cell phone from his back pocket. "I'll call Mom and Dad to see if they've made flight arrangements yet. Their hearts broke when they heard about Paddy. They loved Niall's brother."

He watches as Libby starts a list. She writes, "Connor and Maeve McPherson."

"And I'll call Ian," she says. "He texted that Fiona's coming with him. They're going to drive." She adds their names to the list.

Mick wishes he could see Libby and Niall's son, Ian—his newly engaged nephew—and his fiancée, Fiona, under different circumstances. "Where will everyone stay?" he asks. "All of the cottages are filled with guests."

"Mom and Dad can stay in our guest room. Would you mind if Ian and Fiona stay in the spare room in your cabin?"

"I don't mind, and I know Emma won't, either. I'll call Father Burke at St. Barnabas and make the arrangements there. I expect that just about everyone in the parish will attend."

Reaching down to rough the wiry hair on Hemingway's head, Libby says, "I'll call the florist."

Mick looks down at the pen and notepad on the table in front of him. *I can't believe we're making funeral arrangements for one of the most lively, robust people I know. Why was Paddy killed? Who killed him? Once I figure out the why, it will lead me to the who.*

An hour later, Mick says, "Libby, now that we've each got our marching orders, I'm going to take this big galoot with me to go check on Niall."

"Thank you, Mick. I'll let you know when I've finished with my list," Libby says.

"And I'll do the same," Mick says. "Come on, Hemingway, let's go."

***

Mick and Hemingway follow a path through a wood of Sitka spruce to the bluff; it's the path Libby said Niall took when they got home from the morgue. "Help me find Niall, Hemingway."

Just before they reach the clearing, Hemingway bolts ahead; he finds Niall sitting on the ground, head in hands, with his back against a tree. The dog nudges Niall softly with his wet nose.

Niall looks up. "Well, hello there, buddy," he says to Hemingway. His voice is thick and raw from tears.

Hemingway settles himself against Niall's legs. Sensing his sadness, Hemingway lifts his head and licks Niall's chin.

Petting the dog's big head, Niall says, "What are you doing here?"

Catching up, Mick sees that Niall's eyes are red and swollen. *It's like the light's gone out of them. That look—I know it well. I saw it in the mirror for years.* "He's with me," Mick says. "May I join you?"

Stroking the big dog's head, he says, "I'm not good company right now, Mick."

"I understand."

Mick sits on the ground with his back against the other side of the tree. He hears Niall crying, followed by the muffled sound of Niall's voice talking to Hemingway.

In his mind's eye, Mick pictures Niall with his arms around the big dog's neck, his face buried in his wiry coat.

One of the best therapies known to humanity. That, and the soothing balm of nature, and the quiet presence of a friend.

Mick hears Niall inhale deeply. He, too, fills his lungs with the fresh sea breeze that's wafting up from the bay.

By late afternoon, the sun has drained from the sky. As Mick nears the circular drive of the main house, his steps quicken when he hears Emma's laughter. Rounding the bend, he sees three people standing in front of a dark blue pickup truck. Emma's wrapped in a bear hug by one man, and another man's waiting for his turn.

They must be Eric and Ellery, Mick thinks, two of Emma's brothers. *They've brought her potter's wheel and supplies from her studio in San Diego.*

Not wanting to interrupt their happy reunion, Mick hangs back and watches obvious delight play over Emma's face.

When she spots him, she waves him over enthusiastically, saying, "Mick, I want you to meet my brothers."

Eric, the oldest sibling, steps forward and takes Mick's hand.

Mick notes that his hand is warm and encompassing, his fingers confident in their grasp.

"It's good to meet you," Eric says. "We've heard a lot about you."

Then it's Ellery's turn. He takes Mick's hand in a firm grip, saying, "Don't worry, it's all good."

"It's nice to meet you, too," Mick says.

"Emma told us what happened," Ellery says. "We're sorry for your loss. We're only staying the night; then we head back in the morning because we've both got to get back to work. Ethan would have come too, but he has the kids this week."

"Thank you so much for bringing my stuff up, guys. I appreciate it," Emma says.

"Anything for you, squirt," Eric says.

Mick looks at Emma, eyebrows raised. "Squirt?"

"Don't you dare," she warns him playfully.

Mick holds up his hands. "I know a death glare when I see one." He nods toward Eric and Ellery. "I'll leave that nickname for your brothers to use at their own peril."

Emma says, "Now, watch how gracefully I change the subject." She points to the workshop, saying, "That's where the wheel and supplies need to go."

"I'll help you unload," Mick says, "then show you to the guest room in our cabin. Dinner will be ready soon."

Emma steps next to Mick, and he wraps his arm around her waist.

"Niall answered the gate buzzer when they arrived," Emma says, "then called me. They've set two more plates."

"Come on, Ellery," Eric says. "Let's unload the truck then get cleaned up for dinner. I'm starving."

"You're always starving," Emma says. "And trust me, you're going to love dinner!"

Mick and Ellery stand behind the truck on either side so Eric can see them in the side mirrors. They direct him as he backs up to the large garage-type door on the front of the workshop.

As Eric lowers the tailgate, Mick looks at Emma. Her hands press to her chest in excitement, and there's a grin on her face.

Mick's heart does a summersault.

Her pulse pounding with excitement and camouflaged by the thick trees and surrounding foliage, Pam watches and listens to the family reunion. She reaches behind her and touches the tattoo on her lower back ("Family First"), then uses the camera on her silenced cell phone to photograph the dark blue truck's license plate. *Just in case I need to widen my reach.*

CHAPTER 16

"*Cheat your landlord if you can and must, but do not try to shortchange the Muse. It cannot be done. You can't fake quality any more than you can fake a good meal.*"

—WILLIAM S. BURROUGHS

Megan measures, stirs, and spices, filling the kitchen in the main house with a riot of scent. Tonight's menu is a light hors d'oeuvre of baked brie with ripe melon and berries, followed by a salad of organic greens, black olives, egg, tomatoes, and bell peppers—tossed in a mixture of olive oil and aged pomegranate balsamic vinegar. The main course is mushroom and goat cheese stuffed chicken breasts. And the wine is Viognier, an apricot and peach-scented white, which also pairs well with the dessert, chocolate macaroons.

Niall follows his nose to the kitchen. "May I be your sous chef this evening?" he asks.

Megan sees that he's been crying. She wipes her hands on her apron. "*Je serais ravi d'être à toi*—I'd be delighted to be yours."

Niall gets an apron from the cupboard. After pulling it over his head, he reaches behind and ties the back. "I'm not fit to be head chef tonight." His smile is bruised. "But I'll make a great second-in-command. Please tell me what I can do to help."

The need to work is evident in Niall's naked eyes. Megan understands this all too well. She assigns him a list of things to do, and he begins. She watches as the soothing rhythm of stir this and add that—the normalcy of the tasks at hand—help to ease the pain that's crushing him.

———

Megan notices that even if it's a little subdued throughout dinner, the conversation among the writers seated at the huge pine table flows. They discuss their day's writing wins and challenges, sharing suggestions on how to conquer this obstacle or that bump in the writing road. "Have you tried this? It often works for me." Or, "That method is a sure-fire winner."

The family resemblance between Emma and her brothers, Eric and Ellery, isn't lost on Megan. She watches as they close their eyes when they chew, savoring every bite—the way Emma does. *I love it when people enjoy their food.*

As they adjourn to the Ink Well after dinner, Megan stays back to help clear the table and clean up. She's met with a wall of steely resolve.

"Absolutely not," Niall says.

"And we refunded your retreat fee," Libby says, brooking no argument.

Megan knows full well that she can't win this battle. After thanking Niall and Libby, she joins the others in the Ink Well just as they finish drawing cards from the Observation Deck.

"You're right on time," Emma says, patting the seat next to her.

"It's your turn to draw," Mick says, stepping up with the open box.

Megan pulls a card from the deck and reads it out loud. "Zoom In and Out."

She turns to the supporting page in the book and reads how novelist Amy Tan begins with a single image—like a pair of chopsticks joined by a silver chain. Using her mind as a camera, Tan pulls back from the chopsticks to take in the larger picture—she sees the table on which the chopsticks lie, the dimly lit room in which the table sits, the different people moving around in the room.

"Tan says, 'I focus on a specific image, and that image takes me into a scene. Then I begin to see the scene, and I ask myself, "What's to your right? What's to your left?" And I open up into the fictional world.'"

When she lifts her gaze from the page, Megan wonders why Pam is staring so intently at Emma.

"Will you take Hemingway with you tonight?" Libby asks Mick as he leaves for the cabin where Emma and her brothers have already gone.

Looking toward the stairs to their master bedroom, Libby continues, "Niall's hurting so bad; the last thing he needs is Hemingway nosing him to go out in the dead of night."

Mick taps his thigh. "Come on, Buddy, let's go find Emma."

Hemingway prances back and forth, left to right, at the prospect of being with Emma. His tail whips back and forth.

"I know, Buddy. Me too." Mick hugs his sister to his chest. "You know I love you, right?"

"Yes," she says into his shoulder, "And I love you, too." Pulling back so she can see his face, Libby blinks back tears. "Don't you dare die on me, Sean Braden McPherson. I couldn't bear it."

"I won't," he says. "And if you'd be kind enough to return the favor Elizabeth Ann McPherson-MacCullough, I'd really appreciate it."

Hemingway nudges the pair with his anvil-sized head, wanting attention too.

"Oh, go on, you big lugs," Libby says, shooing them both away. "It's time for bed."

———

Mick hears the muted crash of distant surf as he and Hemingway walk toward the cabin. He turns his attention skyward and sees breaks in the cloud cover where a jet-black night sky peeks through, salted with stars.

He pauses to throw a stick for Hemingway. Looking over his shoulder, he watches the lights go out in the main house—first, the ground level, and shortly after, the second level.

Mick's delighted when Emma meets them on their way. "Eric and Ellery have already crashed for the night. They're getting up early to head back to San Diego."

They walk hand in hand, watching Hemingway. He cocks his leg against a moss-covered tree stump, then proceeds to water every fallen pine needle and cone the rest of the way to their cabin.

"He can't possibly have to go again this evening," Emma says. "If he were a gas tank, the needle would be on empty."

Looking to Hemingway, Mick says, "Clearly, Emma doesn't know you do more than pee in the woods—you're a mighty hunter who loves to stalk his prey at night."

"Hunter?" Emma says, laughing. "I've seen him frolicking with butterflies!"

"Don't worry. *I'll* be the one he cold-noses in the middle of the night. We'll make our rounds without disturbing a hair on your head."

———

They enter the cabin quietly, knowing that Eric and Ellery need to sleep soundly before they get up at sunrise and drive back to San Diego.

"I'm so glad my brothers brought my potter's wheel," Emma whispers. "Thank you for clearing space for it in the workshop."

Mick bows his head and wraps his arm around her waist, pulling her closer to him. As his lips touch hers, Emma closes her eyes, tilts her head back, and puts her arms around his neck. An electric warmth courses through her. As she relaxes into the kiss, Mick envelops her with both arms, wrapping her in his warm embrace.

Emma feels Mick's need against her pelvis. "Me, too," she says, "but not with my brothers in the next room." Standing on her tiptoes, she cups Mick's ear with her hands. "But I guarantee that the moment they're out the front gate in the morning, I'll have my way with you."

"Promise?" he asks.

She nuzzles his chin. "Promise," she says, as she leads him to their bedroom.

Hemingway watches two of his favorite people change their clothes and get into bed. He pads over to Mick's side and stares into his eyes.

"Lay down, Hemingway. It's time to go to sleep."

Hemingway gives Mick the cold shoulder and goes over to Emma's side of the bed.

"Hello, handsome," she coos as she reaches out to scratch under one of his ears.

Satisfied, Hemingway circles and circles the floor and then lies down. He thrusts out his legs in a long, luxurious stretch before burrowing his nose between his paws and settling in.

"You shouldn't have done that," Mick says.

"Why?" Emma asks.

"Because now you're his night buddy."

"You mean—"

"Yep," Mick says. "*You're* the one he's going to cold-nose in the middle of the night." He chuckles as he turns out the light in their bedroom.

Fully dressed, Pam extinguishes the lights in Dickens cottage. *There's no point in going to bed when I have to get up again to retrieve the package that Vito's leaving at midnight.*

On the phone this afternoon, Toni assured her that she warned Vito about the driveway sensor. "He knows to park a quarter of a mile back and walk up to stash the package," she said. "And I was clear that he leave it in the bushes by the stone column on the left side as he approaches the entrance gate to Pines & Quill."

That asshole probably doesn't know his left hand from his right, Pam thinks. *If he screws this up, I'll take great pleasure in cutting them off.*

CHAPTER 17

*"Remember: Plot is no more than footprints left in
the snow after your characters have run by on their
way to incredible destinations."*

—RAY BRADBURY

"Really?" Mick's whispered voice asks Hemingway.
Cracking one eyelid, he turns toward the nightstand
and sees that it's 11:45 p.m. "You're kidding, right?"

Hemingway's wet-nosed, tail-wagging greeting tells him
that he's in earnest.

Mick looks at Emma's sleeping face, bathed in moonlight,
and gently strokes her cheek.

"All right, already," Mick whispers to an increasingly
adamant Hemingway. "Let me pull some clothes on."

Mick slips out of bed quietly, careful not to wake Emma.

———

It's full-on night in the Pacific Northwest, the temperature
has fallen, and thick fog lies like a pall over Pines & Quill.

Its mass is dense. The air struggles to carry its moist weight. Mick's breath steams when he exhales. Walking toward the woods, he looks up at the sky. "You wouldn't know it, Hemingway, but a white moon is buried somewhere behind the fog and clouds."

Not caring about Mick's celestial thoughts, Hemingway runs several feet ahead, leaping with strength and grace over shrubbery. He's preoccupied with the scent of whatever or whoever recently trampled the ground. The dog lifts his head into the faint breeze, sniffs the air, and continues.

Mick sees the last of Hemingway's tail on the path up ahead as the ground-breathed mist swallows him whole. Similar to using high beams in fog, Mick's flashlight makes the visibility worse. He turns it off and follows the trail under the canopy of trees where the forest's litter fall—twigs, seeds, needles—crunches under his feet.

Hugging trees, Pam edges through the cover of darkness toward the entrance gate, intent on retrieving the package as soon after the drop-off as possible. The smell of the damp earth rising in the mist assails her nostrils. The fog of her breath streams out of her mouth, billowing over her nose and cheeks.

Twigs snap, and she freezes. She hears footfalls. Peering around the tree, she can barely make out Mick and that damned dog through the fog heading toward the main entrance gate.

That means Emma's alone. A thin-lipped smile slithers across Pam's face. *Change in plans.* Pam waits until Mick and Hemingway are completely out of sight, then turns around. *I don't know why Toni insists I use a gun. They're great for a distance kill, but I have no problem working up close and personal.*

Vito cuts the headlamps on his tricked-out old black Chevy pickup truck. In his spare time, his head is either under the hood or polishing it. In the rearview mirror, he sees Smith—one of his two Dobermans—pacing back and forth in the bed of the truck. He left Wesson on guard at the wrecking yard.

In the distance, strategically placed uplighting illuminates a massive wrought-iron entry gate. Through the fog, Vito can just make out the overhead sign, WELCOME TO PINES & QUILL.

It triggers childhood memories of the Ponderosa Ranch on *Bonanza* reruns. "You look like Hoss Cartright," his dad told Vito. His brothers teased him. The memory makes him angry. *They didn't think it was so funny when I forced them to play cowboys.* He was the youngest, and they weren't interested. Like Hoss, he was also the biggest and the strongest. Vito runs a hand over his bald head. *It was easy to get my way, even against all three of them.*

Vito cuts the engine on the truck and then removes a clear Tyvek pouch from the glove box and gets out. When he lets down the tailgate, Smith jumps to the ground and runs ahead along the drive. As they reach the entrance gate, Vito walks to the stone column on the left, parts the surrounding bushes in front of it, then tucks the pouch inside the shrubbery as Toni had instructed. "When you're done, leave it looking exactly like you found it," she'd warned. Vito carefully smooths the fronds back together. Smith walks to the column on the right and lifts his leg, liberally marking it as his territory.

Hemingway stops abruptly and lifts his head to sniff the air. The hair on his back morphs into a ridge. He bares his teeth. A rumble comes from deep within his chest.

"What is it, boy?"

Ignoring Mick, Hemingway charges toward the massive, wrought-iron entrance gate at the front of the property. The fog is thick, but Mick knows without seeing him that when Hemingway's running full tilt, his stride and powerful drive eat up the ground. Mick bolts to catch up.

The closed gate isn't a problem for the large dog; he clears it in a single bound and keeps pounding forward.

Smith turns around and stands stock still. A small ridge forms down his spine. His eyes go sharp as onyx.

And though Vito can't see clearly through the fog, a bad feeling, heavy as a stone, hits the pit of his stomach. His mouth fills with the sour taste of fear. Turning to run, he shouts, "Smith, come. *Now!*"

Both man and dog race pell-mell for the truck. The dog outdistances the man.

Close by, Vito sees a gray mass streak past him. He watches in horror as a massive dog downs Smith.

They roll in the dirt snarling.

Grabbing the Ruger from his waistband holster, Vito raises his gun. He waits for a clear shot and then pulls the trigger. But the dogs move lightning fast. There's a sickening yelp, the sound of Vito's guilt, before Smith goes limp.

Hemingway stands over the lifeless body, panting.

Adrenaline slams through Vito's veins. He runs and jumps into the truck. The engine roars to life, the rack of headlamps flare over the top of the cab, and he peels out, fishtailing before his tires gain traction. When he hits the main road, he speeds toward the freeway, hands strangling the steering wheel.

Oh, my God, Hemingway! Razor-edged fear slices at his heart. Mick scrambles over the entrance gate to save time and keeps going. In the distance, he sees fog-smothered taillights careen out of view. When he reaches Hemingway, he finds a dead Doberman with blood pooling under its lifeless body. Its spiked collar has no identification tags.

———

Emma isn't aware she dropped off to sleep until a gunshot splits the night. The ominous sound claws her upright and out of bed. Tottering on unsteady legs, she holds the nightstand for support. Heart galloping and mouth dry with fear, she listens for another shot. Terror immobilizes her legs.

She unfolds the wheelchair between the bed and nightstand and sits down. Arms pumping and heart racing, she rushes down the hallway, wrenches open the front door, and rolls into the night.

The clouds part, but even with the slight illumination, she has no idea which way to go. Emma cups her hands around her mouth and calls out. "Mick! Hemingway!" But the fog absorbs her words. Sitting under a moon pale as bone, Emma feels like she's drowning in time waiting for Mick and Hemingway to return.

———

Like a cat, Pam carefully pads her way toward Mick's and Emma's cabin, all but purring in anticipation. She's surprised when she sees Emma sitting outside in her wheelchair, the moonlight spilling on her face and neck as she looks up at the sky. A heady combination of adrenaline and anticipation floods her veins.

With her target in sight, Pam knows this kill will be easy. *I've got the advantage, Emma's in a wheelchair for fuck's sake.*

Pam flexes her fingers several times, limbering them for the task at hand. Focused on her footfalls, she eases forward stealthily through the trees toward Emma.

Pam's head snaps toward the sound of a footfall. Her gaze narrows into slits.

"Oh, Libby. You scared the life out of me," Pam hears Emma say.

"Did you hear the gunshot, too?" Libby asks. "And where's Mick?"

"It woke me out of a sound sleep to find Mick and Hemingway both gone. I expect they're checking out the noise. Where's Niall?"

"He couldn't sleep," Libby says, "so I gave him a sleeping pill." Looking around, Libby continues, "Where are your brothers?"

"They must still be sleeping," Emma says. "But I don't know how. That gunshot was loud."

Pam withdraws as stealthily as she arrived, vanishing like a shadow in the black night. Statue still, she waits silently behind trees on the path that Mick takes to get home.

CHAPTER 18

*"Write the kind of story you would like to read.
People will give you all sorts of advice about writing, but if you are not writing something you like,
no one else will like it either."*

—MEG CABOT

Rather than climbing back over the gate again, Mick
presses a multi-digit code into the keypad, then gets out
his cell. While waiting for the gate to swing open, he calls Joe
and explains what just happened. Absently, he watches Hemingway sniff and mark, sniff and mark, reclaiming his territory.

"Okay," Mick says. "Once I check on Emma, I'll bring
back the ATV and get the dog's body. I'll drop it off tomorrow
with Dr. Sutton at Fairhaven Veterinary Hospital. It looks like
a pure breed, so he might be chipped."

"Great idea," Joe says.

"If there's a registration number for the dog in the
national database," Mick says, "it's tied to the owner's contact
information. It might be a lead, so it's worth a shot."

Oh, shit! Here they come, Pam thinks when she sees Mick and Hemingway heading back to their cabin.

Aware that the slightest movement, the blink of an eye, will catch the dog's attention, Pam holds her breath and hugs the tree; it hemorrhages the scent of pine. She loves the rush of adrenaline singing through her veins.

Once they pass by, Pam waits until the tempo of her heartbeat eases, then moves toward the entrance gate. *It may be harder than I thought to get Emma by herself. She might be a distance kill after all.*

She heads straight toward the stone column that Toni specified, "On the *left* as you approach Pines & Quill." Spreading the bushes next to the stone column, Pam finds the clear Tyvek pouch containing a Beretta Centurion. It holds fifteen rounds in the magazine and one in the chamber. She smiles when she sees that Toni threw in an ankle carry for good measure—a Sig Sauer P365.

Pam takes her cell phone off silent mode and calls Toni. "I got the guns, but there's a problem."

"What problem?"

"Mick was out walking that damn dog, and he may have seen Vito. There was a gunshot, and then his truck tore away."

"Who shot at who?"

"I don't know. It's not like I had a front-row seat. All I know is there was a gunshot. I heard parts of a phone conversation. I think Mick was talking to Joe Bingham."

"Shit. I'll call the boss and let him know."

When he sees Libby and Emma, Hemingway rushes the welcoming committee.

"Where have you been?" Emma asks the big dog. "And where's Mick?"

"I'm right here," Mick says, coming around the bend. He

reaches up and touches his hair, aware that it's standing on end from raking his fingers through it while trying to figure out what just happened. *Who shot that dog? Why did they have a gun? What the hell were they doing here?*

"What's going on? We heard a gunshot," Libby says.

Mick brings them up to speed on what happened out by the entrance gate, then continues, "Emma, if you and Hemingway head back into the cabin, I'll walk Libby home, then get the ATV and pick up that Doberman. That bullet was meant for Hemingway. And while I'm sorry that a dog has died, I'm glad it wasn't him," he says, roughing the big dog's head.

As Mick leaves Libby at the main house, he reminds her, "I don't know if Niall's aware, but if not, he doesn't need to know that they're doing a postmortem on Paddy's body in the morning."

"But *why* are they doing one?" Libby asks Mick.

"It's because of the nature of his death, Libby. A postmortem is required for murder. It's a normal part of the investigation."

In the early morning, Emma's brothers, Eric and Ellery, wolf down stacks of pancakes that Emma's making as fast as she can. She feels like Lucy Ricardo in the candy factory episode where she couldn't keep up.

Mick sidles up behind her in the kitchen and whispers, "Because neither of your brothers seems to have heard anything out of the ordinary last night, let's not mention what happened."

Emma turns into his arms. "I agree."

The smell of burnt pancakes fills the air.

"What are you two doing in there?" Ellery's voice teases from the dining room.

"You know what Mom says," Emma calls back. "You've always got to sacrifice one for the pancake gods!"

After Mick and Emma wave her brothers off, Mick heads to the morgue for Paddy's autopsy. On the drive to town, he steels himself for what he knows he'll see. *But I want to understand as much as I possibly can about Paddy's death*, he tells himself. *And knowing more about the murder might just help me learn something about the murderer.*

The Whatcom County medical examiner's office is on State Street between Champion and York. Mick pulls into the parking lot and waits until Joe pulls up next to his Jeep.

Both men step from their cars. "Where's Toni?" Mick asks.

"She called this morning to let me know she'd be late. She busted a tooth on a piece of popcorn last night."

Mick presses a hand along his jaw and grimaces. "Oh, man, that's gotta hurt."

"Better her than me," Joe shudders. "I can't stand the dentist."

After Joe signs them in at the front desk, the two men walk down the hallway to the morgue.

The fluorescent lights hum inside the autopsy suite. Mick quickly, instinctively, takes in his surroundings. He sees a woman wearing a surgical gown over scrubs; a clear acrylic shield protects her face. She's standing beneath a surgical lamp suspended from the ceiling. The mixture of antiseptic and alcohol in the air prickles the back of his throat.

Joe introduces Mick to Dr. Jill Graham, briefly explaining his previous experience on the force and his relationship to the man on the table.

"Okay," Dr. Graham says. "Even though you're not assisting in the postmortem, I want you both to put on gowns, shoe covers, latex gloves, and protective masks."

Once ready, she has Mick and Joe stand table side opposite her.

Mick notices how the overhead light glints off various silver tools on a separate portable surface next to the doctor: a saw, what looks like a breadknife and sailmaker's needle, a hammer with a hook and a chisel, an assortment of scalpels, scissors, shears, toothed forceps, and industrial-looking tweezers.

There's a ceiling microphone on a drop cord over the surgical table. Before starting the autopsy, Dr. Graham turns on the recorder. "Today is Tuesday, June eleventh, two thousand twenty-one at 0800h. I, Dr. Jill Graham, am the attending physician and forensic pathologist at the Whatcom County Medical Examiner's office, Bellingham, Washington. I am performing the autopsy on Patrick Joseph MacCullough, a sixty-year-old male. In attendance are Officer Joe Bingham of the Bellingham Police Department, and Sean McPherson, retired law enforcement and relative to the victim."

Then Dr. Graham draws back the sheet, exposing Patrick's ashen face, his bloodless skin.

Mick's thankful that someone had closed the lids on Paddy's lifeless eyes that he knows would otherwise stare into infinity. *Who killed Paddy? In any murder investigation, you have to ask yourself, who would benefit from the death? That's what I need to find out.*

After Dr. Graham determines the nonexistence of trace—fibers, fingerprints, DNA—and defensive wounds, she uses a scalpel to open Paddy's body. She cuts from just above the groin, up to the sternum, methodically diverging in a Y-shape to each shoulder, then peels back the dead flesh with the forceps.

"I had expected there to be more blood," Mick says.

"I'll explain why there's not," Dr. Graham says. "We can see that six bullets entered the body." Pointing, she continues. "Four in the abdomen, and two in the chest. This one," she says, marking a specific area, "nicked the aorta on the way through. Even though he was shot six times, the victim died from a single gunshot wound, resulting in a traumatic aortic rupture. The cause of death—exsanguination."

"In other words," Mick says, "he bled out."

"That's right," Dr. Graham says. "Wounds stop *spouting* blood when the heart stops pumping, but they *seep* for a while. Once the body's inert, time and gravity pool the body's fluids to the lowest points, causing the distinct bluish-purple discoloration known as lividity. As you know, we use that to tell how long someone's been dead."

When the postmortem's complete, Dr. Graham places the sheet back over Paddy's face.

Looking at the doctor, Mick says, "I'm heading to Westford Funeral Home from here. They've asked about the timeline. Do you know when you'll be able to release Patrick's body?"

"You can let them know that the deceased will be ready for transport by ten o'clock tomorrow morning. Please be sure to sign a release form at the front desk before you leave."

Mick thanks Dr. Graham for including him, and the two men leave. On the way out, Mick completes the form.

"What's on your agenda for the rest of the day?" Joe asks.

"After Westford, I'm heading to St. Barnabas to finalize arrangements for Paddy's service; then, I'm going home to hug everyone I love. After that, I'll take the Doberman's body out to Dr. Sutton at the veterinary hospital like we discussed last night. If the dog has a chip, we might find out who the owner is."

"Call me if you get a lead."

"Count on it," Mick says.

"This is going to be a lot more fun than going to the dentist," Toni says to her reflection in the mirror as she steps out of the shower. After considering the clothes in her closet, she decides on civilian clothes—white blouse, black slacks, and blazer—before driving to the wrecking yard.

When Toni pulls up to the locked gate, a snarling Dober-man meets her. *I wonder where the other one is?* Stepping from the car with her handbag, she approaches the gate.

Dressed in oil-stained coveralls, Vito steps out of the doorway of a small shack and over to the gate. Toni can see that he's visibly distressed. "Be quiet, Wesson. Sit," he commands.

"Where's your other dog?" Toni asks.

"He's dead."

"How the hell did that happen?"

Shamefaced, Vito looks down at the ground. When he looks back up, Toni sees surprise bloom on his doughy face before he rocks back on his feet. One step. Two. Then with a thud, he lands supine on the ground with a bullet between unseeing eyes that seem to appraise the early morning sky.

Damn, I hate giving you up. Toni wipes the burner free of prints before tossing it over the fence.

I've given the cops means—the gun. And opportunity— this godforsaken wrecking yard's in the middle of nowhere, there's not a soul around. But they'll be SOL on motive.

Looking at the dead body, she says, "The boss wants me to give you a message. 'Never, *ever* let yourself be seen. I have zero tolerance for mistakes.'"

She gives the barking dog an exfoliating stare, then removes her holdout gun—a Beretta Laramie—from its ankle holster. "Vito told you to be quiet," she says.

A moment later, he is.

CHAPTER 19

"Actors are all about entrances, but writers are all about exits."

—Vincent H. O'Neil

As the morning sun struggles to burn away the coastal drizzle, Joe steps into the foyer of the Bellingham police station and shakes off his wet coat. His stomach's queasy. He's nervous over what he's about to do. Before heading to the chief's office, Joe pours himself a cup of station house coffee—wretched, but welcome.

He walks to a door that's closed and hesitates. The brass nameplate reads CHIEF BRUCE SIMMS. Before Joe can knock, he sees the chief through the slender side window that runs the length of the door. Simms waves him in.

"Bingham," Chief Simms says. "What can I do for you?"

"I accept," Joe says without preamble.

Simms raises his eyebrows. "Why now?" he asks. "You've turned it down twice before. Why are you taking the job now?"

"I discussed it with Marci, and she agrees. She's under the impression that I'm less likely to be in the line of fire."

Simms looks Bingham in the eye. "Oh?" he says. "And how did she come by that impression?"

The tips of Joe's ears heat up. He knows that when he's distressed, they look like he's sure they do now, severely inflamed. Bingham says, "She may have gotten it from me."

Simms fishes through a desk drawer, then standing, places Joe's new identification in his hand.

Joe looks at the laminated photo ID, which reads: INSPECTOR JOSEPH P. BINGHAM, BELLINGHAM POLICE DEPARTMENT. HOMICIDE DETAIL. "How on earth do you just *happen* to have this ready?" Joe asks.

"I never dreamed you'd turn it down the first two times," Simms says.

After speaking with the director at the funeral home, Mick walks briskly to the exit. Once outside, he takes in a huge gulp of fresh air. *I'm glad it's sprinkling*, he thinks. *Maybe it'll wash off the scent of all those fresh-cut flowers—the cloying smell of death.*

Mick stops at St. Barnabas. Walking down the hallway into the administration office, he finds Father Burke sitting alone behind a desk filled with tidy stacks of paperwork covering the surface. The tall, slender priest has a full head of silver hair and a pleasant face with kind blue eyes.

Mick remembers when Paddy said, "Though Burke's pushing seventy, he's a chick magnet!" Mick had laughed at Paddy's terminology.

"I'm not kidding," Paddy said. "A gaggle of women flock around him after every Mass like birds on seed, vying for his attention."

Mick's usual joy at seeing Father Burke is dampened due to the nature of his visit—finalizing funeral arrangements for Paddy.

"It's good to see you, Mick," Father Burke says, shaking Mick's hand. "I'm just sorry that it's under these circumstances." The priest tips his head to the side questioningly and continues. "May I ask where Niall is? Since he's Paddy's brother, I was expecting that he'd be with you."

"I'm sorry I didn't make that clear on the phone," Mick says. "Right now, Niall's feeling nothing but numbness at this loss; he's drawn into himself. To help lift the emotional weight, Libby and I are taking care of the necessary arrangements."

"I can appreciate that," Father Burke says.

The men take a seat on either side of the desk and talk through the details with Father Burke making notes periodically.

Once they finish discussing the arrangements, the priest says, "I was wondering if you discovered yet any reason why someone would want to murder Paddy? It's unsettling that he was killed right here inside these very walls." He makes a sweeping gesture with his hand. Nodding toward the sanctuary, he continues. "We've set up a temporary confessional booth while the one that Paddy was shot in is still being gone over by the police and their team. Once they're done, we're having it replaced."

"Yes," Mick says, "I'm sure the parishioners will feel better. And to answer your question, Father, the only thing we have right now is speculation, and it's thin, at best. I do have a question for you, though."

"What is it?" Father Burke asks.

"Do you happen to know if you have a male parishioner by the name of Vito Paglio? He's a heavyset bald man who works at a wrecking yard, the Scrap Heap, on the outskirts of town."

The priest clasps his chin in his hand. After a minute, he says, "I'm sorry, but the name and description aren't familiar. Then again, St. Barnabas is a large parish, and I don't know every single person. Would you like me to ask the other priests?"

"That would be great," Mick says. "It's a long shot, but worth checking. If you come up with anything, please give me a call." Reaching over to shake the priest's hand, he says, "Thank you again for your time. I appreciate it."

As Mick stands to leave, the finality of the situation hits him. *The next time I'm here, it'll be for Paddy's funeral service.* Walking to his car, he blinks back tears. It doesn't lessen the sting to know that Paddy was beloved in the neighborhood and a staple at St. Barnabas, a Roman Catholic parish and part of the Archdiocese of Seattle. And Mick's willing to bet that there isn't a soul in the Fairhaven/Bellingham area who has a negative thing to say about him.

Mick's stop at Pines & Quill to retrieve the Doberman's body coincides with the arrival of Ian and Fiona—Niall and Libby's son and soon-to-be daughter-in-law. They've just driven from Pullman, Washington, where they're both in their last year at Washington State University College of Veterinary Medicine. A six-hour drive at best but, for two people in their early twenties who shared driving duties, not taxing.

Embracing his nephew in a bear hug, Mick says, "You two are staying in the cabin with Emma and me. I'm excited for you to meet her." Turning to Fiona, Mick takes both of her hands in his. "It's good to see you again. I'm glad you came."

"I love Pines & Quill," Ian says. "But I'm sick about the reason we're here. I can't believe Uncle Paddy's dead—that he was murdered."

"I'm sick about it, too," Fiona says, tears shimmering in her brown eyes.

"I'm glad we're a close family," Mick says. "It helps that we have each other for support." Noticing the luggage in their back seat, Mick says, "I'll put your bags in your room later. Right now, let's get out of this drizzle and head to the main house. If your mom thinks I detoured you, she'll throttle me."

"Are Grandma and Grandpa here yet?" Ian asks. "I'm excited to introduce them to Fiona."

"Their plane arrives in the morning," Mick says. "They haven't met Emma yet either. I'm looking forward to them meeting her, too."

When Mick opens the door to the main house, Hemingway gives a joyful yelp and bounds toward Ian and Fiona, almost knocking them over in greeting. As veterinarian students, they're unperturbed. They appreciate his healthy physique and the enthusiasm of his full-body wag, his way of saying, "Welcome!"

Fiona laughs as Hemingway's large, wiry muzzle sniffs her pockets for biscuits.

"Sit down, mister," Mick says.

While Ian goes to find his parents, Fiona gives a tail-thumping Hemingway liberal scratches behind each ear.

"You can head back to the kitchen," Mick says. "I'm going to run over to the cabin and get Emma before I need to leave again. She's looking forward to meeting both you and Ian. I'll be right back."

By the time Mick takes off for his next appointment, he's introduced Emma to Ian and Fiona. Libby's joined them at the kitchen table. And Niall's making something in the kitchen that smells wonderful. *There's no mistaking the smell of freshly baked bread.* Mick remembers Niall telling him time and time again that the kitchen is his sanctuary and that cooking and baking are his forms of therapy. He said, "Life inhabits our kitchen; it's where sorrows are lightened and burdens are shared."

Mick glances in the kitchen before leaving. Hemingway's by Niall's side, dusting the floor with his tail while waiting for a sample.

After retrieving the Doberman's tarp-wrapped body from the workshop, Mick heads to the vet's office. Dr. Sutton, who was kind enough to fit him into his busy schedule, is expecting him. Mick's hunch is right; the dog's chipped. After Dr. Sutton inputs the registration number in the identification database, they learn that "Smith"—a purebred Doberman—is registered to a Vito Paglio.

Mick notes the contact details, then shakes the vet's hand. "This is helpful. Thank you."

"Do you want me to dispose of the body?" the vet asks.

"Yes, please. But before you do, will you take photos and then remove the bullet? I'll pick them up in the next day or so. You've got my credit card information on file because of Hemingway. Please use it to cover the expenses. And thank you again for squeezing me in."

"Bingham," Joe answers his cell.

"It's Mick. You told me to call if I get any leads. I've got one."

After learning the registration details, Joe says, "Toni's not back from the dentist yet. Want to take a ride?"

"Yes."

"I need to swing by home first; then I'll meet you half-way—at Pines & Quill. If this is the same guy who shot the dog, we know he's armed. You may want to do the same, but you didn't hear it from me."

Mick's waiting outside the front entrance gate, admiring a blue sky with wisps of white clouds receding into space, when Joe pulls up in an unmarked car.

"Well, I'll be damned," Mick says, sliding into the passenger seat and taking in Joe's suit.

A flood of memories washes over Mick. *Sam was killed on a Friday night. On Monday, we would have started our careers as homicide detectives. We'd gone suit shopping earlier in the week after Chief Reynolds called us into his office and said, "As you know, detectives don't respond to the same service calls as a patrol officer; they don't need a uniform that immediately identifies them as law enforcement. In fact," he said, "in most situations, you don't want a uniform that shouts, 'The police are here!' And in cases where homicide detectives respond, people are more likely to talk with someone who's not in a police uniform."*

"Between the unmarked car and the suit," Mick says, "it's clear that you finally said yes." Mick reaches over and shakes Joe's hand. "Congratulations, detective. It's about time. Now let me see your new ID."

Joe fishes in his shirt pocket and then hands the laminated photo ID card to Mick, who reads it out loud. "Inspector Joseph P. Bingham, Bellingham Police Department. Homicide Detail." Turning to Joe, Mick says, "I'm happy for you, Joe. You're going to be great at this."

After running Vito Paglio's name for additional details, they pull alongside the Scrap Heap's chain link drive-through gate and see what appears to be a dead Caucasian man and Doberman on the other side. Both are soaked with rain. "I wonder if this was the guy from last night," Joe says.

"I don't know," Mick says. "But that truck," he continues, pointing at the vehicle, "with the rack of headlamps over the cab, could be the same vehicle that peeled out of there. It was too foggy for me to see any more details than that."

"Look at that," Joe says, pointing through the windshield to a gun near the dead man's feet. Joe pops the trunk, and they walk to the back of the car. While they put on latex gloves, Joe nods to the bolt cutters and says, "You do the honors."

When they're through the gate, Joe picks up the handgun, shows it to Mick, then drops the .380 ACP in a clear plastic evidence bag. "Tamper-Evident Technology" is printed on the front, ensuring that once sealed, it can't be opened without showing visible signs of interference.

Joe takes out his cell phone and starts taking photos, immediately sending them to the cloud for safekeeping.

Squatting down next to the body, they each sit on the backs of their mud-caked heels.

Joe checks the dead man's pockets. There's a set of keys in the front right.

Together they roll the heavy body far enough over to check the back. An IWB—inside the waistband—holster reveals a Taurus TH9 Compact. Joe whistles at the 9mm Luger and then removes a worn black leather wallet from the rear right pocket.

"The driver's license photo matches this guy's face, minus the extra hole in his head," Joe says. Looking closer at the ID, he adds, "The name, Vito Paglio, matches the registration information for the dead Doberman. And now we've got *another* dead Doberman."

As Joe takes more photos, Mick asks, "Why on earth would this man and his dog have been at Pines & Quill? What were they doing, and why was he carrying a gun?"

"That's what we're going to find out, Mick," Joe says.

"We?"

"The more help, the better," Joe says. "You're just as well trained as I am. Hell, probably better. You and Sam were just a weekend away from starting your careers as homicide detectives." Joe looks directly at Mick. "And I know you love this work."

Mick nods.

"You know, your father could just snap his fingers, and you'd be an FBI agent."

"First off, my dad's integrity wouldn't allow for that. Second, I don't want a free ride."

Joe shakes his head and holds up his hands in resignation. "I'm just saying."

Changing the subject, Mick says, "The vet, Dr. Sutton, has Smith, the first dead dog. And like you said, this one makes a matching pair." Nodding toward the Doberman, he continues. "We might as well take him there, too. What do you want to bet his name is Wesson?"

After Joe calls in their findings, he says, "The medical examiner should be here soon. I imagine they'll set up a canopy tent in this weather. While we wait, let's check out the area. I'll take this." He points to a small shack, the door still hanging open. "You take the truck."

Despite the gloomy weather, both men are in their element.

As Libby gets a biscuit for Hemingway, she's heartsick that someone shot and killed a dog outside the Pines & Quill entrance gate last night. A Doberman. Mick's words echo in her mind. *That bullet was meant for Hemingway.*

Reaching over the lower half of the Dutch door, she roughs the big dog's head before giving him the treat, then turns to Ian and Fiona and explains what had happened the night before.

Libby sees outrage on their faces.

"What the hell?" Ian says. "Why would anyone shoot a dog?"

"Do you think it has anything to do with Paddy's murder?" Fiona asks.

They hear Niall's voice from the kitchen. "Hey, you guys, we're going to have a house full of hungry writers any minute. Will you please finish setting the table?"

"I thought the writers in residence eat breakfast and lunch in their cottages," Fiona says.

"While that's usually the case," Libby says, "today, the writers have the option to have lunch at the main house. And each of them—Tom, Megan, Pam, and Linda—indicated that they'll take advantage of the opportunity. Not only because the food's delicious," she nods toward Niall, "but for the opportunity to socialize with others because the rest of the day is spent closeted away in their cottages writing."

As the writers arrive, Libby introduces them to her son, Ian, and her soon-to-be daughter-in-law, Fiona. An easy camaraderie is established as they share a simple meal of olives, freshly baked bread, fruit, and cheese, with a dandelion-leaf salad spiced with yellow nasturtiums.

When Niall excuses himself from the table for a moment, Pam whispers to Libby, "Have you learned anything more about your brother-in-law's death? From the night the police were here, we know that he was murdered in the confession booth at St. Barnabas church. But have they found the killer yet?"

Before Libby can answer, Niall returns with a large pitcher of iced tea. "Who needs a refill?" he asks.

Just then, the sensor outside the main gate sounds a soft buzz in the kitchen, quickly followed by a ringing phone. Libby looks at Niall, whose surprise she knows mirrors her own.

"Excuse me," Libby says, as she leaves the table to take care of the interruption. "Oh, hi. Yes. Please join us for lunch; we just started."

After pressing the button to open the entry gate, she heads to the front door, pausing at the table to quietly tell Niall that Officer Bianco—Toni—is here to offer her condolences in a civilian capacity.

This is a fucking waste of my time, Toni thinks. *Then again, the boss, Giorgio "The Bull" Gambino, is not someone to argue with.* "Stop at Pines & Quill to offer your condolences to Niall after your 'visit to the dentist' this morning," he'd ordered. "It gives you the perfect alibi. You're right under their noses and keeps you above suspicion."

CHAPTER 20

"Don't tell me the moon is shining; show me the glint of light on broken glass."

—Anton Chekhov

When Toni enters the massive eat-in kitchen, she feels all eyes on her, including those of the Irish wolfhound, Hemingway, who's mastered the icy glare. *I hate dogs, and he knows it,* Toni thinks. Fortunately, only his head protrudes over the bottom portion of the closed Dutch door.

"Here, let me take your wet things," Libby says.

"Thank you," Toni says. She turns and smiles at the others. "Is that freshly baked bread I smell?"

"It sure is," Niall says.

Libby reintroduces the group to Toni, saying, "You already know Niall, and you briefly met Tom Gordon, Megan Duprey, Pam Williams, and Linda Washington. But you haven't met my son, Ian, or his fiancée, Fiona O'Meara."

Ian stands to shake Toni's hand. "It's a pleasure to meet you," he says.

"You as well." Turning to Fiona, Toni shakes her hand. "It's so nice to meet you."

"You, too," Fiona says, smiling.

Before settling down at the table, Toni walks over to Niall. Taking one of his hands in hers, she quietly says, "I'm so sorry for your loss. Everyone in St. Barnabas parish loved Father MacCullough." *But the SOB was in the wrong place at the wrong time, and unfortunately, I had to eliminate him.*

"Thank you," Niall says. Clearing the emotion from his throat, he motions to an empty seat at the table and continues. "Please join us. There's plenty of food."

"I don't know how much I'll be able to eat. I just came from the dentist," she says while lightly touching her fingers to her jaw.

———

The warm atmosphere of the main house's sprawling eat-in kitchen is welcoming. As animated conversation resumes around the table—this time, sharing war stories about dental work—Linda notices Toni and Pam exchange a meaningful glance.

Linda's eyes grow smaller, considering, thoughtful. To hide her rumination, she spreads her napkin on her lap and busies herself, flattening out its creases. When she looks up again, she watches Toni cut a slice of warm bread. Fragrant steam wafts toward the beamed ceiling before Toni spreads butter on the soft, golden piece.

Linda turns to see Tom looking at her. She likes that he smiles easily, the right side of his mouth pulling up a little higher than the left. She notices his strong, wide hands with a dusting of dark hair—hands, Linda imagines, that can do any number of things. She glances away, self-conscious of her reaction.

———

When Joe pulls the unmarked car into the circular drive in front of the main house, he says, "That's Bianco's car. I wonder what she's doing here?"

"Let's go find out," Mick says.

Niall's the first one to notice the two men. "Hey, Mick. Joe. Are you guys hungry? We just finished lunch, but there's plenty left."

"I'm starving," they say in unison.

"Bianco, I thought you had a dentist appointment. What are you doing here?" Joe asks as he settles himself in a chair.

After kissing Emma, Mick sits at the table, too.

"I stopped here on my way home," Toni says. "I wanted to give my condolences to Niall as a civilian, not a police officer. Hey, why are you wearing a suit, Joe? What have you two been up to?"

God, I wish I'd brought antacid tablets, Joe thinks. *I can't stand it when Toni's in a snit, and my promotion—correction, her lack of promotion—is going to twist her undies in a tight little green-with-envy bundle.* "It has to do with one of our ongoing investigations," Joe says. "We'll talk back at the station."

Turning to Ian, he says, "It's good to see you again." Then nodding to the young woman at Ian's side, Joe continues, "And you must be Fiona."

"Yes, I am."

Beaming, Ian says, "Joe, I'd like you to meet Fiona O'Meara. Fiona, this is Joe Bingham. He's a police officer and friend of the family."

"Actually," Mick says, smiling, "he's a homicide detective." Turning to the faces around the table, he continues, "That's why he's wearing a suit. He just accepted the promotion this morning."

The phone rings on the heels of a soft buzz announcing a vehicle's arrival at the main gate.

Joe sees Mick raise his eyebrows questioningly at Niall. "Are you expecting others?"

"Not that I'm aware of." He looks to Libby.

"I'll get the phone," she says. "Pines & Quill, Libby Mac-Cullough," she answers. "You're *here?* Oh, my gosh! We weren't expecting you until morning—what a nice surprise. I'll buzz you in. See you in a minute." Then she hangs up the phone.

Joe watches excitement blossom on Libby's face as she rushes past the curious glances.

Over her shoulder, she says, "Mom and Dad are here. They caught an early flight and rented a car."

Mick and Niall excuse themselves from the table. "We'll be right back."

"Not without me," Ian says.

Joe sees Emma and Fiona look at each other and nod. "We're coming, too," they announce in unison as they scramble away from the table.

Toni turns to the remaining guests at the table. "Would you excuse Joe and me for a moment, please?"

Toni and Joe step out the patio door. Once he closes the glass slider behind them, Toni rounds on Joe, and, with a tongue like a kitchen knife, starts in.

"What the fuck! When, exactly, were you going to tell me that you made detective?" She knows that her tone reeks of jealousy, but she continues, uncaring. "What about me?" she says, jabbing at her chest. "You know I've only been here a couple of months from SFPD. I'm new to this precinct, so I won't even be considered for a promotion until I've had a chance to prove myself. What the hell am I supposed to do now?"

"I know—"

"I'm not through," Toni hisses through clenched teeth. "If you were going to say you know my transfer was a disciplinary measure, then let me set the record straight. My being put on administrative leave after shooting that asshole in self-defense was normal police procedure. You," she jabs her finger toward Joe, "would have done the same thing. I was cleared of all wrongdoing. And the reason I was assigned elsewhere is *none of your fucking business.*" Each of the last five words are punctuated with a jab toward Joe.

This yahoo doesn't know, Toni thinks, *that payoffs were made and strings were pulled to get me transferred here.*

"*You stick to him, 'like white on rice,'*" Gambino had ordered Toni.

How the hell am I going to do that now? Toni wonders.

"Are you through?" Joe asks.

When Toni crosses her arms in front of her chest and tosses her head, he continues. "I was going to say that I didn't intentionally leave you in the dark. It's a promotion I turned down twice before you even arrived in Bellingham and only accepted it this morning after Marci and I talked it through."

His wife, Toni thinks. Smiling now, she makes a decision. *I can use Marci to exact the perfect revenge.*

———

Mick watches as hugs and happy tears abound. Sad tears, too, as his mom, Maeve, wraps her son-in-law, Niall, in a hug and expresses her sorrow at the loss of his brother, Paddy.

Taking a deep breath to try and relax, Mick thinks, *I'm stressing because my parents, both retired from the FBI, are here on the heels of two deaths—Jason Hughes, who we now know was an alias for Alexander Berndt and appears to have been a serial killer. And now Paddy, murdered in a confession booth at St. Barnabas.* Mick continues his line of thought. *This is a recipe for disaster. The last time Dad "came out of retirement," he was shot.* Mick puts a hand on his stomach. *It feels like a knife's turning in my gut.*

Connor looks at Mick and Ian. "Well, are you going to introduce us to these fine ladies?"

"Age before beauty," Ian teases his uncle, Mick.

"I'll get you later," Mick threatens, his eyebrows drawn together in a mock scowl. Taking Emma's hand, Mick turns to his parents. "Mom and Dad, I'd like you to meet Emma Benton, my soon-to-be wife."

Turning to Emma, he says, "Emma, this is my—"

Before he can finish, his mom leans down and swoops Emma into a warm hug. Drawing back, she looks into Emma's eyes and says, "I feel like I already know you. Between Mick and Libby, our cell phones are filled with nothing but wonderful things about you. They've even sent a—"

Connor clears his throat. "Are you going to keep her all to yourself, woman?"

Emma stands up from her wheelchair. Mick steps behind her for support as his dad draws her into a big hug. "It's so nice to meet you, Mr. McPherson," Emma says.

His large hands envelop hers. "Please call us Maeve and Connor."

After Emma sits back down, Connor turns to the young woman next to Ian and says, "And you must be Fiona." Maeve and Connor both step forward to meet their grandson's fiancée.

"I'm so happy to meet you finally," Fiona says. "Ian's told me so much about you. Your exciting lives would make a great action movie."

"I don't know about that," Maeve says at the suggestion. "But it's certainly been eventful." She slips her hand into Connor's.

Looking up at the sky, Connor says, "On the drive from the airport, we watched dark gray clouds roll in from the west; they look to be covering most of Whatcom County. That's why we came early. It's supposed to storm through the night and tomorrow morning."

Toni and Joe reenter the kitchen just as Connor, Maeve, and their welcoming committee pour in from the hallway. Loaded down with luggage, Mick and Ian bring up the rear.

Emma and Fiona rejoin the others at the table. While Libby makes the introductions, Toni's appraising eyes take in the tall, slender woman. *Like mother, like daughter,* she thinks. *That's where Libby gets her looks.* She notices that Maeve's silver hair is swept up in a loose chignon, skewered with a carved hair stick. *I bet that's Mick's handiwork. And if everything I've heard is true, I bet she knows how to use it as a weapon.*

Turning her gaze to the man directly behind Maeve, Toni thinks, *He and Maeve are like bookends, perfectly suited to each other.* Tall and handsome, Connor has a whipcord-lean body. She sees where Mick gets his good looks.

Toni's heard plenty of stories about Connor McPherson. *Just invoking his name gives any instructions immediate currency.* Covertly, she stares at him. No elaboration is needed. Connor looks terrifying without even trying.

Toni turns her head to look at Maeve. *Like a tiger, she exudes grace overlying power.*

On his way through to put Connor's and Maeve's luggage in the guest room, Ian teases, "These are heavy. What did you pack, Grandpa? A hostage? Gold bars for a ransom drop?" His voice fades as he continues down the hall.

Pam cocks an inquiring eyebrow. "What on earth?"

Fiona laughs. "Well, in addition to a fantastic imagination, Ian's referring to his grandparents' adventurous lives."

"Do tell." Pam encourages, along with the other eager faces around the table.

Looking at Connor and Maeve before proceeding, Fiona asks, "Do you mind if I share some of your exciting escapades?"

"Fire away," Connor says. "It's old news." Walking over to the Dutch door to greet Hemingway, whose tail is wagging broad sweeps across the mudroom floor, he continues. "Maeve and I've been retired from active service for many years now. I doubt they'll even be interested."

As Maeve opens the Dutch door to release the now-ecstatic dog, Connor snags a biscuit from the jar. "Come on, Hemingway, let's blow this pop stand."

With hands clasped, Fiona's barely contained excitement hints at Maeve and Connor's illustrious past. She looks with anticipation at those around the table, and then stories that Ian's told her begin to tumble from her lips like birds freed from a cage.

"Maeve enjoyed a long and distinguished career as a criminal psychologist, or CP. Her expertise is the *why* behind criminal activity—the motivation—particularly for violent crimes.

"When law enforcement agencies are trying to figure out the identity of a criminal—for instance, a serial killer—they often bring in a criminal psychologist. The CP uses a mix of psychology, pattern recognition, and indicative reasoning to predict a suspect's age, background personality, and other identifying characteristics. The resulting profile is used by law enforcement to narrow down their pool of suspects quickly.

"Maeve worked with the FBI to help solve crimes by developing profiles of murderers, kidnappers, rapists, and other violent criminals. Ian calls his grandma a 'psychological sleuth.'"

Before continuing, Fiona looks around the table to gauge her listeners' interest. And though she's a grown woman, she relishes the limelight like a giddy high schooler. *"Captive audience" is the perfect descriptor*, she thinks. Smiling, she continues.

"Maeve and Connor met at Quantico. She was there training, and so was he. But his area of focus was different. He was there for NAT—New Agent Training with the FBI."

Fiona leans forward and whispers, "He's *highly* esteemed. And from what Ian and Mick say, the man is still formidable. He worked his way up, and by the time he retired, he was the FBI's Special Agent in Charge of Marin, Napa, and San Mateo County offices, and the main office in San Francisco."

From the end of the big kitchen table, Toni exchanges a covert glance with Pam. Raising her eyebrows, she almost imperceptibly tips her head toward the long hallway that swallowed Connor and Maeve just minutes before. Looking around to make sure all eyes except Pam's are on Fiona, she mouths, "FBI."

A foghorn in the bay blares in the distance, its sound echoing off the cliff below the windswept bluff. A warning.

CHAPTER 21

"Substitute 'damn' every time you're inclined to write
'very'; your editor will delete it and the writing will
be just as it should be."

—MARK TWAIN

At the Bellingham Police Station, Joe nods to Toni on his way to the break area. "I could murder a cup of coffee," he says to Chris and Herb, who've just refilled their cups.

"I hear that congratulations are in order, *detective*," Chris says, smiling.

"Ditto that," says Herb.

After shaking hands with both of the officers, Joe fills his mug, then walks back through the hum of the main room where uniforms sit back to back in low-walled cubicles. He remembers the description Chris used regarding the room style—"prairie dog farm." *And it's not too far from accurate.* Joe sits down heavily in the well-worn chair at his desk. He rubs the dark whiskers that dust his jaw.

After tapping his computer out of sleep mode, Joe enters his username and password. He's greeted by the Bellingham

Police logo—an indigo background featuring a snow-covered mountain with green trees in the foreground, the same logo that's emblazoned on every squad car in town.

Toni sits at her desk behind him. Swiveling around, she grunts. "I thought you'd be moving desks now that you're a *detective.*"

In her tone, Joe hears what he knows from short-lived experience as her partner to be barely reined-in sarcasm.

He looks out the window at a wet, tree-laced view of the Bellingham Municipal Court building's southwest side. He watches a little red Fiat parallel park with ease in a tight space that would be difficult for a bigger car. "Naw, one change is enough for now."

"Well, now that we've established that, are you going to tell me?"

Joe's chair creaks as he turns to face her. After taking a sip of coffee, he brings her up to speed on what he and Mick found at the Scrap Heap wrecking yard.

Toni asks, "What do you think this Vito Paglio guy was doing out at Pines & Quill? And with a gun, no less?"

"I don't know. I ran a background check, but nothing out of the ordinary popped. 'Vito Paglio's probably an alias." Joe pauses to inhale the scent of the bitter brew before taking another sip. He watches her over his cup—*Is she hiding something?*—then continues. "Dr. Graham fingerprinted the deceased at the morgue and sent them over. They're running them through AFIS now. If we get a hit, I'll let you know." *There! It was only a fraction, and for only a moment, but her eyes widened. Was it from fear, surprise, or both?*

"Who's Dr. Graham?" Toni asks. "I'm new here, remember?"

"Graham's the CME—the chief medical examiner," Joe says.

Toni stands and walks over to the window. "I recognize the name now."

Joe studies Toni's profile as she looks out the rain-splattered glass. From the side, he sees her jaw clench. *You don't have to be an expert at reading body language to know that her steely grip on the windowsill betrays turbulence beneath her exterior.*

Joe remembers what Emma told him, Mick, and Rafferty when she was in the hospital after being held captive by Hughes/Berndt. "He said, 'Stay wary, for treachery walks among you.'" *And though that's not what I told Chief Simms, that's the real reason I requested to stay at the same desk.*

One of the overhead fluorescent bulbs blinks and clunks, bathing Toni's features in a ghostly pale.

Swiveling his chair back toward his desk, Joe leans back, steeples his hands on his stomach, and thinks, his thoughts cascading one after the other.

———

Libby's mesmerized by the raindrops racing down the window that separates the garden from the cozy chair she sits in while enjoying a hot cup of tea, or "cuppa," as Niall calls it. Her mind wanders to this month's writers in residence. *And while many people use a rainy day as the perfect excuse to sleep in, read a book, or binge-watch their favorite television shows, most writers are "pluviophiles"—people who love the rain. It comes down to rain being a muse, a source of inspiration.*

Unfortunately, writing and procrastination tend to go hand in hand. But once the raindrops start, excuses end. That's why inclement weather is a writer's friend. There's no better time for a writer to work.

In her mind's eye, Libby envisions the writers snug in their cottages. She can practically hear the rhythmic *pat pat pat* of rain on their windows as they sit at their desks or curl up in an overstuffed chair with a laptop, a steaming mug of coffee, tea, or hot chocolate, then put on their proverbial blinders and knuckle down to write.

Heavy drops splatter the window like pebbles bringing Libby back from her mental reverie. *This much-needed break has been nice, but it's time for me to knuckle down, too.* With a grieving heart, Libby gets up from the chair and heads to her office to continue making funeral arrangements for Paddy.

Tom Gordon, in Austen cottage, pulls up to the square oak desk. His brow furrows in concentration as he works on his manuscript, *War-Torn: A Casualty's Manifesto for Peace.* The only sound he hears is wind-driven rain slapping the sun-faded terra-cotta on the smooth-tiled patio. He looks up periodically and sees the wild profusion of potted flowers bowing their pelted heads.

His mind wanders to Linda—*She's beautifully unaware of her own allure.* He smiles when he remembers a line that she shared with him from a recently read book, *The Odds of Loving Grover Cleveland:* "If you're ever feeling lost, remember it's easier to find yourself if other people help you look."

Snug on the window seat in Brontë cottage, Linda Washington's laser focused on her manuscript, *Life after Deaf: Piercing the Sound of Silence with Cochlear Implants.* She mulls over the conversation she had with Tom. When she asked him, "What's your all-time favorite book?" he answered without hesitation, "*Timeline* by Michael Crichton." When she asked him, "Why?" he said, "I love history." Then he shared one of his favorite lines from the book: "Professor Johnston often said that if you didn't know history, you didn't know anything. You were a leaf that didn't know it was part of a tree."

Looking out the window toward the stand of Douglas firs, Linda watches the raindrops meld together and then slide down the glass. She can't shake the feeling of dread. *It's pooled in ruts like the deluge outside, but in the pit of my stomach.* She waits. For what? She's not sure.

Megan Duprey sits in a comfortable chair with her laptop resting on the tops of her thighs. The heat from the laptop warms her legs, but she doesn't want to move to the desk. Between lengthy bursts of rapid-fire typing, she sets the laptop on the side table and stands up to stretch—first mountain pose, then downward dog. After sitting back down, she pulls her legs up to her chest and looks out the south-facing glass wall of Thoreau cottage. Overlooking Bellingham Bay National Park and Reserve, she sees that the tops of the tallest trees are hidden in a fog that rolled in after the temperature dropped.

Pleased with the progress she's made on *One Heaping Teaspoon: Simple, Fresh, and Tasty Meals for a Busy Lifestyle,* she turns back to her manuscript, but not before her stomach growls, reminding her that it's getting close to dinnertime. She smiles in anticipation. *In addition to two chocolate tortes that I made and dropped off earlier, I wonder what else is on the menu tonight?*

In Dickens cottage, Shelly Baker, who's at Pines & Quill in the guise of Pam Williams—the woman whose life she took and now inhabits—waits.

When her burner phone rings, she picks it up, answering with silence.

"His fingerprints popped," she hears Toni say. "They know that Vito Paglio's an alias for Salvatore Rizzo. Bingham's the one who told me. He said, 'Salvatore Rizzo's an underling in the Gambino mafia family, now grown to a formidable syndicate, headed by Giorgio 'The Bull' Gambino—a serious player in the crime community.'

"Playing dumb, I asked him, 'What the hell's the mob doing in Bellingham, Washington?'

"He said, 'With one hundred and fifty-seven miles of coastline, it's an ideal entry and exit for illicit goods. Seattle's just south of us. The Canadian border's a stone's throw to the north. And Bellingham Bay—a gateway to multiple islands, channels, and straits that lead to the Pacific Ocean—is immediately to the west. It's the ideal location for trafficking drugs, guns, and humans.'

"The part I didn't already know is that they're bringing in Sean Rafferty."

"Who the hell's he?" Pam asks.

"Rafferty's an FBI agent from the Seattle office. He was sent in when Jason Hughes, who you knew as Alex Berndt, took Emma hostage."

"Does the boss know he's coming?"

"Yes, he's the first one I told, and after he heard that news, he told me to give you a message."

Oh, shit! Pam thinks. "What's that?" she asks, with just a hint of desperation on the edge of her words.

"Eliminate Emma Benton sooner than later."

"What's the rush?" Pam asks, trying to imbue her voice with calm.

"It's imperative they don't find out there's a dirty cop on the payroll—*me*. As one of the last people Alex spoke to before he died, there's a probability that Emma knows."

"Probability or possibility?" Pam asks.

Pam hears Toni's voice tighten with anger. "Alex told me that when he was holding Emma hostage in the cave, he blabbed to her that I'm a dirty cop. That means that with everything that's happened to her, she just hasn't remembered it yet. Emma needs to be disposed of." Toni pauses before continuing, her voice sharp and commanding. "And it's *your* job to eliminate her from the equation *before* she does."

Pam feels a prickle of adrenaline. Sweat stings her armpits and gathers at the nape of her neck. "Consider it done."

CHAPTER 22

"When your story is ready for rewrite, cut it to the bone. Get rid of every ounce of excess fat."
—STEPHEN KING

"You must have been watching for me," Tom says when Libby opens the door to the main house.

"Megan, Linda, and Pam arrived a few minutes ago. I figured you'd be on their heels," she says.

Cuffing the rain from his eyes, Tom says, "It's really coming down out there. My mom would say, 'It's raining pitchforks and little green frogs.'"

Libby laughs. "I haven't heard that one before."

As she leads the way to the large dining table in the eat-in kitchen, Tom takes an appreciative whiff and says, "It sure does smell good."

"Niall's putting the finishing touches on dinner," Libby says. "We're starting with cream of celery root soup with braised sea scallops, followed by seared beef tenderloin with three-pepper crust in a red wine sauce, served with Jerusalem artichoke gratin, and a chocolate torte—compliments of Chef Megan."

Tom pats his stomach as he rolls up to an empty place at the table. "I'm in heaven."

Linda gives him a teasing look. "If you hadn't gotten here when you did, I was going to eat your share."

"You'd have had to fight me," Pam says. "It smells incredible, doesn't it?"

After Niall and Libby place the soup tureen and platters on the table, Niall sprinkles the soup with a chiffonade of minced basil leaves and says, "*Bon appetite*—enjoy your meal."

"*Vous n'avez pas à demander deux fois*—you don't have to ask twice," Megan says.

Pam looks around the table. "Where's the rest of the group?"

"Emma and Mick are hosting dinner for my parents, Ian, and Fiona, at their cabin this evening," Libby says. "They've got Hemingway, too."

"Oh, how lovely," Pam says. "Will Emma be back in time to draw a card from the Observation Deck this evening? That's half the fun."

"I doubt they'll come out again in this weather," Libby says.

Looking toward the Dutch door, Tom says, "Poor Hemingway, he's missing out."

"Trust me, he's not missing a thing. Emma's an excellent cook. But if Hemingway could clone himself, he'd double dip and enjoy the best tidbits from *both* kitchens."

"I'd be a happy man living off Hemingway's *tidbits*," Tom says.

Under the table, Pam toes her ankle holster. *Well, fuck! Emma's not here. When the boss says, "Sooner than later," he means now!*

Fear clenches her stomach. Wiping her clammy hands on the cloth napkin, she thinks, *I was counting on the storm to cover my tracks and the sound of the shot when I caught her*

alone tonight on her way home. And if Mick was with her?
Oh well, that's the cost of doing business.

———

Mick opens the front door of the cabin to a hearty knock. Waving his parents inside, he says, "Come in where it's dry."

After stashing their umbrellas in the stand by the front door, Maeve and Connor lift their noses. Connor gives an enthusiastic sniff. "It smells delicious," he says to Mick, who's handing their wet coats off to Ian, who arrived just before them.

"Mick and I've been waiting for you two to show up," Ian says. "We're starving, and the smell's been teasing us for *hours*."

"That's a slight exaggeration," Mick says. "But we *are* ready to eat. Emma and Fiona have been busy. Come on." He leads his parents to the dining room.

Emma rolls out from the kitchen. "I thought I heard you arrive. Welcome. I hope you brought your appetites."

Connor pats his flat stomach. "No worries there."

Maeve says, "What's that wonderful smell?"

Just then, Fiona arrives from the same direction as Emma. She sets a large serving bowl on the table. "We're eating family-style tonight. To start with, we have fresh apple salad with sautéed shrimp and crispy brie cheese, tossed with a late-harvest vinaigrette that Niall made with ingredients from his garden."

"Then we'll have the main course," Emma says. "Grilled salmon with fava beans, and roasted portobello mushrooms in a baby mushroom sauce."

Maeve turns to Connor. "We need to visit more often."

"And for dessert," Emma continues, "we have Chef Megan's chocolate torte." Shooting an accusing glance at Mick and Ian, she continues. "Unless these two have managed to sneak even more."

"Who, us?" Ian asks in mock innocence while holding both of his hands up palms out.

"We have no idea what you're talking about," Mick confirms.

Thunder mutters in the distance.

Through the windows, they watch as lightning illuminates the sky and wind tosses tree branches. A wall of bruise-colored storm clouds hunkers behind the tree line like something evil waiting to pounce. Lightning slashes the sky again, like a knife in a canvas. This time, however, it's just outside their windows.

Mick wishes that Libby and Niall were here in the cabin with them. *That would complete having all of my family under one roof—all except for Paddy.*

After everyone helps with the cleanup, they adjourn to the living room to enjoy Megan's chocolate torte paired with red wine. Mick watches his mom walk over to a group of three beautiful pottery pieces. She lightly touches the one on the left first. It's a bottle-shaped piece with a thick "lemon peel" glaze, accentuated with light indigo edges that pool at the foot. Next, her hand hovers over the piece in the center, a vase with two sweeping handles featuring a mottled blue glaze with a russet drip overlay. Finally, her hand touches the piece on the right, an oval-shaped vase with a cream glaze streaked and speckled with soft yellow. "These are breathtaking," she says. "The colors are as if they were tailor-made for the room."

"Thank you," Emma says. "I made them with that in mind."

"Are these *your* pieces, dear? I know you're a potter, but I had no idea just how exquisite your work is."

"I'm glad you like it. I'd love to create a piece for you and Connor. We can talk later about size and colors."

Mick looks around the room. Thanks to Libby's artistic flair, the cabin's interior colors—indigo and cream, with a few splashes of soft yellow—welcome him, and now Emma, too, home at the end of each day.

With reading as one of Mick's and Emma's favorite pastimes, well-worn books fill the built-in shelves. Mick's favorite seat, a French club chair and ottoman with worn leather upholstery, sits on a muted rug facing the stone fireplace. A matching couch and loveseat are paired on the other side of the room. The exposed logs and wooden beams of the rustic interior are restful, a perfect retreat for encouraging the flow of thoughts.

Old habits die hard, Mick thinks, as he watches his parents take a seat—never with their backs to a door or window. *Then again, I don't turn my back on things either. Law enforcement training of any flavor sees to that.*

Hemingway lifts his nose to sniff the lingering aftermath of dinner—grilled salmon—then makes several circles before settling with an *umph* at Mick's feet. He lowers his head onto his paws and tracks the ensuing conversation with his eyes.

"Oh, man, this is delicious," Ian says around a mouthful of dessert.

"I second the motion," Fiona agrees.

Connor turns to Mick. "Son, I understand from Libby that you were at the medical examiner's office for Paddy's autopsy this morning. I'm sorry. That must have been hard."

Mick's hands tighten over the leather on the arms of his chair. "Thanks, Dad, it was. But I want to know everything I possibly can about what happened. It's the least I can do." Looking around the room he can't help but think, *Paddy would love to be here right now.*

Fiona says, "I'm sorry to interrupt, but I thought that *coroners* are the ones who do autopsies."

Turning, Mick says, "That's a great observation, Fiona. Both medical examiners and coroners are responsible for investigating suspicious deaths, identifying bodies, notifying next of kin, and signing the death certificate. However, the qualifications they have and the medicolegal systems in which they work can be quite different.

"A medical examiner is a licensed physician, usually certified in forensic pathology. They're appointed to their position and perform autopsies.

"A coroner is a layperson who typically has little to no medical training. They're elected to their position and oversee the operation of the coroner's office. They hire forensic pathologists to perform autopsies."

"Thank you for the clarification," Fiona says. "They say you learn something new every day. Well, that's my learning for today."

Mick smiles at Fiona. He appreciates her attempt at relieving the sad tension in the room. He watches Ian squeeze Fiona's hand in camaraderie.

"I learned something new, too," Ian says. "I had no idea there was a difference between a coroner and a medical examiner either. I thought the terms were interchangeable."

Shaking his head at an embarrassing memory, Mick says, "I learned the hard way, Ian. Remind me to tell you one day. But right now—" Mick turns his attention back to his parents. "Mom. Dad. Can I bounce a few things off you to get your perspective?"

"Sure, son. What's on your mind?" Connor McPherson says.

Mick tells them what he knows about Alexander Berndt, alias Jason Hughes. "He's the fraternal twin brother of Andrew Berndt, one of the ringleaders who was arrested in conjunction with the drug heist on the night of Sam's death. Andrew Berndt was later found hanging in his prison cell."

Expert listeners, his parents nod without interruption.

"Alexander Berndt is the man who held Emma hostage. He's dead now." Mick details his understanding of Alex's death from a heart attack shortly after a visit from Niall's brother, Father MacCullough, on chaplain duty at St. Barnabas hospital the night of Berndt's death.

Maeve asks, "Do you think that Paddy's death is related to all of this?"

Mick nods. "I think it might be. Maybe Berndt thought he was dying in the ICU and confessed something to Paddy, and whatever he said needed to be covered up. Why else would anyone shoot him six times?"

Connor says, "That's a feasible line of reasoning. Go on."

As briefly as he can, Mick tells his parents about the man at the Pines & Quill entrance gate in the middle of the night. "He shot and accidentally killed his dog while trying to shoot Hemingway."

At the mention of his name, Hemingway lifts his head off his paws and thumps his tail on the hardwood floor. Mick pats his big head reassuringly and continues.

"I took the dog's body to the vet to have the bullet removed so Joe Bingham could run a ballistics report, and also to see if the dog was chipped. It was."

Mick notices Fiona's white-knuckled grip on Ian's hand. From what Ian had said, he knows that she's a glutton for excitement. *She eats it up like dessert.*

Looking back to his parents, Mick continues. "Today, the information from the dog's chip led us to his owner. We found him dead at the Scrap Heap, a wrecking yard on the edge of town. The ballistics report on the bullet the vet pulled out of the first dog is a 9mm—a perfect match to the Luger we found in the waistband holster of the dead guy at the wrecking yard."

"What do you mean by the *first* dog?" Connor asks.

"The dead guy at the wrecking yard had a dead dog lying next to him, another Doberman. That dog was taken to the vet, too. Joe called earlier and told me that the dead man's prints popped. He'd done time for armed robbery. The name on his ID, Vito Paglio, is an alias for Salvatore Rizzo. It turns out Salvatore was 'connected,'" Mick says, making air quotes. "Apparently, he was an underling in the Gambino crime family."

"As in Georgio 'The Bull' Gambino?" Connor asks, one eyebrow cocked higher than the other.

Mick nods. "Yes, that's the one. And the bullet the ME dug out of Vito's head and from the second dog, the one lying next to him, are from two different guns. It appears that Salvatore didn't shoot the dog lying next to him. The ballistics report says that the bullet from Salvatore's head matches the gun we found lying next to his body. But we haven't found a gun to match the bullet that killed the second dog."

Mick continues. "So when you put this all together, we've got the *means*. Salvatore didn't shoot himself. His gun was holstered in his waistband—it's the one that killed the first dog with a bullet that was meant for Hemingway. The killer must have shot both Salvatore and the second dog through the fence, then tossed one of the guns over for us to find." Mick pauses, rubbing his jawline. "And we've got *opportunity*. The Scrap Heap wrecking yard is in the middle of nowhere. There's not a soul around for miles. That leaves the big question of why—what's the *motive*? Why kill Salvatore, and why leave the gun behind?"

Mick looks at his parents. "Do either of you have any ideas?"

"I don't know the motive behind the killing," Maeve says, "but in my experience, intentionally leaving the murder weapon behind is part of a typical cat and mouse game that a psychopath plays. The killer feels invincible. They're saying, 'Catch me if you can.'"

"I intend to," Mick says.

Looking at the faces around the room, he continues, "Consider this your orientation to the underside of the greater Seattle area. Speaking of Seattle, Sean Rafferty, an FBI agent from the Seattle office, will be here tomorrow evening. We've already talked, and though it's a bit unorthodox, I'm going to help him with this case."

Mick watches as his dad stands and walks toward the dining room. He sees him turn toward the table, pull out his cell, and make a call. He speaks quietly. Briefly. Then slips the cell back into his pocket. As he steps back into the living room, his dad looks at his mom and nods in their unspoken shorthand. If he hadn't been looking for it, he would have missed her silent agreement. His mom stands and walks over to join his dad. Mick all but feels electricity crackle in the air—electricity that has nothing to do with the storm outside. *I know those looks*, Mick thinks. *Those two are up to something.*

"Thank you so much for a lovely evening," Connor says. "The meal was delicious."

"Yes, thank you so much," Maeve agrees. Turning, she continues. "Fiona and Emma, it's such a pleasure to meet you both."

Connor agrees. "Yes, welcome to the family."

As Mick helps his mom with her coat, his dad's phone rings. He answers, "McPherson," then listens intently, thanks the person on the other end, and terminates the call.

Before he and Maeve leave, Connor turns around. Looking at each person in turn, he says, "It goes without saying that our conversation this evening stays in this room." Then he and Maeve step out the door into the rain, wind, a flare of lightning, and the tagalong boom of thunder.

"Holy shit!" Fiona says as Mick shuts the door.

CHAPTER 23

"If you are using dialogue—say it aloud as you write it. Only then will it have the sound of speech."
—JOHN STEINBECK

Niall swings his legs out of bed and walks over to the window. This morning, dawn, normally his friend, eviscerates him. He looks away, blinking. A sob catches in the back of his throat, full, wet, and painful where it's lodged. He hears a mourning dove call, the notes haunting, pure, and wide enough to fill the world. The dove calls again, causing the tears in Niall's eyes to spill.

Making his way to the bathroom, Niall passes the chair next to the closet, where he laid his clothes out the night before. The black suit has served him well on many occasions, most of them joyous, none of them as heart-wrenching as today's— Paddy's funeral.

After dressing with care, Niall shoulders his jacket, tugs down the cuffs on his shirtsleeves, and adjusts his tie. A spurt of rage boils up inside him. He straightens to his full height. *I can't believe I'm going to my brother's funeral. He shouldn't be dead. This shouldn't be happening.*

On the north end of Bellingham, early morning mist hovers over dew-covered grass, soaking through Niall's dress shoes with each stride as he veers to cross the churchyard where it borders one of Paddy's favorite trails. He looks up, hoping for a sign from his brother. Church spires pierce the skyline, and potted geraniums hang from balconies. *Nothing.*

The family enters a side door and moves through another set of doors that leads to the worship area. Niall notices the light bounce off the bald spot on the back of a man's head as he and Libby, Mick and Emma, Connor and Maeve, and Ian and Fiona make their way toward the front. He's numb as he notices this, not wanting to think about why they're here.

It's June, and the air inside the sanctuary at St. Barnabas Catholic Church is thick with incense, the cloying scent of funeral flowers, sadness, and hushed reverence. Niall touches each walnut pew on the left-hand side of the nave as they walk down the center aisle toward the altar. The thin, well-worn dark green cushions and stiff wood backs to keep parishioner's attention aren't lost on him. He remembers years of attending this church as a youngster with his family. Their mother called him and Paddy "wiggle warts" because they squirmed on the uncomfortable pews through what seemed to them a "boring waste of time" when they could be outside playing.

People flock in. Every pew is filled, with overflow lined up outside. And though it rained last night, the body heat from the mourners who've come to pay their respects sits like a heavy weight on Niall's chest.

The stained-glass windows are immense and colorful. As he looks toward the front of the church, he sees Jesus hanging

on a cross, mounted to the wall behind the altar. It bothers
Niall. Viscerally.

———————

Libby instinctively wants to ease Niall's burden. Her heart
reaches for his pain. It breaks for him. The deep bruises
beneath his eyes betray a severe lack of sleep. His face is void
of expression. Each minute that ticks by is anguish. She takes
Niall's hand and holds it gently, reassuringly. Heartache seems
to vibrate through the sanctuary—row after row. Turning to
look, it's a tangible thing that clings to the faces of everyone
there—a tsunami of grief.

Her mind turns toward the concept of forgiveness. *It's
such a lovely, generous idea when it's not linked to something
this awful that needs forgiving.* Tears slip down her cheeks.
She knows she'll never be able to forgive this evil.

Libby feels like an eternity passes before Father Burke
begins to wrap up his portion of the Mass.

"Patrick MacCullough understood the importance of
living a life aligned with his values and without regrets, where
the people he cared about most knew how fully they were
loved. Father Paddy lived his eulogy, not his obituary." Father
Burke pauses, taking time to make eye contact with the congregation before continuing.

"An obituary is a public resume of a life. It might include
a person's place of birth, education, work, volunteer com-
mitments, and a list of surviving family members. It's the
end-of-life example of people's favorite question, 'What do
you do?' Or, in this case, 'What *did* you do?'

"If an obituary tells people that you lived, a eulogy tells
them how well. The purpose of a eulogy is to share memories,
stories, qualities, quirks, and characteristics of the deceased.
How did the person impact others? What will be missed about
them? What is their legacy? That said, at this time, I'd like to

invite Patrick's brother, Niall MacCullough, to the pulpit to deliver the eulogy."

———

Niall senses all heads in the congregation turn toward him as he makes his way to the front. He steps behind the microphone situated next to a large headshot of his brother Paddy, known to the rest of the congregation as Father Patrick MacCullough. Niall clears his throat. After two false starts, he begins.

"When I spoke with many of you about my brother, you almost unanimously remembered his epic storytelling and his colorful adventures. I'm not half the storyteller he was, but I shall begin.

"What many of you may not know is that early on, Patrick MacCullough was in the Special Forces. What he experienced during that time didn't dampen his faith. In fact, it made it stronger. It was the impetus for him becoming a priest.

"My brother shared with me that one of the most challenging tests the United States uses for recruiting its Special Forces soldiers has nothing to do with marksmanship or hand-to-hand combat. He told me, 'It's just a simple race. The candidates are told to don full gear and report to the starting point in the morning. Often sleep-deprived and hungry, the recruits are nervous. They don't know how long the course will be, over what terrain, or what obstacles lie in their path.'

"'Some sprint forward. Others pace themselves to conserve energy in the event the race is long. The physical exertion of the test is far less demanding than the mental strain. It's the pressure of not knowing the distance to the finish line that pushes many past their breaking point—the fear of the unknown.'"

Niall feels sweat bead on his forehead. He removes his suit jacket, rolls up his sleeves, and loosens his tie before continuing. "Paddy said, 'None of us knows how long our life will be. None of us knows how painful or how joyful it will be. None of us knows overall how difficult it's going to be. Tasks like this race are often the best way to reveal a person's true character.'

"I'm not going to idealize my brother today. He wouldn't want me to. He was a terrific human being, but he was far from perfect. And that's what made him so utterly approachable.

"Like Old Faithful, Paddy was consistent." Niall chuckles. "During Christmas, our family would always place secret bets on how many times he'd say, 'I have the receipt if you'd rather have something different.' And everyone remembers his trademark statement after any gift was opened. He'd draw out the initial 'Ohhh,' then clasp his hands together and say, 'Now isn't that just perfect?'

"And though he wasn't perfect, it was his imperfections and quirky tendencies that made my brother unforgettable to everyone he met.

"You may not know this, but Paddy could be fierce. Formidable. I'll never forget the time our parents left me in his care. I thought I could get away with whatever I wanted and was being rowdy in the house, nearly breaking some of our mother's precious things. He put me in a chair and sternly told me not to move a muscle. He left and quickly returned with a *shillelagh*—an Irish club our parents used to scare us with. He held it over me, and right before he was about to strike, he leaned in, winked at me, and said, 'Now go change your pants and don't ever behave like that again.'"

Laughter erupts from the pews.

"Paddy believed there were very few situations in life that couldn't be diffused with a bit of comedic ingenuity. He never held a grudge. And even though he knew more about people's lives than they did, he never gossiped. What was shared with him in confidence stayed in confidence. And I never once heard him say 'I told you so' or 'You should have done it my way.'

"He gave nothing but encouragement. He was sharp-witted, and his sparkling sense of humor was contagious. I was always impressed with his ability to turn boring into fun. He was the life of the party and one of the few people I knew who was capable and worthy of being the center of attention. "There was never a dull moment when Paddy was around. But we must remember him for more than his stories and his sense of humor. He was far more than that. The Paddy we were privileged to call family and friend knew better than most the power of relationships, loyalty, faith, kindness, perseverance, and a smile, even when a smile defied the darkness of the moment. From his example, we can learn to give others our undivided attention, to make ourselves available for listening, teaching, and caregiving."

Niall's voice falters momentarily. "Paddy's legacy is what he did with the hand he was dealt. He became Father Patrick MacCullough and safely shepherded every person gathered here in his honor today."

Niall's hand curls around a silver crucifix. Once Paddy's, it's now at home in his pants pocket. "So off you go, Paddy. The race was shorter than it should have been, but I know you enjoyed every moment of it. It was a pleasure to be in your sphere of influence—to be your brother."

Libby gently squeezes Niall's hand when he sits back down next to her. She's so much a part of him that she can taste his grief. She looks around the full sanctuary. People from every walk of life—eyes glistening—fill the pews and stand in the back with the overflow spilling outside.

Her parents, Maeve and Connor, sit on her right. Next to them are Ian and Fiona, her son and his fiancée. Mick and Emma are seated next to them. Libby smiles as she remembers Emma's determination this morning. "I *will* walk down the aisle at Paddy's funeral." And she did with support from Mick.

Libby's eyes gaze across the aisle and take in Joe and his wife, Marci. *A nicer couple you'd never meet.* Seated next to them, she watches as Toni brings a tissue to her face, shoulders heaving. *I had no idea she'd cry like that. I've never seen her show that type of emotion.*

Toni looks around the sanctuary, taking it all in. She brings a tissue to her face to cover her insidious grin. Afraid a laugh will erupt, she bends forward to conceal her mirth, knowing full well that to others, it looks like she's crying.

This—all this—is a result of my handiwork. Mine and mine alone, Toni gloats to herself.

CHAPTER 24

"Don't bend; don't water it down; don't try to make it logical; don't edit your own soul according to the fashion. Rather, follow your most intense obsessions mercilessly."

—FRANZ KAFKA

Niall wants nothing more than for this day to be over. When he looks at his watch, his stomach tightens. *The day's only one-third over, the ninety-minute Mass. There's still the graveside service and then the reception at Pines & Quill.*

The lengthy funeral procession snakes its way between St. Barnabas Church and Whatcom Falls Park to the east. Niall and Libby arrive at Bayview Cemetery, an expansive lush lawn dotted with headstones and surrounded by trees. Amidst the oaks, maples, and colorful shrubbery, the early history of Whatcom County is reflected on monuments bearing the names of the area's founding families. Names like Eldridge and Roeder.

The Eldridge family mansion, the most famous house in Bellingham, originally belonged to the pioneering family who helped establish the area. The site is part of Edward and Teresa Eldridge's three hundred and twenty-acre pioneer land claim that once covered much of north Bellingham. Edward Eldridge, originally from Scotland, came to Bellingham from San Francisco in 1853 with another of the city's founding fathers, Captain Henry Roeder. Eldridge's first enterprise in Bellingham was to open a lumber mill that supplied San Francisco with much of the wood needed to rebuild the city after the city's earthquake-sparked Great Fire in 1906.

Niall and Libby walk to a small tent fixed with rows of chairs set amid headstones.

Family members arrive next, followed by Paddy's closest friends, then parishioners from St. Barnabas. *There must be two hundred people here*, Niall thinks. At least half of them stop and offer condolences before taking their seats.

Bagpipers in full Highland dress play "Amazing Grace" as the pallbearers set the casket on a lowering device over the rectangular hole bordered by synthetic green grass. As Paddy's casket lowers into the ground, the mournful sound of the bagpipes swells the hearts of everyone there.

When "Danny Boy" fills the air, a final farewell to Patrick MacCullough—son, brother, friend, and priest—Niall steps out of the gathering of mourners, picks up a handful of dirt from the pile beside the hole. He drops it on the casket to symbolize Paddy returning to the earth. The sound is loud in the silence. Niall says a tearful, final goodbye and then returns to his place beside Libby.

The other family members and friends follow suit, each throwing a handful of dirt as they say a final goodbye.

Niall's jaw knots as people gather around him. Some kiss his cheek, others give a brief hug. All whisper their heartfelt condolences. He's vaguely aware of floating through the motions, of being propelled from person to person without thought and only automatic reactions.

Toni looks across the distance as mourners wend their way through headstones to their cars. Blending with the shade of a tree, dressed in a dark suit—with two men behind him in sunglasses and suits—is a man in his mid-sixties. A bulbous nose dominates his ruddy face. He has a thick mat of white hair and a matching mustache. An imposing figure, he looks to possess great physical strength. And though she's never met him, Toni doesn't have to be told that it's Giorgio "The Bull" Gambino—head of the Gambino crime family.

The man cocks his head. *Like a raptor considering a rodent in its talons.* After a pause, he gives her a basilisk smile and nods. Then he places a fedora on his head, turns, and walks away.

The other two men close ranks and follow suit. They get in a black Cadillac Escalade and drive away.

When Toni looks back, she sees Mick flip a small tablet closed, click and then pocket a pen before heading over to his brother-in-law.

Mick puts an arm around Niall's shoulder before he gets into the waiting limo. Leaning in, he speaks quietly from personal experience. "You're never going to be the same again, but one day, you'll be okay. Maybe not tomorrow, maybe not next week, but one day you will be."

Mick squeezes his shoulder before walking away, giving Niall the privacy to fall apart.

"I can't even begin to express my gratitude," Libby says to Megan. Both women are on the east side of the property at Pines & Quill, standing in a large, raised pavilion. It has a pagoda-style copper roof, patinated with age, and corners that flare out over Chinese-red supports. Its design is distinctly Asian.

Libby watches Megan, who's packed with energy like a terrier. *This amazing woman's outdone herself with food for this reception.* As she looks around, Libby sees two or so dozen pub-height tables, servicing four people each, covered with understated, cream-colored tablecloths.

On one side of the pavilion is a beverage bar featuring iced tea, hot coffee, wine, and beer, managed by Ian and Fiona. *No wonder they left the graveside service a bit early.*

On the other side is a long buffet table laden with plates, napkins, and self-serve hot and cold meats, salads, and hors d'oeuvres. Stepping closer, Libby sees some of Paddy's favorites: shrimp in phyllo cups, bacon-wrapped water chestnuts, rustic Tuscan pepper bruschetta, and garbanzo-stuffed mini peppers. *Megan must have asked Niall.* All of the delectable offerings are "finger food"—easily transported on disposable plates while their guests mingle and chat with each other.

At first, Libby was adamant that she'd hire caterers, but after Megan outlined her plan, explaining that she'd done this many times before, Libby finally agreed.

Libby sees Niall look with dread at the attendees milling around talking, eating, and drinking. *Paddy's death has torn him in half with a breath-stealing force, leaving him devastated to the core.* "You don't have to be here for this part, Niall."

His dark eye pouches tell of little sleep. "If you don't mind, I think I'll go up to the house. I can't face any more people today."

"You go on up and get some rest. I'll be there as soon as I can."

As Niall makes his way to the house, Libby weaves through mourners with heat-flushed faces. They hold napkins topped with assorted cakes and sandwiches in one hand and drinks in the other. Looking through the crowd, she sees that Mick and Emma, and her parents are all dutifully playing host and hostess to their guests. Making eye contact with each of them in turn, she smiles and mouths, "Thank you." *This is what family is all about.*

Niall's like a flywheel inside, about to let go and spin free. When he enters the main house, he rushes to the bathroom, kicking the door closed behind him. He flips up the toilet seat and vomits. Breathing hard, he steadies himself against the cabinet, waiting for another heave. When it doesn't come, he flushes the toilet and splashes cold water on his face. After rinsing his mouth, he dries his hands and face then heads to the mudroom to get Hemingway, a never-fail source of comfort.

After Niall opens the bottom half of the Dutch door, Hemingway steps through and licks Niall's hand in greeting. *It feels good to be away from the crowd and to be loved by this big four-legged lummox.* "Would you like a cookie?"

Niall gets a biscuit from the glass jar for Hemingway. Turning around, he sees an unopened newspaper along with some mail on the table. *I wonder who brought this in from the entrance gate?* He sits down. His breathing is heavy, and his throat throbs from crying.

Hemingway nudges him for the forgotten biscuit in his hand.

Niall gives him the treat and hears a loud crunch followed by another as Hemingway makes quick work of the biscuit. His wagging tail indicates he's ready for another. Niall pats the wiry hair on Hemingway's anvil-sized head. "That's enough for now, my friend."

He picks up the *Bellingham Herald*. He can smell the ink. *It's so fresh that it's practically still wet.* Paddy's story is on the front page, above the fold. Niall sees a picture of his brother and reads the corresponding piece.

A piercingly beautiful and sublimely musical funeral Mass for Father Patrick MacCullough was held this morning at St. Barnabas Catholic Church in front of a packed house and teary parishioners who have been blessed for twenty years of service by this venerated old-world style priest. Three fellow priests officiated the nearly ninety-minute Mass that included a balcony musical ensemble led by choral director Evelyn Phillips. The priests—Fathers Burke, O'Rourke, and Quinn—paid tribute to their beloved clerical colleague by recalling him as a kind man who led a simple life by way of meals, a shared drink, long walks, and an unstinting devotion to his duties. Father MacCullough was waked in the church for two days and is interred at Bayview Cemetery. This unforgettable Mass will forever be ensconced in the memory of this larger-than-life figure. Another chapter in Fairhaven/Bellingham history has ended today in the hallowed halls of the resplendent cathedral-like church.

Hemingway knows his friend is grieving. He nudges Niall's elbow with his nose. Niall puts his arms around the big dog's neck. Hemingway tucks in even closer as Niall buries his face in his coat and cries until his tears are spent.

Numb with grief, Niall looks around. The stack of mail catches his attention. He absently opens the first envelope, a condolence card. Handwritten on the inside flap, it reads, "I'm sorry. This must be very difficult for you. What can I do?"

He opens another. In slanted script, it says, "I'm so sorry for your loss. May the constant love of caring friends soften your sadness, may cherished memories bring you moments of comfort, and may lasting peace surround your grieving heart."

Niall sits quietly and absorbs the outpouring of love from his friends and family. He startles when the phone rings. "Pines & Quill, this is Niall."

Hemingway senses that Niall's in for the long haul. Resigned, he lies down at his friend's feet, plopping his head across one of his dress shoes.

"Hi, this is Kyle Williams. I believe my sister, Pam, is one of your writers in residence?"

"Yes, she is," Niall says.

"I haven't been able to reach her via email or on her cell," Kyle says. "I'm worried."

"No need to worry," Niall says. "I assure you that she's doing great. I'll be happy to let her know we spoke and ask her to give you a call."

"The thing is," Kyle says. "I'm here. I had unexpected business in Seattle and thought that while I'm out this way, I'd stop by and say, 'hello.'"

"Oh," Niall says, "well, in that case, where are you staying?"

After writing down the details, he assures Kyle that he'll give the message to his sister, Pam, immediately.

Niall pats his thigh. "Come on, Hemingway. Let's take a little walk."

Stepping next to Niall in a heartbeat, Hemingway doesn't need a second invitation.

They leave through the mudroom door and head north to Dicken's cottage. It's a beautiful afternoon. The sky is open and blue, guileless in its beauty. Once they clear the copse of big-leaf maples, they see Pam sitting in the Adirondack chair on the covered front porch.

Niall sees surprise light her eyes when she notices them. She abruptly ends the call she's on and sets her cell phone down on the table next to her chair.

Niall stops Hemingway from bounding forward. "Sit. Stay." Niall continues without Hemingway.

———

Shit! Pam knows that the smile on her face is saccharine, but she's been caught off guard. "To what do I owe this surprise?"

"Your brother's here," Niall says.

What the fucking hell? A thousand thoughts race through Shelly's mind as she runs through taking over Pam Williams' life. *I completely forgot about her brother, Kyle.* "He's here? At Pines & Quill?"

"No, not here." Niall indicates the area around them. "Apparently, he had unexpected business in Seattle and wants to stop by to say 'hello' while he's in the area. He said he hasn't had any luck reaching you by phone or email and that he's worried."

Niall leans forward over the rail and hands her the note he'd written. "He's staying at the Shoreline Hotel in Bellingham. Here are the details."

"What a lovely surprise," Pam says. "Thanks so much for delivering the message. I appreciate it."

"You're welcome."

As Niall turns to go, Pam says. "I just want to say again how sorry I am for the loss of your brother. Please accept my condolences."

"Thank you." Patting his thigh, he says, "Come on, Hemingway."

As Pam watches the two figures return through the big-leaf maples, she picks up her cell phone. *Time for another disposal.*

CHAPTER 25

"Every sentence must do one of two things—reveal character or advance the action."

—KURT VONNEGUT

The sun set long ago. The sky is now that deep velvet blue that speaks of midnight or close to it.

One would never suspect that under cover of night, two black-clad marauders with slender-profile backpacks are scaling the side of the building to a room on the third floor. Their tools make entry easy and soundless.

In the lobby of the Shoreline Hotel, the decor is old-world elegance. Potted palms and diffused lighting soften the marble floors, vaulted ceiling, and white columns. The tiers of the central fountain are arrayed with glass-covered candles, and the flower arrangements—dusky green, ivory, and muted pinks—are artfully understated.

The first ski-masked figure slips in through a window and drops with cat-like ease to a squat.

The second one follows suit.

They both do a tactical scan, spotting the man—Kyle Williams—asleep in bed. They nod in affirmation, then start working quickly.

After dousing a cloth with chloroform, one of them presses it across Kyle's nose and mouth.

The other one straddles his chest and arms to minimize the fight response.

Kyle's eyes open wide, bulging with fear. His voice, urgent, is muffled behind the fabric. The struggle is short.

There's a soft knock at the door.

After glancing at their watches, the first person silently gives the okay sign.

The second one pulls a gun from a bellyband before looking through the peephole and opening the door to a man wearing a hotel uniform.

The uniformed guy nods, then enters the room, pushing a linen cart in front of him.

The three of them work with efficiency under the cloak of silence. Their latex gloves don't slow them down.

The garrote ensures a bloodless kill. They strip the body and wrap it in a sheet before placing it in the linen cart along with the victim's repacked possessions. Folded towels are placed on top.

Kyle's wallet, keys, plane ticket, and car rental paperwork are tucked into one of the backpacks.

They check and recheck the space to ensure that nothing of his or theirs is left behind.

Nodding, the man in the hotel uniform retraces his steps through the door with the cart.

The other two exit the window, keeping to the shadows as they make their way back down the side of the hotel.

In the parking lot, the man dressed in the hotel uniform changes into black clothes, along with a pulled-up hoodie that covers his baseball-capped head. The visor on his cap puts his face in shadow, offering further concealment from security cameras.

After placing the uniform and the victim's possessions in his car's spacious trunk, the other two help him lift the body in as well. The previously uniformed man gets into the car and pulls away. His destination is a homeless encampment known as the Jungle, under I-5 near Airport Way South and South Atlantic Street south of downtown Seattle. He'll dispose of the body there. It will be a long time before it's identified.

One of the two remaining people locates the rental car. After getting in, they start the engine and give a thumbs-up signal.

The other person gets into a different vehicle and pulls up behind the rental car at the parking lot exit. They head to the airport to drop off the rental at the self-return, where they slip the completed contract and keys into the drop box. This extra step serves to stave off a stolen vehicle report and subsequent search for the renter.

Mick gives the Jeep a once-over by habit before placing the wheelchair in the back.

"I don't think we need to bring the wheelchair," Emma says.

"It's not for when we're on the boat," Mick says. "The boat has stairs to walk up for boarding. It's for afterward when you're exhausted. You're making fantastic progress. You've got your 'land legs' now," he says, looking down and waggling his eyebrows. "But this afternoon, when we're underway, and the deck is pitching and swaying, I'll hold on to you."

Emma leans in closely. She looks up into his green eyes and bats her eyelashes. "It's a tough job, but somebody has to do it."

"Damn straight," he says, enveloping her with both arms, wrapping her in his warm embrace. "If we don't go now," he growls into her hair, still wet from this morning's shower, "we'll never get going." He steps back, but her scent lingers— *fresh and citrusy, like lime, with a hint of vanilla.* Shaking his head to clear the teasing thoughts, he fobs the Jeep open with a beep and a flash of lights, then opens the passenger door.

"All right," Emma agrees. She peels herself from him, slides into the seat, then fastens the seatbelt. Once Mick's behind the wheel, she continues. "I know we were supposed to go last month when whale watching season opened, and the narrated tours were only on the weekends. The boats probably weren't crowded in May. Now that it's June and they've reached full traction, do you think it's going to be packed?"

Mick looks up at the clear sky. He sees dawn struggling to break over the Cascade Mountains. "It's going to be a beautiful day. I suspect it'll be a full tour. But not to worry, I made reservations. We have a spot."

"I'm excited to see the San Juan Islands," Emma says. "What kinds of whales do you think we'll see?"

"The San Juan Excursions are part of a local whale spotting network. They look for resident and transient orca, humpback, and minke whales. And on rare occasions, gray and fin whales. Not always, but many times guests on the tour boats also see bald eagles, seals, harbor porpoises, and sea lions. I take the tour at least once a season, and I've never been disappointed."

Patting her cell phone, Emma says, "I hope to get lots of great pictures. And since Sean Rafferty doesn't arrive until this evening, after we're back from the cruise, we'll have time to wander around the seaside port. You said it's filled with shops, art galleries, and brew pubs, and that it's even got the largest whale museum in the Northwest."

"I hope I didn't oversell it." Mick smiles. "It's just something I enjoy, and I want to share it with you."

Apron clad, Libby watches the writers in residence seat themselves around the big pine table in the eat-in kitchen of the main house. She and Niall rarely have to cover for each other, but breakfast is up to her this morning. *I know that grief takes an incredible amount of energy. Understandably, losing his brother has hit Niall like a freight train. The shockwaves have immobilized him. They keep rolling over him again and again, relentless and debilitating. He's so heavy with grief that some days, he can barely lift his head. Then out of the blue, like a pendulum, he swings back to his normal self.*

Pam stifles a yawn. "Excuse me," she says, covering her mouth with her hand.

"Did you pull an all-nighter?" Megan asks.

"You could say that," Pam says, nodding. "I got a lot done." Using her arms, she makes a satisfied, cat-like stretch.

Megan asks. "What smells so good?"

"Bacon-asparagus crescents," Libby says. "Niall and Hemingway are having a bit of a lie-in this morning. I knew we had the ingredients for these bad boys. They're fast, easy, and delicious."

"I'll wash the dishes if you share the recipe with me."

Libby laughs. "There's no need for that, Megan. It's nothing more than placing a slice of cooked bacon on a square of puff pastry, followed by three to four stalks of asparagus and a generous sprinkle of Parmesan cheese. You wrap the bacon around asparagus and cheese, then wrap the puff pastry around the bacon-asparagus bundle, overlapping the puff pastry ends to seal. Pop it in the oven until the pastry is golden and puffed—about twelve minutes in a 425-degree oven."

"That's it?" Megan asks.

"That's it," Libby says, wiping the palms of her hands on her apron. "And you don't even have to wash the dishes!"

Libby watches Tom pour sweet cream into his coffee, the pure dark color of it turning milky. Across from him, she sees Linda wince at the sacrilege of it all.

"What?" he asks. Putting on a posh tone, he holds up his cup. "The fats in cream enhance a cup of coffee's 'mouthfeel.'"

Linda rolls her eyes. "Oh, brother. The fats in cream do nothing more than cover up the robust texture."

Libby enjoys watching their early morning banter. Since Paddy died, she misses sharing that with Niall.

"Do I sense some coffee snobbery going on here?" Pam asks. Looking around the room, she continues. "We could take a vote, but we're not all here." Ticking them off on her fingers, she asks, "Where's Maeve, Connor, Ian, Fiona, Emma, and Mick this morning?"

"My parents and Ian and Fiona are eating at Mick's and Emma's cabin before the kids head back to school in Pullman," Libby says. "It's a six-hour drive, so they're getting an early start. But Mick and Emma aren't here. They left at zero dark thirty to go on a whale watching tour."

"That sounds interesting," Pam says. "It might be fun to do while I'm here. Where's it at?"

"San Juan Excursions has two locations at the ferry landing in Friday Harbor. The upper office is on Spring Street, and the lower office is on Front Street."

Her interest piqued, too, Megan asks, "Where's Friday Harbor, and how do you know which location to use?"

"Friday Harbor's on San Juan Island," Libby says. "And we use both locations; they're equally good. Mick and Emma have reservations from the lower office today."

"I take it they're not driving since it's on an island," Pam says.

"You're right. There are only two ways to get there. The fast way and the slow way." Libby grins. "The fast way is the ferry taxi. It takes about two and a half hours to get from Bellingham to Anacortes and from there to Friday Harbor."

"If that's the *fast* way," Megan says, "what's the *slow* way?"

"The long way is the shuttle ferry. It takes about five hours, but you have your vehicle."

"Did Emma and Mick take the short way or the long way?" Pam asks.

"They took the short way," Libby says.

"Are the boats wheelchair accessible?" Tom asks.

"The only wheelchair-friendly whale watching boat is out of Anacortes. It's with Island Adventures." Libby taps her fingers on the table. "Now that you've got me thinking," she says, pausing, "there are actually *three* ways to get there. Friday Harbor has an airport. A person can take an air taxi from Bellingham International, but then you miss the fun of being on the water." At the sound of a buzzer, Libby says, "The bacon-asparagus crescents are ready."

All talk of whale watching vanishes when Libby's hot-mitt-covered hands set two baking sheets on large cork trivets on the table. The savory smell of the bacon mixed with the yeasty dough makes a heady combination that elicits a chorus of *oohs* and *aahs*.

"Dig in while they're still hot," Libby says.

———

Back in the privacy of Dickens cottage, Pam takes out her burner and makes a call. It's met with silence on the other end.

Pam relays her newfound information staccato-style. "Today is ideal for the hit. Mick and Emma are taking a whale watching tour on San Juan Excursions. Their boat leaves from the lower office location. The fastest way to get there is from Bellingham International."

CHAPTER 26

"People say, 'What advice do you have for people who want to be writers?' I say, they don't really need advice, they know they want to be writers, and they're gonna do it. Those people who know that they really want to do this and are cut out for it, they know it."

—R. L. STINE

M ick's behind Emma as they board the *Odyssey*. Her navy-blue slacks, white blouse, and wide-brimmed straw hat are perfect for the day's outing, as are Mick's khaki pants, a button-down shirt, and Sperry Top-Siders.

Gulls squawk as they fly tangent, their breasts opened to the wind. Mick's gaze is drawn from Emma skyward. He inhales deeply, remembering. *Last year after the whale watching tour, I saw my therapist. I couldn't enjoy life because it felt wrong. I felt guilty about being alive—guilty about my role in Sam's death. We flipped a coin to see who'd drive the squad car that day. If the day's coin flip had come up tails, I would have been the driver. Not Sam. I would be dead. Not Sam.*

Once all of the passengers settle, Captain Pete introduces himself, then says, "Before we get underway, I'd like to welcome you aboard the *Odyssey*. As you know, we're currently about sixty miles north of Seattle in Puget Sound. Today's adventure includes some of the most beautiful natural areas in the world. And of course, orcas. What many people don't realize is that orca whales are the largest of the dolphin species.

"We're heading to the west side of San Juan Island—the side the orcas frequent the most. The ferry ride is about an hour and a half long, allowing you to relax and take plenty of photos.

"The *Odyssey* is sixty-five feet long and can accommodate up to eighty passengers. She's the most comfortable whale watching boat available in the San Juan Islands. A classic motor yacht, she has comfortable indoor lounge-style seating and heated cabins to keep you warm, two restrooms, a snack bar, large windows for inside viewing, and a small library with books and coloring for the kids.

"Outside, the *Odyssey* offers large, wraparound decks with comfortable, padded seating on two levels, along with outdoor speakers for hearing information from our naturalists, listening to the orcas on our hydrophones, and for music during the trip. The *Odyssey* was built in 1941 as a naval air/ sea search and rescue boat, then converted into a charter craft in the mid-1980s."

To look at them, no one would know that the person walking casually down the street is an elite shooter—no one, perhaps, but another marksman or -woman.

Their thoughts are laser-focused. *When a sniper takes a shot, there are countless variables to consider before squeezing*

the trigger—wind speed, wind direction, range, target move-
ment, mirage, light source, temperature, barometric pressure,
and that's just the beginning. The work that goes into getting
an excellent position to take a shot is immense. By the time the
Odyssey pulls back in, I'll have found mine.

Captain Pete continues, "Most of you met my wife, Erin. She loves working on the boat as a naturalist and is a member of the Salish Sea Association of Marine Naturalists. Still, her main passion is working in the office with you, our guests, helping you to plan day trips to Friday Harbor or weeklong vacations to the San Juan Islands and Washington State. She won't be on board with us today.

"With that in mind, I'd like to introduce you to Melisa. She started working with us in 2010 and is a certified marine naturalist and orca identification expert. She also works at the Center for Whale Research and has interned at Cascadia Research Collective and the Whale Museum. She's lived on San Juan Island her entire life, and in 2017, she graduated from Evergreen State College with a bachelor of science in marine biology and ornithology. Melisa is ready to answer any questions you might have about the Salish Sea and its amazing wildlife."

A beautiful Searay Sevilla—*Sea Ya*—slips past the *Odyssey* as they get underway from the Friday Harbor Ferry Terminal. Captain Pete gives a friendly honk and wave of acknowledgment and tells his guests, "That's Hank Cimeron's boat. She's his mistress—a twenty-one-footer. She has a cuddy cabin, a rebuilt V-6 170 horsepower Mercruiser, and glides like a dream."

There's a faint smell of diesel as Captain Pete guns the engine and steers the *Odyssey* into the open water.

Pausing now and then, like any other tourist, the sniper appears to take photos with their cell phone. Their mantra is precisely as they'd been trained—*I'm adept in stealth, camouflage, infiltration, and observation techniques.*

Not missing a beat, they continue. *The wind and shooting position are just as critical as distance. Remember that wind isn't constant. The most important wind consideration for a sniper is the wind at two-thirds of the way to the target. There can be multiple wind directions and speeds between me and a target. I have to recognize these and make the right adjustments.*

———

Seagulls soar overhead as the *Odyssey*'s guests feel *Sea Ya*'s wake lap against their boat. Mick wraps his arms around Emma as she sways on the rocking deck. The air is cool and salty. The sea produces a brine perfume that permeates their skin and clothes.

Mick's mind wanders to a recent conversation with his therapist, who said, "Survivor's guilt is an endless loop of counterfactual thoughts that you could have or should have done something different, though, in fact, you did nothing wrong. Yet survivors think they could have done something to prevent the tragedy from happening, when, in most cases, they could not."

But what if ours wasn't "most cases"? And what if Paddy's and Vito's deaths are linked to Sam's?

Mick leaves his mental reverie when he hears a mother calling, "Sammy. Sammy!" as her young daughter flits from passenger to passenger like an unabashed social butterfly. *Oh, to be carefree like that child.* A slow smile builds as he continues to watch Sammy. *Today's a respite from sad thoughts*, he tells himself. *Today is for fun.*

Mick leans down and whispers in Emma's ear, "It's clear that 'stranger danger' isn't part of Sammy's vocabulary. She's taking full advantage of having a captive audience."

Emma chuckles. "My mom used to call me Chatty Cathy. I, too, am a people person, just not quite that gregarious."

Mick's strong arms brace Emma as they watch Sammy's shoulder-length brown hair lift in the wind. While holding the rail around the afterdeck, the girl squints at the horizon and scans the islands.

"All she needs to complete the picture is a tricorn hat and a telescope," Mick whispers.

"That, and a parrot on her shoulder," Emma whispers back.

As the *Odyssey* slices through the chop, Captain Pete says, "Major shipping channels surround the San Juan Islands. Haro Strait, along with Boundary Pass, is the westernmost and most heavily used channel connecting the Strait of Juan de Fuca and the Strait of Georgia."

It's Melisa's turn on the PA system. "Have your cameras ready, folks, because shortly, we have a photo op coming up. The Lime Kiln Light is a functioning navigational aid located on Lime Kiln Point overlooking Dead Man's Bay on the western side of San Juan Island. It guides ships through the Haro Straits and is part of Lime Kiln Point State Park, which offers tours during the summer months."

Looking around at the passengers' faces, Melisa says, "I see that some of you are looking a little green around the gills. If you feel like you're going to throw up, please do it over the side. There may be sympathy pukers on board today, and that will help to minimize the problem.

"That said, where we're heading today, we'll likely see whales breaching. A breach is when a whale leaps mostly or entirely out of the water. It's the most spectacular and popular of the humpback whale's many moves. While other species of whale breach, the humpback whale is the world champion of this breathtaking behavior. Breaches often occur in a series, creating excellent photo opportunities.

"Humpback whales are baleen whales. Rather than teeth, they have two hundred and seventy to four hundred fringed, overlapping plates hanging down from each side of the upper jaw, called baleen plates. The plates are made of keratin, which is the same thing human hair and nails are made of. Baleen plates are black and about thirty inches long."

Melisa interrupts herself to direct everyone's attention to a trio of Dall's porpoises leaping along the port side. All the passengers turn in unison with their cameras at the ready.

Sammy's enthralled. Her father locks his arms around her waist, then turns to his wife. "Just making sure she doesn't fall in accidentally or leap in on *porpoise.*"

Everyone around them, including Emma and Mick, laughs at his joke.

Emma turns to Mick. "It's easy to see where Sammy gets her exuberance."

He nods in agreement.

Mick watches the water for telltale spouts and splashes. It's not long before Captain Pete—who knows the region, her history, her mysteries, and her secrets—spots a pod.

"A pod is a social group of whales with the bond between mother and calf being the strongest," Captain Pete explains. "Members of a pod may protect one another. The toothed whales travel in large, sometimes stable pods. They frequently hunt their prey in groups, migrate together, and share the care of their young."

Jumping up and down with excitement, Sammy counts eighteen orcas while her father hangs on tightly.

As Mick looks around the deck, he hears cell-phone cameras and traditional cameras click away. Some of the passengers are even taking videos. The *Odyssey's* filled with happy whale watchers. He turns and focuses his attention on a delighted Emma. *Even with wind-whipped hair and sea spray glistening on her face, she's beautiful.*

Dressed in a generic utility uniform, the sniper on top of the barn-red building with white trim—the Cheesecake Cafe & Bakery—is in the classic position: prone, feet turned out, a rifle on a bipod pointed forward.

Two fucking days in a row? And this hit in broad daylight? You've got to be shitting me. Unbelievable!

While using the rifle sight as a telescope, every nook and cranny in the ferry terminal is visible. *The Odyssey's pulling back in.* Looking at the photo on the cell phone one more time, the sniper confirms the target—Emma Benton. *Everything's set. This is going to happen quickly.*

The boat rises and dips. The sniper lets the air out of their lungs, and with steady hands, moves the sight to Emma's heart. Their right index finger gently squeezes the trigger.

Delightfully exhausted, Emma leans back against Mick. They're standing on the forward deck, facing the bow, with the galley wall and windows supporting both of their weight.

A sleek and cheeky seal, sunbathing on a nearby buoy, peers at the gawking passengers. Behind it, sunlight glints on white caps.

In the distance, Mick sees a combination of old and new homes with toeholds in the sloping banks. Some appear imposingly important. Some speak of nonchalant elegance, while yet others are small and eclectic.

"It's been a good day, hasn't it?" Mick whispers in Emma's ear.

Before Emma can answer, Sammy starts toward her and points at her chest. "That's cool! How'd you get that dancing red dot on your shirt?"

Sammy's mid-step when Mick pushes Emma facedown on the deck and covers her body with his. There's a whipcrack noise, and the galley wall splinters. Then pandemonium breaks loose, eliminating all opportunity for another clear shot.

———

The sniper sets the rifle down and looks at the time. *I promised Gambino that the job would be done within five minutes of the target's arrival, and I fucked it up.* Reaching behind, they touch the fabric just below their belt—at the small of their back. *"Family First."* Yeah, right. *A lot of good this tattoo's going to do me now.* Descending the building, the sniper looks around. *No witnesses.* Long, calm, terrain-conquering strides take them down Spring Street past Cask & Schooner Public House & Restaurant, Blue Water Bar & Grill, the China Pearl Restaurant, and the Crow's Nest Coffee Shoppe—away from the ferry terminal.

The use of a frangible bullet ensures that ballistics experts won't have a projectile, but even that won't help me. I made a pact with the devil and failed. I'm as good as dead.

CHAPTER 27

"Writing is about hypnotizing yourself into believing in yourself, getting some work done, then unhypnotizing yourself and going over the material coldly."
—ANNE LAMOTT

After ensuring that none of the passengers are hurt, Mick speaks with Captain Pete in the wheelhouse who's maneuvering the *Odyssey* into Friday Harbor.

"That bullet was meant for my fiancée. If it's okay, I'd like her to stay here at the helm with you for just a few minutes. It's the only enclosed space that's not crowded with passengers."

"Absolutely," Captain Pete says. "What the hell was that about anyway?"

"I'd like to know the same thing," Mick says. "Excuse me. I'll be right back." Even with the salt-flavored breeze of the sea, sweat beads on his forehead. He's filled with an unwieldy combination of nerves, adrenaline, and anticipation. But anticipation of what? Mick isn't sure. *If I knew, I'd be able to plan for it.* The only thing he's sure of is his responsibility to keep Emma safe. *You've got to stay calm,* he tells himself. But dread grips his heart, increasing its already ragged tempo. Mick returns to the wheelhouse carrying an exasperated—albeit visibly shaken—Emma. "I'm not taking any unnecessary chances with you," he says.

Emma presses a shaky palm to her sternum.

"I'll be back in just a few minutes," Mick says. "I promise to stay in view. You'll be able to see me the entire time."

Mick walks aft of the upper deck for a semblance of privacy. From here, he and Emma can see each other through the windows of the wheelhouse. After scanning the area, he locks his gaze on her. Mick has three calls to make.

His first call goes straight into voicemail. Checking his watch, Mick realizes that Special Agent Rafferty is midflight between Seattle and Bellingham. He's coming to Bellingham to help investigate the death of Salvatore Rizzo, aka Vito Paglio, an underling in the Gambino crime family. It's only a hundred-mile drive, but flying is faster than driving in the notoriously gridlocked traffic in this area.

He leaves an urgent voicemail. "Rafferty, it's Mick. Call me when you land. Someone tried to kill Emma." Frustrated, he gazes at the water stretching to the horizon, unbroken and blurred in the distance at the place where the ocean meets the sky.

Mick rubs a hand over his face and calls his dad. When Connor McPherson picks up the phone, Mick summarizes what happened. He appreciates the way his dad listens—one hundred percent. He knows from years of experience that his dad's eyes are narrowed in concentration as he absorbs the information. Now and then, Connor makes a sound of acknowledgment, letting his son know that he's taking it in.

When Mick finishes, he says, "Dad, you know it's situations like this that made me join the force in the first place. I want to help stop it."

"Mick, there's no reason you can't go back into law enforcement."

Mick kneads the top of his thigh. "After the accident, Chief Reynolds placed me on indefinite medical leave."

"Yes, but that was *before* you learned to walk again, to run again. *Before* you expressed interest again," his dad says.

"I haven't expressed interest because I walk with a limp. I run with a limp. Hell," Mick says, "I'm considered *disabled*. Who's going to take me on?"

"If I'm not mistaken, Special Agent Rafferty of the FBI has requested your help."

Alarm fills Mick's voice. "Dad, you didn't pull any strings, did you?"

"Son, you know I wouldn't do that."

Mick's shoulders relax as relief floods his system. "Thank you. I just needed to be sure. Can I talk with Mom for a minute, please?"

Connor hands his cell to Maeve. After a short back and forth between mother and son, Mick says, "Thanks, Mom. See you soon," then disconnects.

Mick's third call is to Joe Bingham, a personal friend and homicide detective at the Bellingham Police Department.

"Bingham," Joe answers.

After bringing him up to speed with the day's events, Mick says, "My mom's making dinner at the cabin tonight. I'm inviting Rafferty, too. That way, we can analyze the situation and make a plan. Oh, and Mom said to be sure to bring Marci."

"I'll be there," Joe says. "But Marci's at an away game with the girls. I was wondering what I was going to do for dinner. Now I know. I'll see you tonight."

Mick's attention is caught by flashing blue, white, and red lights bouncing off the surrounding buildings and boats, their reflection shimmering on the water. Then he feels the

Odyssey shudder as it moors. He heads to Emma and Captain Pete in the wheelhouse.

Having come from just blocks away on Second Street, officers from the San Juan County Sheriff Department are already on the pier. In the gathering crowd, Mick watches a man in the stranglehold of a professional-looking camera strap. The attached camera has a large telescopic lens attached. *He's got to be a reporter. Probably from the San Juan Islander.*

Once the *Odyssey*'s secured to the pier, two uniformed officers board the boat. After ensuring that no one's hurt, one of them uses the PA system. "Hi, folks, I'm Officer Bailey. We need everyone to remain on the *Odyssey*. You'll disembark one at a time as we take a statement from each of you. Thank you in advance for your patience and cooperation."

The man who looks like a reporter cups his hands around his mouth and yells up to the passengers on deck. "Does anyone know who the gunshot was meant for?"

"That lady," Sammy shouts, pointing up to Emma Benton in the wheelhouse.

Like "the wave" in the stands at a stadium game, heads turn to gape at Emma.

Mick clenches his muscles, holding his body firm and still, in hopes of keeping his worry contained.

On the drive back to Pines & Quill, Mick says, "Emma, I know you were frustrated with me when I left you in the wheelhouse. But I couldn't stand it if anything happens to you again."

"I appreciate that, Mick. But I'm not fragile. Look what I've been through." Emma turns to him. He sees determination in her moss-green eyes. "If the opportunity ever presents itself, I'm going to save your bacon, Mr. McPherson. Just like you saved mine."

Mick holds out his hand. "It's a deal," he says. "There's no one I'd rather have covering my back." Mollified, Emma shakes his hand, and their conversation shifts to the call he had with his dad. "I know you've told me before, Emma, but please tell me again *everything* that Berndt said and did when he held you hostage in that cave. *Nothing* is too small or irrelevant."

"Mick, we've gone over this what seems like a hundred times."

"I know. But Dr. Timmerman said that with all the trauma you've gone through, you may not have remembered everything—*yet*. She said it's possible that with time, something more may surface. Like the trauma of being shot seems to have triggered your ongoing recovery from transverse myelitis. Maybe today's near-miss shook something loose in your memory."

"Okay. If you think it'll help." Emma leans her head back against the leather headrest and closes her eyes. She brings the cave to the forefront of her memory. "Jason said that he was using me as bait. I asked him to explain. Before speaking, he took a long time to think. I could tell his right arm was hurt by the way he held it across his chest. He tapped an empty bottle of Jack Daniels on the top of his thigh. But now and then, he'd raise it to his nose and inhale deeply. I could see he relished the fumes.

"When he finally spoke, he sneered at me. 'So you want me to explain why I'm using you as bait. Is that right?'

"I nodded and said yes.

"That's when he looked me in the eyes. It felt like his reptilian stare pinned me like a snake does with its prey."

Mick sees Emma shiver. She rubs her arms up and down with her hands before continuing.

"He said, 'It doesn't matter what you know because you're going to be dead shortly. And I'm the one who's going to kill you. You're the ideal bait because I've seen how Lover

Boy looks at you. Once he realizes you're gone, he'll come looking for you. And I'm going to derive a great deal of pleasure watching Mick crumple as I slit your throat. You'll be the second person I kill that he cares for.'

"'Who was the first?' I asked. He said, 'His name was Sam. Poor, unfortunate bastard. He was McPherson's partner.'

"I told him that I didn't understand. To which he responded, 'A little slow on the uptake, aren't you? Five years ago, my brother and I orchestrated a heist for Giorgio "The Bull" Gambino. It involved well over ten million dollars in heroin. The problem was, the goods were in the SFPD evidence lockup. But Gambino had someone on the inside helping us—a dirty cop.' That's when Jason winked at me and said, 'Stay wary, for treachery walks among you.'"

Mick's grip tightens on the steering wheel, and his heart accelerates when Emma says, "Georgio 'The Bull' Gambino." *This is new information. She's never mentioned him before.* Outwardly, his demeanor remains the same—cool and calm. He doesn't want to interrupt her train of thought.

Emma resumes. "Jason said, 'The only thing we had to do was empty the stationhouse. Police are predictable creatures. When an officer falls, they rally. Every one of them. All we had to do was kill a police officer—*any* cop would do.'

"'We used a diversionary tactic to draw a squad car to a bridge. And that's when I got the driver in my sights and squeezed the trigger. *Boom!* Sam was out of the game.'

"I said, 'I don't understand why you want to kill Mick. He's off the force. And you got your drugs.'

"'That's where you're wrong,' Jason said. 'I didn't get the drugs. My brother was one of three people who got caught. He's the one who stashed the drugs. He's the only person who knows their location.'

"'Why won't your brother tell you where they are?' I asked him.

"He said, 'Dead men tell no tales. My brother was killed in jail before he could tell me. So I'm out ten million bucks, and McPherson's going to pay.'

"'But why Mick,' I asked. 'You said *any* police officer would do, and you shot Sam. So why Mick? Why now? Why five years later?'

"'Consider it tying up loose ends,' he sneered. 'Just like I'm going to do with you.'"

Emma opens her eyes and turns to look at Mick.

Even though she's emotionally bruised and exhausted, she's beautiful, Mick thinks. He takes her hand.

"Mick, when I was in the hospital, Dr. Timmerman and I talked about what happened when Jason held me hostage in the cave. She said that even though it's not her specialty area, she studied psychology in medical school, including the difference between psychopaths and sociopaths. She said, 'Between a psychopath and a sociopath, the psychopath is more dangerous because they don't feel shame or experience guilt in connection with their actions. They point blame instead.' She added, 'Psychopaths and serial killers don't need a motive. They're obsessed with what they do. They can't stop themselves.'"

Emma's physical shudder at the memory of the events in the cave runs through him. Just then, his cell phone rings. Using the hands-free option, he says, "McPherson."

"It's Rafferty. I just landed and got your message. Who tried to kill Emma? Where are you?"

"We're in my Jeep on the way back to Pines & Quill. I don't know who tried to kill Emma. It was from onshore. We were on a whale watching excursion in the San Juans. When our boat, the *Odyssey*, pulled back into Friday Harbor, a little girl asked Emma about a dancing red dot on the front of her shirt.

"Rafferty, we both know that reflex sights are optics that use a single point of reference—a red dot—for sight acquisition. It was 'dancing' because the boat was rising and dipping. I pushed Emma onto the deck, and then a bullet ripped through the galley wall right where we'd been standing.

"We gave our statements to the sheriff's deputies. The problem is, Emma and I were facedown on the deck, and no one else saw anything. With the number of shops, houses, locals, and visitors, the deputies have no idea where to start looking. And frankly, I don't know if the San Juan County Sheriff's Island Office is equipped to handle something like this. I'm afraid the sniper's long gone by now."

"We need a drone," Rafferty says. "They cover a lot of territory—*fast*. But I can't make it happen quickly enough. I know who can, though."

"Who?" Mick asks.

"Your dad, Connor McPherson. Will you send me his cell number?"

Emma releases Mick's hand and texts the information to Rafferty.

"What's your ETA to Pines & Quill?"

Mick punches the accelerator. "We're about forty minutes out. We'll meet you there. Joe Bingham's coming, too. And Rafferty," he adds before ending the call, "my mom loves to feed people. Plan to stay for dinner."

After picking up his rental car, Sean Rafferty heads to the Moon-Dance Inn, his favorite place to stay when he's in Bellingham. Nestled amid towering forests and majestic mountains, with scenic views of Lake Whatcom, the MoonDance Inn provides a relaxing escape from the busy world. It also offers a place to exorcise ghosts.

He shakes his head. *Not this trip—thinking about my son's death is for another time.*

CHAPTER 28

> *"The main rule of writing is that if you do it with*
> *enough assurance and confidence, you're allowed*
> *to do whatever you like. (That may be a rule for*
> *life as well as for writing. But it's definitely true*
> *for writing.) So write your story as it needs to be*
> *written. Write it honestly, and tell it as best you*
> *can. I'm not sure that there are any other rules.*
> *Not ones that matter."*
>
> —Neil Gaiman

Linda enjoys Tom's company in front of Brontë cottage. They agreed to meet after a day of writing and before heading to the main house for dinner. Previously, she noticed that steps are still hard for Tom to maneuver with his new prosthetic legs. Before he arrived, she moved the Adirondack chairs down to the area in front of the porch.

Side by side, they each take a seat.

After pulling her legs underneath her, Linda says, "It's slow work, but my manuscript's coming along. How about you?"

"I had a sluggish start today. But then I gained traction and made some serious headway."

"If you don't mind sharing, I'd like to hear it sometime."

"I'd enjoy that," Tom says. "I'd like to hear yours, too. I'd also like to see some of your photos. I read about your work online. It's impressive."

Linda feels the blush of pleasure as it steals up her neck and cheeks. And she knows it's a nervous habit, but she can't help twirling her hair with a finger. *I promised myself I wouldn't get flustered and that I'd remember to tell Tom about Pam and Officer Bianco.* She exhales deeply. "This might sound like a strange question, but have you noticed anything odd about Pam? Or for that matter, Officer Bianco, when she's been here?"

Tom's lips purse in thought. His head tilts slightly to the side. "Odd? What do you mean, exactly?"

"Maybe odd's not the right word. 'Off' might be better. Or 'sneaky.' It's as if they know each other but don't want anyone to know."

"What makes you think that?"

"I've read lips since I was a child," Linda says. "And some of their conversations indicate that they already knew each other before 'meeting' here. But if that's the case, why wouldn't they say something? Why would it be a secret?"

"Those are great questions," Tom says, rubbing the back of his neck. "I haven't noticed anything out of the ordinary, but now that you shared that, I'll pay closer attention."

Linda absently touches one of her cochlear implants. *Is that skepticism I hear in his voice? Maybe I should have told him that I saw Officer Bianco tell Pam, "Don't let that wheelchair fool you. You'd be surprised at just how capable Emma is."*

"Of course, I may be mistaken," Linda says, feeling awkward and wishing that she hadn't brought it up. Stretching both arms over her head, she takes a deep breath of fresh air. "I love being outside. Last night when I was sitting on the porch, I thought I saw fireflies, but I wasn't sure if they have them in the Pacific Northwest. After checking online, I learned that there *are* some fireflies on the West Coast of Washington State." She stretches both arms over her head and takes a deep breath of fresh air.

"If you see a firefly here," Tom says, gesturing to the Douglas fir tree around them, "you know it's a female."

"How on earth do you know it's a female?"

"Because I thought I saw fireflies last night, too, and did a little research myself. I read that fireflies in Washington State don't flash *unless*"—he lowers his voice and adds a spooky inflection—"they're females hoping to trap a guy as a meal."

"That's gruesome," Linda says, wrinkling her nose.

Tom looks at his watch. "Speaking of meals, I think it's time we head over to the main house. I'm starving. I wonder what's for dinner?"

Linda releases an appreciative sigh. "No matter what it is, it's going to be wonderful. I think Niall could make cardboard taste delicious!"

Linda's relieved that she and Tom seem to be back on an even footing. *From now on, I'm going to keep my observations to myself.*

After resting for most of the morning, Niall's in a better frame of mind—a mind to cook. Cooking is something he's always found to be therapeutic. Slipping an apron over his head, he checks this week's menu board and nods in remembrance. After gathering the necessary items for the main dish, he begins, stopping only when Libby enters the kitchen.

"I just spoke with Mick on the phone," Libby says. "Joe Bingham and Sean Rafferty are meeting them here shortly. They're eating at the cabin with Mom and Dad. Mick already talked with Mom, and she's making dinner. He said to tell you that he's sorry for the last-minute change of plans. But Niall, I'm telling you that something's wrong."

"What do you mean?" Niall asks.

"It's Mick's voice. It sounds stressed."

Niall's squishes his eyebrows together in thought. "After a relaxing day of whale watching? Libby, that just doesn't make any sense."

"I know my brother, Niall. Something's wrong, and he doesn't want to worry me." She walks into the prep area, slips an apron over her head, and while tying it at the back of her waist, asks, "Where's Hemingway?"

"He's at Mick's cabin with your folks."

"Then he's in good hands." Standing up to her full height, Libby salutes. "Sous chef reporting for duty, sir. What can I wash, chop, or peel?"

Just as Libby knows Mick, Niall knows Libby. *I know she's looking for a diversion from her worry.* Opening the refrigerator and pointing to the crisper drawer, Niall says, "If you're game, that's what you'll be chopping and shredding. The side dish it's going in is packed with fresh summer squash, radishes, carrots, scallions, cabbage, lettuce, and cucumbers."

"It sounds like it's going to be delicious."

"I've planned an Asian themed meal for tonight," Niall says. "The side dish is *hiyashi chuka*—cold ramen salad. It's a new-to-me recipe, so in preparation I already cooked and chilled the noodles and ginger."

"You can't go wrong with fresh ginger," Libby says.

Niall turns and opens the oven door. "Take a whiff of that," he says as an intoxicating aroma fills the kitchen.

"Oh, my gosh," Libby says. "Is that the main dish?"

"Yes, it's coconut milk-braised chicken. What you smell is the sauce." Careful not to burn himself, Niall dips a clean spoon into the pan, then blows on it before cupping a hand under the enticing offering and holding it to Libby's lips. "Here, have a taste."

Libby mouths the spoon, then closes her eyes and moans. "Mmm, it's wonderful."

"I thought you'd like it," Niall says. "It's a combination of coconut milk, curry paste, lemongrass, ginger, and garlic. After the chicken's fully baked, I'll top it with coconut flakes and cilantro, then serve it with lime wedges."

"Are you pairing it with wine or serving something else?" Libby asks.

"I thought about sake, but decided to pair it with a snappy, high acid Joseph Phelps Estate Grown Sauvignon Blanc. Its refreshing vibrancy will be a great counterpoint to these aromatic flavors."

"Our guests are in for an incredible treat," Libby says.

Niall waggles his eyebrows suggestively. "Maybe you and I can enjoy *dessert* after everyone leaves."

"There, that's taken care of," Connor says to Maeve as he joins her in the kitchen. "Something sure smells good. What's for dinner?"

Maeve's face blossoms with a smile. "Thank you. We're having old-fashioned comfort food—lasagna with my home-made sauce."

"I do love your sauce," Connor says, winking.

"Go on with you, now," she says. "There'll be six of us—you, me, Mick, Emma, Joe Bingham, and Sean Rafferty. Will you set the table for me, please?"

"I'd be delighted." When Maeve turns back to the stove, Connor quickly reaches for a dessert-laden plate—but not quickly enough. Wooden spoon in hand, Maeve gently smacks Connor's hand away from her freshly made lemon bars.

"Ouch," he says, shaking his hand in mock pain. "Do you have eyes in the back of your head, woman? I just released a drone on San Juan Island, but I can't even sneak a taste in the kitchen?"

"It's not my fault if your reflexes aren't as fast as mine," Maeve says.

Hemingway wakes from his nap and walks into the kitchen to see what all the teasing is about—and more importantly, to see if there might be handouts. His nose is counter height, ideal for scoping out the culinary situation.

"I swear that dog's smiling," Connor says.

Maeve takes a biscuit from the treat jar and hands it to Hemingway. "Aren't you a handsome boy?" she coos.

As she dotes on Hemingway, Connor peeks in the oven. The delicious aroma of Maeve's lasagna fills the kitchen. His stomach growls in response. "Lord, woman, you're killing me. After I set the table, would you like me to help make some salad or garlic bread?"

With Maeve's back still turned as she talks to Hemingway, Connor takes his opportunity and sneaks a lemon bar, placing it under the napkins on the stack of plates in his hand.

"That would be lovely," Maeve says, turning to face him. "I'll make the salad and you make the garlic bread."

"Deal," Connor says as he swiftly heads to the dining room, knowing full well he has a Duchenne smile on his face.

A tail-wagging conspirator, Hemingway follows closely on his heels.

Rafferty remembers the first time he stayed at the MoonDance Inn. A friend had told him about it. When he checked it out online, he'd read:

Conveniently located just minutes from downtown Bellingham—the gateway to the North Cascades, San Juan Islands and the Inside Passage, Mt. Baker recreation area, and British Columbia, Canada.

Combining contemporary amenities with old-world charm, Innkeepers Gary and Linda Fuller have created an ambiance reflective of their artistic craftsmanship and European style in restoring their 1933 lakeside home. Appreciation of quality and detail permeates every feature of the MoonDance Inn. Mesmerizing campfires and soft waterscapes enhance your experience.

The Fullers hadn't oversold it, and he'd been here several times since then.

After placing his Dopp kit in the bathroom, Rafferty unpacks his few belongings. He remembers his dad's words of wisdom, *Travel light, travel fast.* They still serve him well.

Picking up the remote, he turns on the television and flips through the channels to the news. He watches as a local newscaster talks about the shooting on San Juan Island earlier in the day.

"A shooting was reported on the deck of the *Odyssey*, a San Juan Excursions whale watching boat as it pulled into the ferry landing at Friday Harbor on San Juan Island this afternoon around three pm. The San Juan County Sheriff's Department says the shot came from off the boat and that no one was injured, but there is damage to the vessel. No one is in custody. Stay tuned to this station for an update of this story as more details become available."

When Connor returns to the kitchen to start making garlic bread, Maeve looks at him and bursts into laughter.

"What?"

"You're the epitome of what my mother said when I was a little girl."

"What's that?" he asks.

"When I got caught doing something that I wasn't supposed to, Mom would say, 'Be sure your sins will find you out.' And yours just did, Connor O'Rourke McPherson."

"All three names?" he asks. "Oh, Lordy, I must be in trouble."

"Here, let me show you." Maeve walks Connor to the bathroom and flips on the light. When he looks in the mirror, he can't help but laugh, too. His mouth and chin are covered with powdered sugar that Maeve dusted the lemon bars with.

"If you'd covered your tracks," Maeve says, "you'd have made it scot-free."

"I must be getting old," Connor says.

"Well, I'm glad that we've got each other to grow old with."

"Speaking of having each other," Connor says, "I've got something I want to tell you about Rafferty. Everyone's going to be here soon, so I'll tell you while we finish the preparations."

Back in the kitchen, Connor continues. "I wanted to know as much about Rafferty as possible before we meet him tonight, so I did a little checking. His son, Drew, was killed in a car accident just before his sixteenth birthday. Understandably, he and his wife, Pamela, were inconsolable.

"Drew was a passenger in his best friend's car. The friend, Jack, had just turned sixteen and gotten his driver's license. They were just two young guys—radio on, seat belts on, no one was drinking, and no drugs were involved. Drew was in the front passenger seat, and somehow, without any reason they were able to discover, Jack lost control of the car, and it flipped over and smashed into a tree. Drew was killed on impact. His friend, Jack, committed suicide six months later. The survivor's guilt he felt became too heavy for him to carry, to live with."

Stunned with sorrow, Maeve bites down on her bottom lip and shakes her head. "That's awful," she says. "I can't even begin to imagine."

"Yes, it is, and neither can I," agrees Connor. "Rafferty and his wife both took an emotional beating. Unfortunately, it led to marital stress and, eventually, divorce."

Taking her husband's hand, Maeve looks into his eyes. "My heart breaks for him. How long has it been?"

"Not quite three years," Connor says. "From what Stewart told me—"

Maeve gives him a questioning look.

"Stewart Crenshaw is Rafferty's commander in the Seattle office."

Maeve nods in understanding, silently urging Connor to continue.

"Stewart said, 'Rafferty pours his life into his work. He excels at everything he does.' Maeve, I share this with you because I want you to have the same information as me. More importantly, you pick up on more things than I do—subtle, intangible things. Body language. Unspoken signals. Having this knowledge will help you read the signs and urge him to share further."

"You're a good man, Connor McPherson."

He gathers his wife into his arms. "What I am, is lucky to have hitched my wagon to your star, Maeve."

CHAPTER 29

"I'm always pretending that I'm sitting across from somebody. I'm telling them a story, and I don't want them to get up until it's finished."

—JAMES PATTERSON

Mick tucks his cell phone back into his pants pocket. "That was Libby," he says to Emma and his parents. "Rafferty's here. He just buzzed from the entrance gate." Turning to Hemingway, Mick taps his thigh. "Come on, boy. Let's go get him."

When he opens the front door, Hemingway bolts outside; Mick follows at a more leisurely pace.

Hemingway's exuberance flushes sparrows from a nearby bush.

Mick paces back and forth in front of the cabin, absently rubbing his brow. *I wish Emma hadn't become another layer in the Salvatore Rizzo investigation. Today's near miss by a sniper was way too close for comfort. I can't lose her. I just can't. This,* he understands as his stomach twists, *is what real fear feels like.*

When Sean Rafferty opens the driver's door and steps out of the rental car, Hemingway circles him with full-body wags and licks his hand. "It's good to see you, too," Rafferty says. Once Hemingway settles, Rafferty kneels and scratches his chin and back. "If I didn't travel so much, I'd get a pal just like you."

Satisfied, Hemingway trots away to sniff a nearby tree trunk.

When he stands, Rafferty wipes the dust from his pants legs then extends his hand to Mick. "And it's good to see you again."

"You, too," Mick says. "I've got to tell you, Emma getting shot at today has my gut in a knot. I'm glad you're on the case. Thank you for asking me to tag along."

"I read your file and appreciate what you've got to offer," Rafferty says. "Your observation and deductive skills, combined with your time with Alex Berndt and your experiential knowledge of the area, gives you a leg up, making you a valuable asset."

"I appreciate your confidence."

Mick turns and whistles. "Come on, Hemingway, it's time for dinner."

The big dog joins them. Tail wagging nonstop, he tilts his head to look up at the two men, causing his ears to flip.

Mick's cell phone rings again. When he answers, Libby tells him that Joe Bingham just arrived. "Are you sure everything's okay?" she asks.

Mick hears worry in his sister's voice.

"Yes, I promise to bring you up to speed as soon as I can. Better yet, Mom and Dad can do it tonight when they get back to the main house."

Hemingway cocks his head and then bolts down the drive.

"He's coming up the drive now," Mick says into the phone. "Yes, you too. Bye."

A moment later, Joe's car comes around the bend with a four-legged escort. Hemingway barks in greeting as the vehicle pulls to a stop. When he steps out, the real welcome ensues.

Hemingway circles him excitedly and prods his hand. Joe returns the love with strokes to the dog's sizeable head.

After Mick shakes Joe's hand, Rafferty steps forward and shakes his hand, too. "I understand that congratulations are in order, Detective."

"Thank you," Joe says. "It's been on the back burner a long time."

"Speaking of 'burner,'" Mick says as Hemingway herds the men toward the cabin, "let's go eat."

Emma, Maeve, and Connor enter the living room as the four guys—Mick, Rafferty, Joe, and Hemingway—step into the cabin. Mick says, "You both already know my fiancée, Emma Benton."

Emma gives each man a quick hug and busses their cheeks. "It's good to see you again."

"Joe, you already know my parents," Mick says.

Connor and Maeve step forward. Connor shakes Joe's hand, Maeve hugs him, and they both offer their congratulations on his promotion.

Turning to Rafferty, Mick says, "These are my folks, Maeve and Connor McPherson. Mom, Dad, I'd like you to meet FBI Special Agent Sean Rafferty."

"It's a pleasure to meet you," Rafferty says, extending his hand. "I've heard a lot about you both."

Connor's and Rafferty's hands meet in a firm grip. "I've heard nothing but good things about you," Connor says.

"And the same is true for me," Maeve says, stepping forward to take Rafferty's extended hand. "By the way, do you prefer to be called Sean or Rafferty?"

"Rafferty, please, Mrs. McPherson."

"And we're Maeve and Connor," she says. "I hope you brought an appetite, Rafferty."

Wanting attention, too, Hemingway steps forward and licks Maeve's hand.

"I know *you* brought *your* appetite, big guy," she says to Hemingway. "Now go lie down. We won't forget you. You'll get your dinner soon."

Hemingway lies on the floor by the couch and puts his head on his paws.

"Don't pout, Hemingway," Mick says. "It doesn't suit you."

The six of them sit down at the table to eat. "Tonight's meal is family-style," Maeve says to Joe and Rafferty. "Please help yourselves."

"It smells delicious, and I'm not shy," Rafferty says, reaching for the platter of garlic bread.

"I'm not either," Joe says, picking up the salad bowl.

Mick leans forward and rests his arms on either side of his plate. "As you know, the reason we're all here is because a sniper tried to kill Emma today."

———

At the kitchen table in the main house, Pam's cell phone vibrates in her pocket. Discreetly, she reads the text from Toni. *That FBI agent, Rafferty, and Joe Bingham are at Mick's cabin for a confab with Mick's parents, Connor and Maeve McPherson.*

Pam manufactures a smile and turns it on her hosts and the other writers. "Will you excuse me for a moment, please? My mom just texted, and I need to speak with her."

After pulling the front door shut behind her, Pam calls Toni. "What the fuck do you want me to do?" she whisper-shouts into the phone. "Join them in the cabin?"

"Don't. Get. Pissy. With. Me." Toni snaps each word like a whiplash. "That order's from 'The Bull,' not me. Use your head. It's the middle of June. The windows are probably open. See if you can hear anything from outside, then call me. And for God's sake, remember, they've got that damned dog with them. Don't make a sound."

Pam silences her phone. *This is one fucking huge risk; the payoff better be worth it.* She looks over her shoulder before ducking into a wooded area, stealthily slipping from tree trunk to tree trunk.

The cabin, nestled in a grove of pine trees, seems to be simultaneously growing out of the earth and swallowed up by the woods.

She sneaks across a small clearing and crouches under a side window near the front of the building. *Nothing.* She takes a cautious peek. *The window's open, but the living room's empty.*

Staying low, she moves to the back of the cabin, where she hears voices rise and fall through another open window. Remaining statue-still in a squatted position, she absorbs the conversation within.

———

"Dad, were you able to get a drone to look for the sniper that shot at Emma?" Mick asks.

"Yes, son. I was."

"Thank you, Connor," Rafferty says, "because *that's* how we hit pay dirt. On the drive over, I was notified that the drone located who they presume to be the sniper. Unfortunately, he's dead. Someone put a bullet in the back of his head. Right now, his body's at the Snohomish County Medical Examiner facility in Everett. They took his prints, and they're running them now. They'll call the minute they've got something."

Mick turns to Emma. "Do you remember in the Jeep when I asked you to tell me again about what happened when Berndt held you hostage in the cave?"

Emma nods. "Yes, I do."

"Do you remember telling me Hughes told you that five years ago, he and his brother orchestrated a heist for Giorgio 'The Bull' Gambino that involved well over ten million dollars in heroin?"

Mick sees her brows knit together. "Yes, Mick. But why are you asking me this?"

"Emma, in all the times you've told me, the police, and the FBI about what happened in the cave, today's the first time you said anything about Giorgio 'The Bull' Gambino."

"It is?" She hears surprise and disbelief in her own voice.

"That's right," Mick says and then turns to the others. "Dr. Timmerman told us that with all the trauma you've gone through, you may not have remembered everything yet. She said something more might surface. I think today's near-miss jogged your memory."

"But how can that be? It doesn't *seem* new to me. It's like I've always known it," Emma says. "Like it's always been part of what happened in the cave."

"That's because it *is* part of what happened in the cave," Mick says. "Only you just now remember it."

What else haven't I remembered yet? Emma wonders. Beneath the table, she places a hand on her belly. *This morning's pregnancy test was 'inconclusive.' Oh, my God! What if Alex Berndt raped me when I was his hostage in the cave? What if I'm pregnant and the baby's his?*

Sick at the thought, Emma says, "Will you excuse me for a moment, please?" She barely reaches the bathroom in time to lift the lid and vomit into the toilet.

CHAPTER 30

"Give the reader at least one character he or she can root for."

—Kurt Vonnegut

Mick's cell phone vibrates with a text from Niall. *Libby's worried, and frankly, so am I. When you guys come up for air, will you please tell us what's going on?*

Mick sends an affirmative reply then replaces the cell phone in his pocket.

Looking at the faces around the table, he says, "We have a lot of information to process. As soon as Emma gets back, we'll recap the events so we're all on the same page."

The group nods their agreement.

In Emma's absence, Mick says, "We've *got* to find out what's going on. This is the *second* time in as many months that someone's tried to kill Emma." He clears his throat to regain control of his voice.

"Can I get anyone some coffee?" Maeve asks.

Mick knows it's his mom's attempt at giving him a moment to collect himself.

"I'd love some," Connor says.

"Me, too," both Joe and Rafferty say.

When Emma returns, Mick asks, "Are you okay, honey?"

"Yes," Emma assures him, smiling. "I just drank a lot of tea this afternoon."

"Okay, then." Turning back to the group, Mick says, "To recap, everything points to having started five years ago when my partner, Sam, was shot as a diversionary tactic. We now know that Alex Berndt, alias Jason Hughes, was the trigger man. The 'officer down' call from that incident nearly cleared the SFPD stationhouse, giving Andrew Berndt, Alex Berndt's twin brother, the opportunity to steal over ten million dollars in heroin from the evidence lockup."

"That's right," Joe says. "Andrew was one of three people caught. He was killed in prison before he could tell his brother where he stashed the heroin. That pissed Alex off because psychopaths don't like to fail. And they don't like loose ends. So he came gunning for you," he says, looking at Mick.

"And from what Emma remembered on the drive home today," Mick says, "Alex and Andrew were working for Georgio 'The Bull' Gambino. We don't know if he was under Gambino's orders when he came to Pines & Quill to kill me, or if it was a personal vendetta. Either way, he took Emma hostage and used her as bait to get to me.

"When we found them in a cave in Devil's Canyon, he shot Emma in the back. I shot him in the chest, but he didn't die. He died while recovering in the ICU at St. Joseph Hospital. Patrick MacCullough was on chaplaincy duty that night. We think that he was the last person to speak with Alex before he died."

"And I was the last person to speak with him before he was shot," Emma says. "He told me that they had someone on the inside at the SFPD—a 'dirty cop'—and he said, 'Stay wary, for treachery walks among you.' Then Paddy was shot and killed. What if when Alex Berndt was on his deathbed, he was confessing to Father MacCullough—divulging information someone didn't want anyone else to have?"

Mick picks up the verbal baton. "Then Salvatore Rizzo, alias Vito Paglio, came to Pines & Quill with one of his Dobermans, Smith. We still don't know why he was here. I took Hemingway out for a midnight walk. That's when he picked up the Doberman's scent and gave chase. Salvatore tried to shoot Hemingway but killed his dog, Smith, instead."

At the mention of his name, Hemingway enters from the living room, noses Mick's shoulder, and lies down with a *harrumph* behind his chair.

"After that," Joe says, "Mick and I find Salvatore and his other dog, Wesson, dead at the Scrap Heap, a wrecking yard on the edge of town. The ballistics report confirmed that the first dog was killed by a bullet from the gun we found on Salvatore. The bullet from Vito's head was from the gun we found on the ground by his body. But the bullet from the second dog, Wesson, the one lying dead on the ground next to Salvatore, was from a gun we haven't found yet."

"We'll find it," Mick says.

———

Rafferty's cell phone rings. "This may be the information we're waiting for." He removes the cell phone from his pocket. "Rafferty." After a minute, he says, "Thank you. That's very helpful," then disconnects.

"The initial identifiers they can tell us about the dead guy the drone found are that he's Caucasian, has black hair, is somewhere in his late twenties or early thirties, and has a single tattoo on his lower back. It reads, 'Family First.'"

———

Aware that his eyebrows are practically in his hairline, Joe says, "Hold on a minute. The morning that Niall and Libby met me at the morgue to identify Paddy's body, I stayed after they left. I wanted to speak with Dr. Graham. Her assistant, Dr. Hargrove, had been on vacation, and she was bringing him up to speed regarding a female corpse on the table.

"Dr. Graham said, 'I'll begin with the obvious. The victim is a female in her late twenties or early thirties. The most conspicuous identifying mark is a tattoo on the small of her back. It reads 'Family First.' She told me, 'This is the second one of these tattoos we've seen. I don't know, but maybe it's gang or even mafia related.'

"That's when she directed me to three sealed bags. One had the victim's clothing, one had her shoes, and one had her small personal effects. When I asked about the victim's purse, Dr. Graham said, 'There isn't one, but look closely at her personal effects and tell me if you see anything odd.'

"When I picked up the clear bag, I saw a half-empty pack of menthol cigarettes, a Bic lighter, a stick of Dentyne gum, a lipstick tube, and what at first glance looked like a folded brochure. I turned the bag over and saw that it was a bulletin from St. Barnabas—Father Patrick MacCullough's church."

Rafferty looks at Hemingway. "I'm going to get my laptop from the car. There's something I want to check. Want to come with me?"

Hemingway stands and dances with excitement. His tail lashes back and forth like a turbo-boosted metronome.

"We'll be right back," Rafferty says as the two of them walk through the living room and out the front door. Before Hemingway breaks away to go sniff, Rafferty says, "We may be onto something here, buddy."

———

Pam plasters herself against the cabin and holds her breath. *Oh, shit!*

Poised for flight, she listens intently. Just around the corner of the cabin, she hears prolonged rustling. *Is the damned dog rolling in something?*

———

Emma has no appetite. Her stomach churns. Something niggles at the edge of her memory. Her mind reaches for it, but it eludes her. It's just out of her grasp. She lowers her head in concentration and closes her eyes in an effort to reach it.

"Is everything okay, dear?" Emma hears Maeve whisper.

"Yes, I'm fine," she whispers back. "I'm trying to remember something." She shakes her head in dismay. "But just when I think I've almost got it, it vanishes."

"I hate it when that happens," Maeve says.

"Me, too," Emma says. "And it seems to be happening more often."

———

Pam, standing to the side of the window and ready to bolt, hears a loud whistle.

"Come on, boy," Rafferty calls to Hemingway.

After the front door opens and closes, she collapses against the side of the cabin and takes a deep gulp of air. *I didn't even realize I was holding my breath.* She crouches back down and continues to listen.

———

Rafferty's heart pounds with excitement as he boots up his laptop and logs into a database that will provide the information he wants.

"Good Lord," Connor says. "What's that smell?"

Everyone's gaze turns to Hemingway, who looks quite pleased with himself.

Mick gives him a stern look. "Did you do something bad?"

Hemingway averts his eyes, drops his head, and looks guilty.

"Dad, open the door, will you? I'm collaring this guy and booting him out. He rolled in scat!"

After the front door closes, Rafferty taps the laptop screen with his hand. "I thought that tattoo sounded familiar. His autopsy report says that Alex Berndt had three tattoos. The one on his lower back read, 'Family First.'"

Reluctant to break Rafferty's concentration, everyone listens as his fingers fly across the keyboard. He looks up with a tight smile. "Bingo! Guess who else had a 'Family First' tattoo?" Without waiting for an answer, he says, "Alex's twin brother, Andrew."

Rafferty holds up his hand to stem what he knows is a tsunami of conversation. "Let me do one more search." Again, his fingers fly across the keyboard. He looks up with a grim smile. "Salvatore Rizzo also had a 'Family First' tattoo on his lower back."

Rafferty's interrupted by his cell phone. "Rafferty." He stands. "Yes, I understand. Thank you," he says, then disconnects the call.

"The dead guy the drone found, presumably the sniper who shot at Emma, was Adrian Padula." He looks around the room. "Does that name mean anything to any of you?"

Joe says, "It sounds vaguely familiar, but I don't know why."

"It turns out that Mr. Padula served in Afghanistan as an Army Ranger. He was a sniper. And his most recent employment was as a Bellingham Police officer."

When Rafferty says, "police officer," something inside Emma's memory clicks. "Oh, my God." She turns to Mick. "Remember the night Toni questioned me on the patio of the main house about being held hostage in the cave by Alex Berndt?"

Mick nods. "Yes."

"Toni dropped the pen she was using to take notes. When she bent over to pick it up, candlelight flickered across the exposed skin where her shirt had come untucked from the waistband at the small of her back. It was hard to tell in the low light, but I read one word clearly. It was beneath another word whose letters were mostly covered by the hem of her shirt. I didn't think anything of it at the time; it was just interesting. After all, lots of people have tattoos." Emma grips the edge of the table. "The word I saw was 'First.'"

Inside the cabin, silence reigns for a moment. Then, like a murder of crows, the occupants start talking all at once.

There's no need to remain quiet now. Shelly, aka Pam, takes off at a dead run.

CHAPTER 31

"Creativity is a habit, and the best creativity is a result of good work habits. That's it in a nutshell. . . . In order to be creative you have to know how to prepare to be creative."

—TWYLA THARP

She wants to play!

Hemingway launches pursuit of Pam. It's not often he gets to chase a human full bore through the woods, but his people aren't here to stop him, and he loves to run.

———

Hearing a noise behind her, Pam looks over her shoulder. She nearly trips and falls on a tree root but manages to keep running. When she reaches the circular drive in front of the main house, the door opens.

"Hemingway!" Libby shouts.

Hemingway screeches to an abrupt halt and sits on his rear. His tail frantically swishes the ground behind him.

Hands on knees, Pam bends to catch her breath. Her panting is loud and labored.

The pearlescent moon skims the trees, and a chilly fifty-eight degrees keeps the crickets quiet.

"Pam, I was just coming to look for you," Libby says. "In the moonlight, it's hard to tell if you're scared or having fun."

Use this to your advantage, Pam tells herself. "Oh, we're just having fun. I was talking with my mom on the phone and wandered off the beaten path. Hemingway found me, and we decided to race each other back." Pam turns around and looks at Hemingway. "I won!"

"That's a relief," Libby says, placing a hand on her chest. "I'm glad you were having fun. Now come on in. We kept your dinner warm. The others are already in the Ink Well enjoying dessert."

"Thank you," Pam says. "But I was just stopping by to apologize for being gone so long. If you don't mind, I'll take a raincheck on dinner. While I was walking, I had a great idea for a chapter, and I want to get it out of my head and onto paper before it vanishes."

Libby nods. "I've been there myself and understand completely." Turning to Hemingway, Libby says, "Come on, you big lug. Before I feed you, I'm going to text Mick and find out if you've already eaten. No double-dipping for you."

Pam manages a chuckle, then says, "Please give my regrets to the others. I'll see you tomorrow. By the way, will there be tai chi in the morning?"

"Yes, six thirty at the pavilion," Libby says.

"I'll be there."

On the walk to Dickens cottage, Pam pauses on the pathway and looks up. She surveys the sky and sees that night is gathering intensity in the east. The air is lightly flavored with salt from the nearby bay. Pursing her lips in thought, she squints into the shadows. Nothing moves except for leaves rustling in the soft breeze.

It may not have been about a chapter, but I really do have an idea. I'll tell Toni about the drone, Padula's body, and that they know he was recently hired as a Bellingham Police officer. I'll let her know that Emma remembered something Berndt told her that ties him and his brother to Gambino. And I'll also tell her that they know about the tattoos—all of them. Except hers. Let's see how Miss 'Don't Get Pissy with Me' reacts when the boys in blue find out that she's a dirty cop.

A hint of a smile cracks the corners of Pam's mouth.

Rafferty looks at the newly promoted homicide detective, Joe Bingham. "How long were the two of you partners?"

"Going on three months," Joe says. "Bianco transferred here after she was put on mandatory leave for a weapon's discharge. She arrived in Bellingham with a chip on her shoulder. In an effort to set the record straight, she told me, 'My being put on administrative leave after shooting that asshole in self-defense was normal police procedure. You would have done the same thing. I was cleared of all wrong-doing. But the reason I was assigned elsewhere is none of your business.'"

Rafferty looks at the faces of the people in the living room of Mick's cabin. He's glad to be in the company of good people who will help him investigate Vito Paglio's death and the Gambino crime family—Mick and Emma, Mick's parents, Connor and Maeve, and Joe Bingham. After making a note on his cell phone, he says, "In the morning, we'll scour her record and the reason for her transfer. We also need to canvass the tattoo studios in Fairhaven, Bellingham, and the surrounding area, although I doubt the 'Family First' ink is being done in a shop by a tattoo artist. It's more likely they're being done by a scratcher. But some of the legitimate tattooists may know where that custom ink's being done."

"What's a 'scratcher'"? Emma asks.

"It's someone who tattoos without any training or concern for health code regulations or the proper use of equipment. Many of them cause damage to the skin of the people they ink." Rafferty says.

"You might also want to check prison records for the 'Family First' tattoo," Connor says. "Someone on the inside may have intel and be willing to talk *if* there's something in it for them."

The horror of who Toni *really* is sends shards of ice through Joe's veins. "I just can't believe this. I've never been accused of being oblivious, but I've been duped. I should have seen something."

"Don't beat yourself up," Mick says. "She's been out to Pines & Quill many times. She's eaten meals with us, and none of us caught on either." Mick rakes a hand through his hair. "For Christ's sake, she came to Paddy's funeral."

"Well, we know now," Joe says. "Or at the very least, have a strong suspicion that Bianco's the dirty cop Alex Berndt warned Emma about when he said, 'Stay wary, for treachery walks among you.'"

"Shelly just reported in, sir," Toni says into her burner phone.

"And?"

"She said that an FBI drone found Padula's body and that they know he was recently hired as a Bellingham police officer."

"I'm aware of that," Gambino says.

Toni knows better than to ask how "The Bull" had already come by that information. "Emma remembered Berndt told her that he and his brother orchestrated the SFPD heroin heist under your orders. They also know about the 'Family First' tattoos."

"And you're certain that Shelly was immediately outside a window when she heard this?"

"Yes."

"And the occupants in the cabin—Connor and Maeve McPherson, Sean McPherson, Joe Bingham, Sean Rafferty, and Emma Benton—were a mere stone's throw from her?"

"Yes, within feet."

"And yet she didn't take advantage of the situation or show any initiative to take them out?" His voice has grown angrier, louder. "She had a Beretta Centurion. It holds fifteen rounds in the mag and one in the chamber." His serrated accusations continue. "She could have taken them out in one fell swoop. It would have been a coup."

"Yes, it would have."

"It's time to eliminate her from the equation. Do you understand?"

"Yes, sir." *With pleasure.*

Rafferty's cell phone rings. "Rafferty. Yes. Yes." He listens quietly, nodding at certain points. "And you're certain there aren't any? Not even a partial? What about on the unspent bullets? Okay. I appreciate it. Thank you."

After disconnecting, Rafferty says, "The drone led the San Juan County Sheriff's Department to a dumpster where they found a Colt Canada C8."

"That's the type of rifle Special Forces used in Afghanistan, isn't it?" Mick asks.

"Yes," Rafferty says. "A distance shot with that type of rifle means a professional. And it had frangible bullets in the chamber—all wiped clean. That explains why the ballistics experts couldn't find a projectile on the *Odyssey*."

"What's a frangible bullet?" Emma asks.

"It's a bullet that breaks into tiny fragments," Mick says. "It doesn't deform or expand like a hollow point. Instead, it shatters or disintegrates upon impact with the target."

"Whoever planned this," Connor says, "is sophisticated, focused, and organized."

"I still can't believe someone wants to kill me," Emma says. "What's the motive? Kill me on the off chance that Alex Berndt told me something they don't want anyone to know?"

"Psychopaths and serial killers don't need a motive," Maeve says. "They're obsessed with what they do. They can't help themselves."

"That's why we need to pick Bianco up now," Rafferty says, pulling the cell phone from his pocket. "If she's a dirty cop, we need to find out if there are others, like Padula, and clean this up."

"Rafferty, before you make that call," Maeve says, "may I make a suggestion?"

"Of course," Rafferty nods.

"This may sound a bit unorthodox, but it just might work in our favor." She looks at the faces around the table. "You've seen *The Godfather Part II,* right?"

"Yes," Rafferty says, nodding.

Maeve sees his brow furrow slightly. *He doesn't know where I'm going with this.* "In it," Maeve continues, "Michael Corleone says, 'Keep your friends close, and your enemies closer.'"

Maeve looks at Connor. She sees him smile when "the penny drops," and he realizes what she's leading up to.

"I propose that we don't do a thing about Toni—*yet.* Instead, we feed her information that we want her to have."

"Use her," Connor says. "Manipulate her to our advantage."

"Track and monitor her movements," Mick says, on board with the idea.

Joe rubs his hands together. "We can tap her home, her phones and cars—both personal and work—and use tracking devices as well."

By the faint creases etched in parentheses around Rafferty's mouth, Maeve already knows his answer to her question, but asks it anyway. "What do you think, Rafferty?"

His eyes crimp at the corners as he smiles. "It's brilliant!" he says.

"I thought you might like it," Maeve says.

"We'll need to get signoff from a federal judge," Rafferty says. "First, though, we need to show probable cause of organized crime and drugs or violent crimes, including serial murders. And we've got it all! I'll get an appointment with Judge Watson. I've worked with him before."

"What about Bruce Simms, the chief of police?" Joe asks.

"Let's keep him out of the loop for now," Rafferty says. "Until we know who's clean and who can be trusted, the plan doesn't leave this room."

CHAPTER 32

*"Keep a small can of WD-40 on your desk—away
from any open flames—to remind yourself that if
you don't write daily, you will get rusty."*
—GEORGE SINGLETON

Libby and Niall sit at the kitchen table nursing fresh-brewed coffee when Maeve and Connor return to the main house.

Hemingway trots over in greeting, then lies at their feet, belly up, hoping to have it scratched.

"I just washed my hands, mister," Connor says. "You're going to have to wait."

"It's after midnight," Libby says. "What on *earth* is going on?" She knows she sounds surly. "I'm sorry, but we've been sitting here worried sick. When I talked with Mick on the phone earlier, I could tell that something was wrong, but he wouldn't tell me. He said that you two would tell us when you got back tonight." Libby turns and looks pointedly at the clock. "And it's practically tomorrow."

"I'm sorry we worried you, dear," Maeve says, touching Libby's hand. "But we had a lot to discuss."

Ever the courteous host, Niall offers his in-laws fresh coffee and dessert.

"No, thank you," Maeve says. "We ate at the cabin."

"What did you have to discuss?" Libby asks.

Connor tells them about the sniper who tried to kill Emma on the *Odyssey* when it pulled back into Friday Harbor.

Libby's knuckles go white as she grips her mug. "This is the second time someone's tried to kill Emma."

"Mick, Rafferty, and Bingham are going to get to the bottom of this," Connor assures his daughter.

"Does this have anything to do with Paddy's death?" Niall asks.

"We think they're connected," Maeve says.

"We can talk more about this in the morning," Connor says, stifling a yawn. "But not in front of the guests. Everything we shared this evening is confidential."

"We understand," Libby says. "That yawn is contagious, Dad. I have a tai chi session at 6:30, so I better get some sleep. I'm sorry that I crabbed at you earlier."

"I would have crabbed at us, too, dear," Maeve says. "Like mother like daughter, patience was never our strong suit."

Libby walks around the table and gives each of her parents a warm hug. "I love you both. Good night."

As Connor and Maeve slip beneath the summer-weight covers in the guest bedroom, Connor says, "Maeve, do you think it's a good idea that we didn't tell Niall and Libby about the tattoos and Toni Bianco?"

He feels Maeve squeeze his hand.

"Yes, Connor, we all agreed that it might even save their lives. Unlike our old poker faces, our daughter and son-in-law wear their hearts on their sleeves. They'd act differently around Toni Bianco, and she'd be suspicious. It's better that they don't know."

"You're right, dear," Connor says.

———

Bianco parks the vehicle she "borrowed" two miles away from Pines & Quill so that it's nowhere near the property. The walk gives her plenty of time to think. Slipping quietly into the forest, she feels as if she's left the wider world behind.

For tonight's "target practice," she muses, *I'm using my FNX 45 Tactical. Most of the standard ammo for a .45 is already subsonic, so it's quiet. Well, quiet as gunshots go. And I love the factory sight.* She pauses to caress the gun, enjoying the touch of cold steel. *It's tritium-powered and tall enough to see over every suppressor I've put on it so far.*

Toni holsters her gun to adjust her night-vision goggles. *It was pretty cool when Joe and I watched Mick climb down the mountainside effortlessly in the dark to find Emma. And all because of his night optics.* Satisfied with the adjustment, she pats her newly acquired pair. "Thanks for the tip, Mick," she barely whispers to the surrounding trees.

Toni unholsters her gun again and checks the silencer a final time. The Osprey 45 has served her well on many occasions. *It not only looks sexy, but the rectangular shape of the suppressor keeps the width of the overall package about the same as the slide.* She smiles. *Best of all, it comes with an optics-ready frame making it easy to add a Trijicon RMR up top. The dot clears the suppressor body, so it makes an excellent sighting option.*

———

Apart from the great horned owl perched on a high limb in one of the big-leaf maple trees surrounding Dickens cottage, no one else is aware that Pam is about to have company.

The owl watches the woman with short, dark, curly hair step with care between tree trunks, stopping periodically to look around. After pressing his needle-sharp talons into the tree's flesh, he rotates his head on his flexible neck to get a better look with his large yellow eyes.

The owl isn't the only one schooled as a predator. The woman approaching the cabin, as well as the woman inside, are both well-versed.

———

Toni keeps her back to the cottage as she eases up to a side window. With her gun in a two-handed grip, she tracks left and right in sync with her gaze. She stops to listen before cautiously peering inside. The lights are out, but with night optics, she sees that the living room and kitchen are unoccupied.

Toni continues to the back of the cottage. After rounding the corner, she pivots and crouches, then edges her way to the open window. She drops to a squat with the gun tucked close to her chest. Statue still, she listens for movement, for noise, for anything.

The maple leaves whisper when the breeze touches them.

Toni inches up and looks through the window screen. She sees Pam lying on her side, facing the far wall. Toni trains her optics on the target. A red dot locks into position on the back of Pam's head.

Toni squeezes the trigger. *Bingo! A perfect headshot.*

Aware that suppressors lower damage at range, Toni's second shot severs the spinal cord at the nape of Pam's neck.

Fuck! Toni spins and aims at a muffled sound in the trees. Through her night-vision goggles, she sees a bird—an owl with an impressive wingspan—glide through the branches into the night sky.

Toni collects the two spent casings before she, herself, disappears into the night.

"No," Mick moans as he reaches to stop the six o'clock alarm.

"I second the motion," Emma mumbles as she rolls over, covering her head with a pillow.

Mick rubs his eyes and blinks his surroundings into focus. "Even though I don't want to either, we're going."

"But I don't want to," Emma's voice is faint through the pillow.

"You've made too much progress to slow down now, Emma. Consistency is key with tai chi. Come on," he coaxes. "Get up."

Emma pulls the pillow away from her head.

Mick looks through the window. "You've got to see this."

Emma joins him. "It's beautiful," she says as she watches the first light of morning dapple the gauzy clouds in the sky.

Mick smiles and locks his hands behind Emma's back, drawing her closer. As he angles his head down to kiss her, he whispers, "And so are you."

Libby can't help but be pleased with the morning's turnout. Everyone, including her parents, is at the pavilion. Everyone except for Niall, who's doing the prep work for breakfast. And Pam.

Libby joins Mick and Emma, who are toeing off their shoes. Taking her soon-to-be sister-in-law into her arms, she whispers, "I heard what happened, and I'm so sorry. But Dad promises that Mick, Rafferty, and Joe will get whoever's behind this. And if I know my parents, they won't sit quietly on the sidelines."

"Thank you," Emma whispers, returning the hug. "We better get started. I need to move before my buns freeze."

Athletic and capable, Libby walks to the front of the class. "The last thing Pam said to me last night before heading to Dickens cottage was that she'd be here this morning."

"She probably hit the snooze button like we almost did," Connor says. "You guys do this every day?" he asks, incredulous.

"You bet." Libby smiles at her dad, knowing full well that her parents get up at zero dark thirty.

"Let's go ahead and get started," Libby says. "Pam can join in when she gets here."

They begin with gentle warm-up exercises that include walking around slowly, clenching and unclenching hands for a couple of minutes, and letting go of everyday thoughts to prepare to focus on tai chi.

With Libby's guidance, they do two stretches for each part of the body, beginning with the neck, then working to shoulder, spine, hip, knees to toes, doing each one five times on both left and right sides.

She encourages them to hold each stretch for fifteen seconds. This allows the muscles to relax until they're near seventy percent of the full range.

Libby watches Tom in his wheelchair, making each move from the waist up. *It reminds me of when Mick was in a wheelchair recovering from his near-fatal accident.*

Unlike many instructors who expect their students to give one hundred percent, Libby works with the principle of only using about three-quarters of a person's energy. The rest is reserved to avoid overwhelm.

At the end of the class, Libby thanks everyone for coming. "You've got about a half hour to shower and change, then head to the main house for breakfast. Niall's making a treat you don't want to miss—peach bourbon French toast."

"I'm there!" Tom says.

"Me, too," Linda and Megan agree.

After the writers in residence leave the pavilion, Libby says, "I'm concerned about Pam. She said she'd be here this morning."

Mick looks at Connor. "Dad, let's head over to Dickens cottage to make sure everything's okay. I'm sure Pam's chipping away at her manuscript."

Libby nods. "She *did* say that she had a great idea that she didn't want to lose. But I'd feel much better if you check to make sure."

"Will do," Connor says. Leaning forward, he kisses the top of his daughter's head. "We'll be up to the house soon. Don't let Niall serve anything to anyone without us," he growls. "I don't want to miss out."

Libby flexes a muscle. "I'll hold them all back until you get there."

On their way to Dickens cottage, Mick says, "Dad, thanks for last night. And thanks for making the drone happen. I know you and Mom are going back to Seattle tomorrow, but it's been great having you here."

"Son, it's been wonderful to be here. I'm just sorry that it was for Paddy's funeral. I'm also sorry that someone's tried to kill Emma—again. But you, Rafferty, and Joe have a great plan."

"It was Mom's idea."

"Yes," Connor says, smiling, "she's always been 'the brains' of the outfit."

When the two men arrive at the cottage, Mick knocks on the door. They wait a minute before Mick knocks again, louder this time. He calls out, "Hello, Pam!"

Connor looks at Mick with a furrowed brow. "It's strange that she's not answering."

"Let's head around to the back," Mick says.

When they reach the bedroom window, they see the holes in the screen.

They cup their hands and peer in.

"Good Lord," Connor says.

"I see two entry wounds," Mick says. "One at the back of her head, the other at the nape of her neck." As an ex-cop with many years on the force, he's no stranger to violence, but the gruesome scene still makes his stomach clench. Mick pats the front of his legs. "I don't have my cell. Do you have yours?"

"No, I didn't think I'd need it for tai chi."

"We'll use the phone in Pam's cottage," Mick says over his shoulder as he runs to the door.

Mick calls Libby and gives her the bare-bones details. "Pam's been killed. She was shot twice." He continues before she can ask an avalanche of questions. "Libby, we don't know any more than that at the moment. Dad and I don't have our cell phones with us. Please call Joe Bingham and ask him to call Rafferty. Tell him that one of the writers in residence was shot and killed in her bed sometime in the evening or early morning. Let him know that Dad and I will wait for them at Dickens cottage."

After the call, the men enter the bedroom. They're careful not to disturb anything. Eyes closed, Pam's head rests on a blood-soaked pillow.

The sun, now risen, pours through the window and over the scene in a clear, clean radiance, highlighting the grizzly wounds.

"She didn't even know it happened," Connor says. "This hit went down like an assassination—like it was business."

Mick cocks an eyebrow. "I wonder if it was 'family' business?"

CHAPTER 33

*"A good plot draws its energy from a reader's curiosity.
As you write your story, keep asking yourself, 'And
then what happens?'"*

—JANET EVANOVICH

In an unmarked car, Joe rounds a bend on the outskirts of the historic Fairhaven district of Bellingham and stops at a massive wrought-iron entry gate. The overhead sign silhouetted against the morning sky beckons, WELCOME TO PINES & QUILL. Aware that a sensor has alerted the main house that a vehicle is here, he uses the intercom system to let Libby know it's him.

When Libby buzzes Joe through, she whispers, "Mick and Connor are at Dickens cottage. Go straight there."

"Why are you whispering?" Joe asks.

"Because the writers are sitting just through the doorway at the dining room table, having breakfast. They aren't aware yet of what's happened to Pam. She wasn't at tai chi this morning. And now she's not at breakfast. Soon, they're going to start wondering what's going on."

"Okay, Libby. I understand. I'll do my best to fly under their radar. But you know that once I assess the scene, I've got to call in a CSI unit. And while I may go unnoticed, their arrival's going to be obvious."

"This is just awful, Joe. I can't believe that Pam's dead, murdered. Who on earth would do such a thing. And why?"

"I don't know, Libby," Joe says, "but we're going to find out. By the way, is Rafferty here yet?"

"Not yet. I'll buzz him through when he arrives and send him straight to Dickens cottage."

"Thanks, Libby. I appreciate it."

The lane to Pines & Quill is lined with tall, sentry-like trees. As Joe looks up through the windshield into their canopy, a part of him feels an oddly comforting connection to this place. *Even though I'm here to investigate a crime, I always feel good when I come here.*

Mick and Connor meet Joe on the front porch of Dickens cottage. "Thanks for coming so quickly," Mick says.

"What have we got?" Joe asks as the three men head toward the bedroom in the cottage.

"One of our writers in residence, Pam Williams, was shot twice," Mick says. "Once in the back of the head, the other in the back of the neck. It looks like her killer took the shots from outside that window," Mick says, pointing. "When Pam didn't answer the cottage door, we went around back and found two holes in the screen. We looked in and saw her lying there. The entry wounds are obvious."

From his peripheral vision, Mick thinks he sees movement on the bed. He looks closely at Pam. *Yes, she's dead.* He remembers speaking with a medical examiner when he was on the SFPD. She told Mick, "Since we living people are used to seeing motion in other living people—breathing, blinking, eye movement—you kinda start seeing movement in dead bodies, too."

Mick shakes himself from this mental reverie.

"What made you come to the cottage in the first place?" Joe asks.

"When Pam didn't show up for tai chi this morning, Libby got worried and asked us to check on her. Libby said that last night Pam confirmed she'd be at tai chi this morning."

Mick, Joe, and Connor turn their heads when Rafferty steps into the room. "Well, I'd say good morning," Rafferty says, "but it sure doesn't look like it for her." He nods his head toward the dead woman on the bed. "I got here as quick as I could," Rafferty says. "What have I missed?"

"Not much. Joe just got here, too." Mick brings Rafferty up to speed on what they've discussed so far.

All four men—Mick, Connor, Joe, and Rafferty—are well-schooled in crime scene etiquette. They don't touch anything and look carefully before taking steps.

"What did Pam do for a living?" Rafferty asks. "Anything that would piss someone off to this extent?"

"As a civil rights attorney," Mick says, "she might have made some enemies of the people her clients sued. Maybe one of them saw her as an obstacle—one that needed to be removed."

Joe flips a page in his notebook, then asks, "Where's she from?"

"Pam flew in from New Orleans. Libby has all of her information on file," Mick says. "Including her emergency contact information."

"I'm going to call in a CSI unit," Joe says. "While we wait, let's cordon off the area. I'll be right back. I've got tape in the trunk."

While they cordon off the area with yellow crime scene tape, Rafferty says, "The writers in residence are considered potential witnesses. Will Libby be okay with having her guests interviewed?"

"She'll be okay," Connor says. "Growing up with parents in the FBI, she knows what to expect. She might not be happy about it, but she knows that it has to be done. For that matter, the rest of us need to be questioned, too. Presumably, we were all on the property when this happened."

"Joe," Mick says, "if you two want, Dad and I will go to the main house and let everyone know that Pam has passed away. We won't give any specifics. I'll inform them that as a matter of routine, they'll be asked some questions."

"That would be very helpful," Joe says. "Thank you."

"Do you want them to stay there as a group," Mick asks, "or do you want to speak with them individually in their cottages?"

"It'll be easier if they all stay there," Joe says. "If it becomes necessary, I can speak with them individually in the Ink Well if that's okay."

"I'm sure it'll be fine if it comes to that," Mick says.

The delectable aroma of peach bourbon French toast and bacon greets Mick and Connor when they enter the large eat-in kitchen in the main house. Mick's stomach rumbles with hunger as he looks at the faces around the table.

Libby looks back at him questioningly, concern written on her face.

The others, Niall, Maeve, Emma, Tom, Linda, and Megan—almost finished with their meal—are unaware of what's happened.

Mick takes a seat in the empty chair next to Emma as Connor sits next to Maeve.

"Why such solemn faces?" Megan asks.

"I'm afraid we've got some bad news," Mick says. "Pam wasn't at tai chi this morning because she passed away."

Like a burst dam, a wave of words takes center stage at the enormous pine table. Everyone speaks at once. "I can't believe it!" "We just saw her last night!" "What happened?"

Mick sees Hemingway stand up on the other side of the half-opened Dutch door to observe the commotion. The look on his bearded face suggests he's not happy with what's happening at the table.

Mick scoots his chair back and walks toward his four-legged friend. On the way, he gets a biscuit from Hemingway's "cookie" jar. "There you go, big guy," Mick says, handing him the treat. "Everything's going to be okay." He scratches Hemingway behind a floppy ear before heading back to the table.

Retaking his seat, Mick holds up his hand to stop the unleashed flow of conversation.

"I'm not at liberty to share the little that I know," Mick says. "However, Homicide Detective Joe Bingham and FBI Special Agent Sean Rafferty will be here shortly and share what they can. They've asked that you please remain at the main house so they can speak with you."

Tom lets out a soft whistle. "A homicide detective and an FBI agent. That means that Pam was murdered, doesn't it?"

Mick feels a prickly tension in the air. "Again," he says, in a calm, even manner, "when Bingham and Rafferty get here, they'll share with you as much as they possibly can. In turn, they'll ask you a few questions either individually or collectively in the event you might have seen or heard something—even if you don't think it's of consequence—that might help them put the pieces of Pam's death together."

When the CSI unit arrives at Dickens cottage, one of the first things Detective Bingham says is, "After you're done with the body, and before you bag it, will you please expose the small of her back? We're looking for something specific."

"Because she's already on her side," one of the team says, "there's no reason we can't do it right now." Using forceps, the crime scene technician gently pulls the blanket and sheet down, then lifts the pajama shirt's hem, revealing a "Family First" tattoo.

Joe looks at Mick, Connor, and Rafferty to make sure they see it too. The men nod confirmation.

Joe turns to the photographer. "Will you please take a shot of the tattoo?" Then Joe hands him his card and asks him to send the photo to his cell phone number.

The photographer takes several digital shots and sends them to Joe.

"Thanks," Joe says. "I appreciate it."

Singling out the team leader, Joe says, "We're heading up to the main house now. We were careful not to disturb anything inside the cottage. And the only outside activity was just below the bedroom window," Joe says, pointing to the screen. "That's how the body was discovered. The two men who found her have law enforcement backgrounds and knew not to disturb anything."

On their walk to the main house, Joe says, "Rafferty, the 'Family First' tattoos are pivotal. First, there was the female corpse at the morgue. The ME said it was the *second* one she'd seen. Alex Berndt and his twin brother, Andrew, both had them. Salvatore Rizzo had one. The sniper on San Juan Island had one." Looking back over his shoulder, Joe adds. "And Pam has one. That makes seven 'Family First' tattoos."

"In addition to that tattoo," Rafferty says, "the other thing those seven people have in common is that they're all dead."

Shaking his head in disgust, Joe says, "The only other person we know of who has that tattoo is Toni Bianco, my cubicle mate at the station."

CHAPTER 34

"Reading fiction is important. It is a vital means of imagining a life other than our own, which in turn makes us more empathetic beings. Following complex storylines stretches our brains beyond the 140 characters of sound-bite thinking."

—Ann Patchett

Mick meets Joe and Rafferty at the front door of the main house. He glances up and sees the sun flirting with wispy clouds in the cerulean sky. He feels sick at this morning's gruesome discovery and that Pam's never going to see another beautiful June morning.

"It might help save time if you divide and conquer," he says. "One of you can take half of the group into the Ink Well, and the other half can stay at the kitchen table. Will that work?"

"Sounds good," Rafferty says.

"Yes, it *sounds* good. But what *smells* so good?" Joe asks.

"Niall made peach bourbon French toast and bacon for breakfast," Mick says. "Would you like me to ask him to save some?"

"Yes," they both say.

When the three men reach the dining room table, Mick makes the introductions. "This is Homicide Detective Joe Bingham. And this is FBI Special Agent Sean Rafferty."

Mick turns to the group at the table and says, "You already know my sister and brother-in-law, Libby and Niall MacCullough, my parents, Connor and Maeve McPherson, and my fiancée, Emma Benton. Let me introduce you to Megan Duprey. She's a chef who owns La Mandarine Bleue, a French restaurant in Boise. And this," he says, indicating the next person, "is Tom Gordon. He's a bass player in Resilient—a band of wounded warriors in Philadelphia who are healing through music." Gesturing to the next person, Mick continues, "And this is Linda Washington, a professional photographer from Chicago whose work is exhibited throughout the States."

Joe steps forward. "It's a pleasure to meet you. I believe you're aware that routine dictates we ask a few questions in the event you saw or heard anything, even if it seems unimportant, regarding Pam Williams. It might help us understand what happened to her. And to save time, I'd like to ask this half of the table," he points to the nearest side, "to come with me to the Ink Well. Agent Rafferty will talk with the rest of you right here."

Connor, Libby, Emma, Megan, and Tom follow Joe into the Ink Well.

Maeve, Niall, Mick, and Linda, stay at the table with Rafferty, who takes a seat.

As the other group heads into the Ink Well, Mick leans toward Niall. "Joe, Rafferty, Dad, and I haven't eaten yet, and the smell from your peach bourbon French toast and bacon is making my stomach growl. Do you think there might be enough leftovers for us to have afterward?"

Niall pats Mick's shoulder. "I can make that happen."

"I know I can always count on you," Mick says to his brother-in-law.

⸻

In answer to one of Rafferty's questions at the kitchen table, Linda shares that she noticed what seemed to be something strange going on between Pam and Officer Bianco on the few occasions Bianco had been to Pines & Quill while she's been a guest.

"What do you mean?" Rafferty asks. "Please be specific."

"I think 'sneaky' might be a better word than strange," Linda says.

"What makes you say that?" Rafferty asks.

"When they were introduced, it looked like they already knew each other but didn't want anyone to know."

"How do you mean?"

Linda turns her head and points to the cochlear implants above and behind each ear. "I just got these," she says. "I've read lips since I was a child. And some of their conversations indicated that they already knew each other before 'meeting' here." She pauses for a moment. "But if that's the case, *why* wouldn't they say so? *Why* would it be a secret?"

"Those are good questions," Rafferty says. He's glad for the information Linda offers. He remembers Tina Schwartz and knows how valuable this kind of knowledge can be. *Schwartz works as an expert forensic lip reader, assisting law enforcement in solving crimes. She's listed on the Expert Witness Register and won a prestigious award at the Expert Witness Awards.*

"And there's something else," Linda adds. "I also saw Officer Bianco tell Pam, 'Don't let that wheelchair fool you. You'd be surprised at just how capable Emma is.'"

Rafferty glances at Mick to gauge his reaction to this new information. *His eyes are blazing. And though I can't see*

Mick's hands, I suspect they're clenched beneath the table. I'd be angry, too, if someone was talking about a person I love behind their back. Especially if I thought they were going to try to use or hurt them.

Rafferty knows his own brow is deeply furrowed as he writes in his notepad. He remembers the death of his fifteen-year-old son, Drew. *That was an accident, and I'm angry. If I thought it had been intentional . . .*

Afraid of what he's capable of, Rafferty reins his emotions back in.

"Thank you, Niall," Mick says to his brother-in-law as he sets heaping breakfast platters on the table between him, Connor, Joe, and Rafferty. The table is flanked on one side by father and son, Connor on Mick's left, and on the other side by Joe Bingham with Sean Rafferty on his right.

"This looks delicious," Connor says, reaching for the crispy bacon slices mounded between him and Rafferty. "Thank you."

"Yes, thank you," both Rafferty and Joe say as they pile their plates with thick slices of peach bourbon French toast.

"I'll leave you to it then," Niall says, setting a pot of freshly brewed coffee on the table. "Libby asked for my help in the office." The rich aroma of coffee—lightly caramelized and almost nutty—fills the air.

"Before you head off, Niall, do you happen to know where Mom and Emma are?" Mick asks.

"Yes, they headed to the workshop. Maeve wants to see the commissioned piece that Emma's working on."

"That's great," Mick says. "Thanks again." He watches as the men dig into their food. *It seems that murder heightens the appetite—all except mine.*

Mick sips his coffee while doing mental triage on his

nerves. He feels the caffeine seep into his brain, ratcheting up his anxiety to the snapping point. *Is this the right time to tell these guys my news, or not?*

"What's the matter, son?" Connor asks Mick. "You look like something's wrong?"

Not just yet, Mick thinks. Instead, he tells his dad what Linda shared. "She lip-read Toni telling Pam, 'Don't let that wheelchair fool you. You'd be surprised at just how capable Emma is.'"

"Well, I'll be damned," Joe says, shaking his head. "I wonder if she's behind Pam's death?"

"Speaking of Pam's death," Mick says, "someone's got to call her emergency contact and deliver the news. Libby checked Pam's application. It lists her parents, Walter and Maxine Williams, as her emergency contact."

Mick, Rafferty, and Connor all look at Joe.

"Yep, it's on me," he says, reluctantly. "And they'll need to ID the body. Do you suppose they know about their daughter's tattoo and that she's somehow connected to the Gambino crime family?"

Joe takes a bite of French toast and washes it down with a swig of coffee. "It just doesn't make any sense. She's a civil rights attorney, for Christ's sake."

"I don't think most people would share that kind of information with their folks," Connor says. "Would you?" he asks Mick.

"No way," Mick says. "But there *is* something I'd like to share with the three of you."

Mick shoves a hand through his hair as he looks at each of their faces. *The opinion of these three men means the world to me.* His stomach roils. "I'm going back into law enforcement—" He holds up his hand at their pleased expressions. "But I'm doing it with a twist."

"What do you mean?" his dad asks.

"The three of us," Mick indicates himself, Joe, and Rafferty, "make a darned good team." He turns to Joe. "If I went back on the force, and it's a pretty big *if* that they'd even have me," he says, patting his leg, "it would be a long while before I made detective."

He looks at his dad and Rafferty. He's encouraged by the intrigue on their faces. "And if I went into the FBI, I'd have to go to Quantico for an extended period of time, and I'd have *zero* say in where they send me from there. That's why I've applied for my Washington State armed private investigator license."

Joe says, "That's gr—"

"Wait," Mick says, holding up his hand. "I've got to get this all out first, please." He takes a big gulp of his coffee, then continues. "We all know that PI's often assist in criminal investigations and can even be found working alongside law enforcement in certain instances.

"We also know that under the law, a police officer has restrictions on their actions that a PI may not be bound by. As a PI, there are fewer restrictions, protocol, and no red tape. I meet all of the requirements, and Emma's already onboard. The next step is to complete the exam."

Famished now, he reaches for a strip of bacon and smiles. "When I'm supposed to be working on my manuscript, I study instead. I should find out today or tomorrow when the exam is. It's soon, and I'm ready."

Connor stands next to Mick, pulling his son with him. He engulfs him in a bear hug, squeezing so tight Mick feels his father's warmth seep through his shirt. Mick's heart nearly bursts with joy as he returns the hug.

Joe and Rafferty come around the table. Mick smiles through their hearty back slapping, handshaking, and congratulations. *These two men are the closest I've come to having brothers since my best friend, Sam, died.*

Mick looks at each man in turn. "An FBI agent, a homicide detective, and me—a private investigator. We each have *different* levels of authority, access, and accountability. And we each bring different skill sets to the table. But the thing we have in *common* is the desire for justice.

"Crime is hitting way too close to home, and innocent people are dying," Mick says. "Paddy's dead. Sam's dead. There've been two attempts on Emma's life. And we've learned that Bellingham's got dirty cops—one's dead on San Juan Island, and there's at least one in the Bellingham precinct. And it all points to Georgio 'The Bull' Gambino's crime family.

"And that's something we can all work on together to bring to justice."

CHAPTER 35

*"When in doubt, make trouble for your character....
Protagonists need to screw up, act impulsively, have
enemies, get into trouble."*

—Janet Fitch

E mma's hands are clammy and her shoulders tight as she walks with Mick's mother, Maeve, from the main house to the Pines & Quill workshop. *Just because the pregnancy test was inconclusive doesn't mean that I'm not pregnant. What if I'm pregnant with Alex Berndt's baby from when he held me hostage in the cave? I wish I could remember more than just pieces of what happened.*

Emma's stomach twists with angst. *Did he rape me?*

———

Maeve's nostrils detect a beguiling rose-like scent when she and Emma enter the workshop. She's drawn to Mick's workbench where she admires her son's latest creation—a walking stick with a bald eagle grip intricately carved from rosewood.

Next, Maeve walks to the table adjacent to Mick's work-bench, where she sees a lovely pink-and-green tea set specially sized for small hands. On the walk over, Emma shared that Sally McGuinty, the owner of Hyde and Seek, a gift shop in downtown Bellingham, commissioned it for her seven-year-old granddaughter.

Maeve turns around to tell Emma how beautiful it is but remains quiet. The sun pours through the mullioned windows highlighting Emma's shoulder-length auburn hair as she sits at her potter's wheel, biting her lip and pinching the skin at her throat.

"What's the matter, dear?" Maeve asks, stepping forward.

"It's my memory," Emma manages to say before her face crumples, and she covers it with her hands. In the thick silence of the workshop, her tears pour unchecked.

Maeve places a hand on Emma's shoulder. "Maybe I can help, even if it's just to listen. Sometimes talking about what's wrong lifts the weight of it."

Emma removes her hands from her face. She looks at Mick's mother through a sheen of tears. "Maeve, you know how I've slowly been remembering pieces of what happened when Alex Berndt held me hostage in the cave?"

"Yes." Maeve nods encouragingly.

"I'm worried about what I *don't* remember."

"What do you mean?"

Emma places a hand on her belly. "Yesterday morning I took a pregnancy test and it came out inconclusive. It makes me wonder what else happened in that cave? If I'm pregnant, what if the baby is Alex Berndt's?"

Maeve kneels on the floor in front of Emma and takes her in her arms. "Oh, honey. Alex Berndt didn't rape you," she assures her.

Emma looks up. Her face fills with hope. "How can you know that?"

"When a victim's hospitalized after being assaulted," Maeve pats Emma's hand, "it's standard procedure for them to have a sexual assault forensic exam. Once permission's obtained, the doctors use what's commonly referred to as a 'rape kit.' The sooner the exam's done, the more evidence can be collected."

"I was unconscious when I was admitted to the hospital. That's probably why I don't remember anything about the exam. I don't know if it was done before, during, or after the emergency surgery to remove the bullet from my lung. I'm sure they obtained my permission. I just don't *remember* it."

"Yes," Maeve nods. "The doctors would have had to receive your permission before performing that important procedure. It's vital because rape kit evidence can aid the prosecution of a suspected assailant. But it can also be used to exonerate the wrongly accused."

Maeve takes Emma's hands in hers. "The first thing Mick told us when you came out of surgery was that you'd pulled through, and your prognosis was good. The second thing he told us was that you hadn't been raped."

Maeve shakes her head. "What I don't understand is why your doctors didn't tell you this."

"I'm sure they did, Maeve. I just don't *remember* it. Dr. Timmerman said that my memory issues are from the physical and emotional trauma I suffered. But she assured me that part, if not all of it, would most likely come back with time."

Emma wraps her arms around Maeve. "Thank you for telling me. You have no idea how scared I was."

Both women start when they hear Mick. "Scared of what?" he asks, stepping into the workshop with Hemingway.

Maeve wipes the knees of her pants as she stands. Wanting to give the two of them privacy, she says, "Oh, hi honey. I'm going to go start packing. Your dad and I leave tomorrow morning, and neither of us is even close to being ready."

Maeve looks at Hemingway and taps her thigh. "Come on, big guy. I know where there's a treat with your name on it." Hemingway prances back and forth, his tail whips back and forth at the prospect of food.

Maeve ruffles the wiry hair on the tall dog's back as they walk through the workshop doorway and head up the path to the main house.

———

Mick pulls up a stool and sits next to Emma, taking her in his arms. "Why have you been crying?" he says into her thick hair.

When she doesn't answer, Mick eases back to look into her green eyes. "Are you scared that someone's going to try to kill you again?" He wipes a tear from her cheek.

"Not nearly so much as something else." Emma proceeds to tell him about the conversation that she and his mother just had.

"It never occurred to me that you didn't know," Mick says when Emma finishes.

"Well, now I do, and that's what matters. It's amazing how a person can go from worried sick to deliriously happy in a matter of minutes," she says, smiling.

"What's this?" Emma touches an envelope sticking out of Mick's shirt pocket. Raising her eyebrows, she offers a questioning gaze. "Did you walk out to the front gate to check the mail without me?"

"Yes," Mick pats his shirt pocket. "I'm sorry. Hemingway and I got it just a bit ago."

Emma tucks a loose strand of hair behind her ear. "I'm supposed to walk with you to the mailbox as part of my daily therapy."

"You were in here talking with my mom," Mick tucks a strand behind Emma's other ear. "I didn't want to interrupt your girl time, but I didn't want to wait, either." He pulls the envelope from his pocket and smiles. "I received the date for the private investigator exam. It's this coming Monday."

After opening the envelope, Mick pulls out the enclosure and unfolds it. "Almost half of the exam will cover how Washington State law applies to private investigators. The rest of it includes federal laws, court systems, legal procedures, and definitions. And a small portion will be on the use of resources and public information in databases and the internet."

Emma's voice matches his excitement. "How long will it take to get your results?"

"It says that I'll receive them within five business days after the exam."

Emma places a hand on each of Mick's shoulders and leans back a bit. "Do you feel ready?" She narrows her eyes.

"I'm ready," Mick scoots Emma from her stool onto his lap. He cups a hand behind her neck and weaves his fingers into her hair, then presses his lips against hers. "Let's go to the cabin, and I'll tell you what else I'm ready for."

He picks Emma up and carries her over the workshop threshold, shutting the door behind them with his boot.

Joe parks his car in short-term parking at the Bellingham International Airport. He looks up to admire the blue sky while listening to the voice on his cell phone. *The third week of June in Washington State rarely falls below sixty-one degrees or exceeds eighty-four degrees. Today's high is expected to reach a perfect seventy-five.* He takes a deep breath, savoring the moment, before entering the massive structure. His nostrils catch the smell of jet exhaust, fast food, and the heady mixture of perfumes and colognes that hang like an invisible cloud over the crowd of bustling people.

"Mr. and Mrs. Williams have a lot on their plate right now," Bellingham Police Chief Bruce Simms reminds Joe. "In addition to their daughter's death, their son, Kyle Williams, hasn't been seen or heard from since he left a business meeting at Microsoft in Seattle a week ago."

Ever vigilant, Joe mentally notes people's hair color, facial expressions, body language, tattoos, jewelry, clothing, footwear, and baggage details. "Talk about adding insult to injury," he says, shaking his head. "That's got to be rough."

He pauses, listening to the chief, then ends the call with, "I'll let you know how it goes after we leave the morgue."

Joe checks the arrivals board. He notes that the Williams' flight from New Orleans is about to land. Within minutes, a crowd of people with luggage draped over their bodies and pulling wheeled carry-ons flow like an incoming tide toward the baggage carousels.

Joe raises a nameboard with "Williams" printed clearly on it. Before long, a couple in their late fifties or early sixties approach him.

Joe lowers the board. "Maxine and Walter Williams?"

The neatly dressed gentleman steps forward, extending his hand. "Yes, I'm Walter Williams, and this," he says, turning toward his wife, "is Maxine."

"It's a pleasure to meet you," Joe says. "I'm sorry that it's under these circumstances."

Maxine pulls a tissue from her black leather purse and dabs under her eyes. "I still can't believe that our daughter's dead. *Murdered*. And that we're here to identify her body. I feel like I'm in a nightmare and will wake up any moment now."

"I wish that were the case," Joe says. "I'm truly sorry for your loss."

———

The scent of pine needles fills Mick's nostrils. It immediately conjures the feeling of "home." *Dorothy was right*, he thinks, *there's no place like it. It's comforting to know that a cozy bed, loving arms, and perhaps even a cookie or two are waiting for me at Pines & Quill. Even so, my gut's in a knot every time I walk to the mailbox to see if my Armed PI exam results have arrived. What if I fail? How will I ever be able to face Emma, my family, Joe, and Rafferty?*

"Whoever said 'time flies' clearly never waited for exam results," Mick says, squeezing Emma's hand as they walk down the tree-canopied lane on this gorgeous June day toward the mailbox at the front entrance gate. "The third week of every month—the last week for the writers in residence—usually goes by fast. But this week seems to be taking an eternity."

Mick's stomach lurches. "Emma, it's been five business days since I took the exam. They said that's how long it would take for me to receive the results." *Please, God, let me pass the test.* "It *has* to be here today."

Hemingway prances, trying to wedge himself between Mick and Emma. He wants to be the *center* of attention.

"Settle down, you big lug." Mick pats the top of Hemingway's head. "There's no sense in both of us being antsy."

Mick and Emma both look up as a helicopter chops across the blue sky.

"We're having a rash of gorgeous days," Emma says. "And I think the icing on the cake will be receiving your test results."

"I sure hope so." Mick playfully tugs one of Hemingway's ears. "I've always thought of myself as being patient, but I guess I'm not. I wonder why they still use snail mail to notify people of their private investigator exam results?"

"It would be easier to send an email," Emma says. "But it wouldn't be nearly as exciting." She scratches the area between Hemingway's shoulders. "Are you nervous about the results?"

"I don't know why, but yes. I studied hard, I did my best, and I felt confident afterward. Now, I'm second-guessing myself."

When they reach the massive entrance gate's stone column, Mick stares at the mail retrieval door like it's a shark with razor-sharp teeth.

Hemingway settles back onto his haunches and lifts his face.

Mick understands Hemingway's familiar loose tail wag, relaxed ears, and wide panting mouth. He pulls a treat from his back pocket and gives it to the now-ecstatic dog.

"Emma," Mick says, pointing to the mailbox, "this is a double-door, front and rear access mailbox. It's pretty cool how the delivery person can leave mail in the box from outside the gate, and we can get it from inside the gate."

Emma laughs. "Quit stalling, Mr. McPherson."

"It might not even be here today." Mick's heart is pounding. *I've been here at least twice a day for the past four days. That makes eight times. Ten if you count Saturday, which isn't even a business day. But I came—twice—anyway. And now I'm here again—the fifth business day.*

"That's possible," Emma agrees. "But you won't know until you look."

Mick exhales deeply, opens the mailbox door, and then pulls out a handful of mail. The envelope he's been waiting for is third from the top.

CHAPTER 36

"The first chapter sells the book. The last chapter sells the next book."

—MICKEY SPILLANE

Joe ushers Mr. and Mrs. Williams into the foyer of the Whatcom County Morgue. The expression on their faces is obvious—they're trapped in a nightmare.

Joe shows his creds at the front desk and signs in the three of them. "We'll make this as quick as we possibly can," he assures the grieving couple.

"That won't be necessary," Walter says. "We know we could have identified Pam through photographs, but we *want* to see our daughter in person."

"Yes, we want to say our goodbyes," Maxine says, tears brimming her eyes.

Their shoes echo on the industrial flooring as Joe leads the way. He pulls on his lower lip reflectively. *The last time I was here was when Niall and Libby came to identify Paddy. Their hearts were broken into pieces of unutterable grief. I wonder if the Williamses are going to be able to withstand this kind of trauma?*

After passing through two sets of heavy double doors, they turn left down a hallway and stop in front of another door; its brass plate indicates they've arrived at the autopsy suite.

Joe turns to the couple. "If you would wait here just a moment, I'll let them know that we're here."

When he enters, Joe's eyes sweep the room, taking in the sterility of it all. Dr. Jill Graham and her assistant, Dr. William Hargrove, are wearing blue scrubs, shoe covers, latex gloves, and transparent face shields over surgical masks. There's a half-covered male corpse on the table between them.

Joe clears his throat to gain their attention.

They turn in unison. Dr. Graham nods. "*Detective* Bingham. Congratulations on your promotion." Then turning to the clock, she continues. "You're right on time."

"Thank you," Joe says. "Maxine and Walter Williams are waiting outside the door."

"Give us just a moment," Dr. Graham turns and covers the body. Then she and Hargrove pull off their gloves, drop them into a biohazard container, and remove their masks. They don thigh-length white lab coats and button them to cover their blood-spattered scrubs.

"Thank you," Joe says, heading toward the door.

———

Mick fist-pumps the air then whoops as he lifts Emma off the ground and twirls her in a circle.

Hemingway barks at Mick's excitement.

Emma laughs with happiness.

Mick sets her down and pulls her close. His mouth finds hers, and they lose themselves in a lingering kiss until Hemingway nudges himself between them.

Emma pats Hemingway's head. "You want to help me give this to Mick?" she says, indicating her back pocket.

"Give me what?"

"Just a little something Hemingway and I got you." Emma pulls a small box from her pocket and hands it to him. "It's a small sampling from a much larger box."

Mick removes the lid to find business cards. *Sean McPherson—Private Investigator.* Beneath that is his phone number.

"Classic and masculine, like the man himself," Emma says.

Mick is speechless for a moment, then swallows a lump in his throat. "Thank you for believing in me, even when I didn't believe in myself."

"Sean McPherson, I'll always believe in you." She takes him in her arms and kisses him soundly before leaning back. "Mick, call your parents and share the good news. Then text Joe and Rafferty. You can tell Niall and Libby in person at the main house. Invite everyone to the cabin tonight for a celebration."

Mick pulls out his cell phone. He knows he's grinning like a kid, and he doesn't care.

Before Joe reaches the door to usher the Williamses in, his cell phone vibrates. He reads the text from Mick. *Passed PI exam. Celebration tonight. Details later.* Joe slips the cell phone back into his pocket and clears the smile from his face before opening the door.

Joe introduces Maxine and Walter Williams to the medical examiner, Dr. Jill Graham. He watches, impressed, as Jill conveys genuine sympathy. *She's extremely good at her job.*

Turning to the man beside her, Jill introduces her assistant, Dr. William Hargrove.

"I'm sorry to meet you under these circumstances," Dr. Graham says. "Detective Bingham said you were coming. I have the body ready for identification."

Joe steps behind the couple as Dr. Graham walks them to a waist-high table. On it, there's a white cloth covering; the outlines indicate there's a body underneath.

The room is silent except for the hum of the ventilation system.

Joe watches the ME's hands lightly grasp the top edge of the sheet. "In a moment, I'm going to expose the face," she tells them. Her voice is soft. "Please let me know when you're ready." Dr. Graham gives them time, honoring their evident emotional pain.

Joe sees Maxine slide her hand into her husband's and squeeze. "We're ready," she says.

Dr. Graham pulls back the covering to just below the clavicle bones.

"Oh, Lord Jesus," gasps Maxine before burying her face in her hands.

Mr. Williams shakes his head.

Joe's heart feels like a vice is crushing it. He can't begin to imagine the horror if anything ever happened to one of his daughters.

Seconds go by before Mrs. Williams removes her hands from her face. Tears glisten her cheeks. "That's not our daughter," Maxine says, her relief evident. "This person looks a lot like her, but that's not our Pam."

Joe's stunned at Maxine's words. The last thing he expected to hear was, "That's *not* our daughter." Joe looks at Walter.

"No, sir, that's not our daughter."

Dr. Graham steps closer. "Death and time have a way sometimes of changing a person's features. Are you *certain* that's not Pam Williams?"

"I'm absolutely certain," Mrs. Williams says. She points to the other end of the table at the body's covered feet. "Lift the sheet and look at the right foot."

Joe sees Dr. Graham pull back slightly. "Well . . ."

"When our daughter was a child," Mr. Williams says, "she was riding her bicycle barefoot, and the big toe on her right foot got caught in the spokes. The doctors couldn't save it. She only has four toes on her right foot."

Dr. Graham walks to the other end of the table and pulls back the sheet exposing the corpse's right foot.

Everyone steps closer to look.

"Five toes," Maxine says. "That's *not* our daughter."

Detective Bingham looks at the ME. "Then who the hell is this?"

"Thank you for your understanding this evening," Libby says to Tom, Linda, and Megan as she hands them each a festively wrapped portable dessert. "Once you get to your cottages, we hope you enjoy one of Niall's specialties—caramel-dipped popovers with chocolate mousse."

"This," Megan says, holding up the package, "on top of beet salad, tenderloin of beef, roasted sweet potato pavé, and pan-seared Brussels sprouts? *Il n'y a pas besoin de s'excuser*—there's no need to apologize. We're in heaven." She brings her thumb and forefinger together, kisses them, then separates them—a chef's kiss—a gesture made by cooks of European descent indicating perfection.

Libby turns when Niall joins her at the front door. Together they watch the writers in residence head through the twilight toward their cottages until they disappear from view.

"With us not gathering as a group for dessert in the Ink Well tonight," Niall says, "what do you think they'll do this evening?"

Libby turns her face up to her husband's. "I think that Tom will play his guitar and work on his manuscript a bit. I suspect Linda's going to look through the photographs she's taken while here and concentrate on those with Tom in them.

And I imagine that Megan will enjoy her dessert, all the while sharing today's events with Adrien's ashes."

"You think so?" Niall asks, his brows shooting upward.

"That's what my gut tells me," Libby says. "I'm just sorry that no one's heading to Dickens cottage tonight."

"Me, too," Niall says, squeezing Libby's shoulder.

"Even though Pam Williams turned out to be nothing like the person I spoke with on the phone when she booked her stay," Libby says, "I wouldn't have wished her any harm."

"Yes," Niall says. "I still can't wrap my head around it. But," he bends at the waist and flourishes his arm through the open doorway, "it's time to go celebrate some *good* news."

"Oh, wait," Libby says, looking over her shoulder. "Emma invited Hemingway, too."

When Libby opens the bottom half of the Dutch door, Hemingway bolts.

"Well, here's your hat, and what's your hurry?" Libby laughingly calls after his backside as they watch their four-legged companion run down the lane toward Mick's and Emma's cabin, stopping periodically to sniff the ground, a rock, a leaf, following a scent known only to dogs.

Tom Gordon eases himself into his wheelchair in Austen cottage, takes off his artificial limbs, and massages his stumps. *I came here to finish my manuscript,* War-Torn: A Casualty's Manifesto for Peace. *And while it's not complete, I made considerable headway.*

He scratches his chin. *Linda told me she lip-read a conversation between Libby and Emma and learned that Mick and Emma are getting married soon and plan to honeymoon in New Orleans. Apparently, it's one of the top ten honeymoon destinations in the United States. I wonder if they could use a stand-in handyman while they're gone? I'd like to stay a bit longer, maybe even finish my manuscript.*

Linda Washington studies her reflection in the mirror as she brushes her teeth in Brontë cottage's bathroom. *When I came to Pines & Quill, I wanted to write* Life after Deaf: Piercing the Sound of Silence with a Cochlear Implant. *But, I think I'll set that aside for the time being and work on a coffee table book of photos—one that includes pictures of Philadelphia. Oh, that's right.* She grins at herself. *That's where Tom lives. I guess I'll just have to drop by to say hello when I'm there.*

She touches the area behind and slightly above one of her ears. *In the three weeks that I've been here, I can feel that my hair's grown a bit. And while I don't regret for a moment my decision to have cochlear implants, I'm glad that I had years to learn to read lips. That skill continues to come in handy.*

Megan Duprey snuggles into her pajamas in Thoreau cottage. After placing the urn with her husband's ashes on the bed pillow next to hers, she gets a spoon from the kitchen and opens the festively wrapped box of caramel-dipped popovers with chocolate mousse.

"Adrien," she says around a mouthful of decadent flavor, "this writing retreat was worth every minute away from La Mandarine Bleue. The restaurant staff got a chance to prove themselves without me. I got protected time to work on *One Heaping Teaspoon: Simple, Fresh, and Tasty Meals for a Busy Lifestyle.* And I'm going home with several new recipes, compliments of Niall MacCullough."

"Thank you, everyone, for coming to celebrate with us," Mick says. Looking at the faces around the dining room table, he sees his sister and brother-in-law, Libby and Niall

MacCullough. Next to them are Detective Joe Bingham and his wife, Marci. Emma's to his immediate right, with Hemingway on his left between him and Special Agent Sean Rafferty. And two couples join them via online video—his parents Connor and Maeve, and Ian and Fiona, his nephew and his fiancée.

"Oh, man. That's so not fair," Connor says as he watches Emma set a huge tray of Asian pear prosciutto appetizers on the table. "I can practically smell it through my laptop screen."

"Aw geez, I wish we were there," Ian says.

"Do you want some cheese with your *whine*?" Joe teases before he leans forward and taps a spoon against his glass. "I'd like to propose a toast to private investigator—"

Rafferty interrupts him. "*Armed* private investigator."

"Oh, we mustn't forget that," Joe says, grinning. "To Mick, *armed* private investigator."

Glasses rise in celebration. "To Mick, *armed* private investigator."

"Thank you," Mick says, raising his glass toward his friends and family. "And I'm pleased to share that I've got my first clients."

Nodding toward Joe and Rafferty, he continues. "I'm assisting in the criminal investigation of two missing persons—the adult children of Maxine and Walter Williams, Pam and Kyle."

"Cheers!" Everyone raises a glass.

"June." Libby shakes her head. "What an incredible month it's been." She puts an arm around Niall's shoulders. "First, we had Paddy's funeral. Then a sniper tried to kill Emma. And Pam was murdered right here at Pines & Quill."

Joe nods in agreement. "Don't forget, Pam Williams wasn't Pam Williams after all. It was someone impersonating her, someone with a 'Family First' tattoo who's now dead. We need to find out who she is and who killed her. And Mick's got to find the real Pam Williams and her missing brother, Kyle. Where are they? What's happened to them?"

As conversation erupts around the table, Mick and Emma slip into the kitchen. After all, there are guests to feed and glasses to fill. Mick collects Emma into his arms and kisses her slowly. "I love you, Emma. Thank you for this evening." he says against her mouth.

"I love you, too. And you're welcome." She sighs contentedly.

Mick feels a nudge at the back of his waist. Turning, he discovers they've been trailed by an ever-hopeful Hemingway, whose eyes trim into smiles at the corners.

"And I love you, too, mister," Mick says, ruffling the top of Hemingway's massive head. "I don't know what I'd do without you, buddy."

"And let's not forget," Emma says, laughing, "he's a constant source of entertainment." She scratches underneath Hemingway's bearded chin. "Yep, life's better with a dog."

"You heard the lady, Hemingway. Now let's go take care of our guests."

When they enter the dining room, the drinks on Mick's tray are perfectly balanced despite his limp. As he starts to replace Joe's drink with a fresh one, Joe rescues his glass. "The first thing you must learn when working with us," he says, nodding toward Rafferty, "is *never* waste marinated ice cubes."

"Oh, brother." Mick shakes his head in amusement and slips Hemingway a treat as celebratory laughter fills the room.

Turn the page to read an excerpt from
Impervious: A Sean McPherson Novel, Book Three

PROLOGUE

"Murderers are not monsters, they're men. And that's the most frightening thing about them."
—ALICE SEBOLD, *The Lovely Bones*

Georgio "The Bull" Gambino sits in closed-eye contemplation, his thoughts a nonstop loop of his sinister achievements, his invincibility, his criminal genius. The only visible movement is in his hands. They rest on his stomach, where his thumbs circle the middle distance between his laced fingers.

Professor Moriarty and I are similar in that we're both Machiavellian criminal masterminds. His creator, Arthur Conan Doyle, once said of the professor, "He sits motionless, like a spider in the center of its web, but that web has a thousand radiations, and he knows well every quiver of each of them. He does little himself. He only plans."

Gambino reflects on their similarities.

Moriarty wields power over a London-based crime web. He controls and benefits from crimes committed by those in his hire.

I wield power over New Orleans, San Francisco, and my latest acquisition, Seattle-based crime webs. I control and benefit from crimes committed by those in my hire.

So gradual and widespread is my infiltration, it's far too late for anyone to stop me. I'm impervious to my enemy's efforts. Untouchable.

Like a self-satisfied spider, Gambino mentally circles the prey trapped in his sticky web. In his mind's eye, he injects his quarry with neurotoxic venom. *It will immobilize my victims and ensure cooperation; it will dissolve their backbones, making them spineless creatures. Making them mine.*

He stops circling his thumbs. Raising both hands before his slit eyes, he envisions them as pincers. He flexes them. *Where to inflict pain next?*

Gambino picks up his cell phone and makes a call. Low and menacing, he utters three words, "Make it happen," then disconnects and goes back to his ruminations.

A faint smile appears on his line-bracketed face. Experiential knowledge informs him that his bidding is as good as done.

Officer Toni Bianco pulls into a space in the employee parking lot at the Bellingham Police Station just as "The Bull" ends the call. She cuts the engine, collects her things, and exits the car. Intent on the task at hand, she barely notices the vapor trails crisscrossing the electric-blue June sky. *Just a little over a week until the Fourth of July. But there'll be plenty of fireworks before then.*

Fobbing the car locked over her shoulder, she scans the lot as she crosses it. The hydraulic whoosh of the building's door bids her entrance to an air-conditioned hallway, its icy draft a relief. Toni heads toward the "prairie dog farm"—the bullpen where uniforms sit back to back in low-walled cubicles.

"Hey, Bingham," she says as she sits in her chair.

Joe raises his mug of home-brewed coffee. "Hey, Bianco."

"I wish I'd had time to bring coffee from home. Now I've got to drink that sludge." Toni nods toward the coffee station down the hall.

Toni stows her things in the bottom desk drawer and taps her workstation out of sleep mode. After entering her username and password, she's greeted by the Bellingham Police logo—an indigo background featuring a snow-covered mountain with green trees in the foreground, the same logo that's emblazoned on every squad car in town.

Toni turns toward Joe. "I still can't understand why you didn't change desks when you were promoted to homicide detective."

"I told you," he says, swiveling his chair to face her, "one change is enough for now."

Turning back to her desk, Toni opens the center drawer and rummages her hand inside. "I'm heading to the supply closet. My Post-it Notes keep growing legs. Need anything?"

"No, I'm good." Joe sips his coffee. "But thanks."

On the way back from her errand, Toni stops to pour herself a cup of station house coffee—wretched, but welcome.

Walking down the hallway to her cubicle, she makes one more stop. To the casual observer, it looks like she's dropping a block of yellow Post-it Notes on Officer Accardi's desk.

Toni smiles at Emilio and nods as she sets them down.

"Hey, thanks, Toni," he says, fanning the little stack.

Emilio sees that they're blank—nothing is written on them. But the message is loud and clear. It's the pre-arranged signal that sets everything into motion.

It reminds Toni of playing the game Mouse Trap with her cousins when she was a kid. *Like the boot kicking the marble,* she thinks. She pushes off from Emilio's desk and heads to her own. *It was fun collecting and stealing cheese from the other players. But in this case, the end game's different. Gambino will have all the cheese, and the other players will all be dead.*

Toni sits down in her desk chair and catches her reflection on her computer screen. She looks immensely pleased with the destruction she just engineered.

I hope you enjoyed reading *Iconoclast* and the sneak peek of *Impervious*.

If you did, please consider leaving a review for *Iconoclast* on Amazon, Goodreads, or BookBub.

A review can be as short as one sentence. And your opinion goes a long way in helping others decide if a book is for them.

ACKNOWLEDGMENTS

First and foremost, thank you for choosing to read *Iconoclast*, book two in the Sean McPherson series. I hope you enjoyed it. If you did, please tell everyone!

To be the first to hear about *Impervious*, book three in the series, please subscribe to my quarterly newsletter at www.lauriebuchanan.com, where you're always welcome to stop by and say hello.

I'm fortunate to work with a fantastic publishing team at SparkPress. Thank you to Brooke Warner and Lauren Wise. I'm proud to be listed among your authors. And thank you to the design team—a special shout out to Mimi Bark—for the beautiful, eerie, and atmospheric cover.

Thank you to Vickie Gooch, detective in the Major Crimes Unit of the Idaho State Police, Rylene Nowlin, DNA specialist at the Idaho State Police Crime Lab, Dr. Glen Groben, forensic pathologist, and Danny R. Smith, private investigator and author of the Dickie Floyd Detective novels. Your insight is invaluable. Any inaccuracies in law enforcement or medical processes and procedures are my own.

Thank you to Christine DeSmet for your professionalism, kindness, and humor. I'm eternally grateful that you always have my back when shaping a story into a relentless suspense piece that keeps urging the reader forward.

Thank you to Candace Johnson; I can't overstate how grateful I am to have you in my corner. Your sharp eyes and fierce determination made everything better.

Thank you to my sister, Julie, for being a patient sounding board, a kind reader, and a constant source of encouragement.

Thank you to my husband, Len, the chef and sommelier in our family. If you enjoy reading about the food and wine pairings in the Sean McPherson novels, he's the one to thank.

Last but not least, a heartfelt thank you to Willa, who was our four-legged friend and constant companion for almost fourteen years. You will always be the real-life inspiration for Hemingway.

"Until one has loved an animal, a part of one's soul remains unawakened."

—ANATOLE FRANCE

ABOUT THE AUTHOR

photo © Len Buchanan

A cross between Dr. Doolittle, Nanny McPhee, and a type-A Buddhist, Laurie Buchanan is an active listener, observer of details, payer of attention, reader and writer of books, kindness enthusiast, and red licorice aficionado.

Her books have won multiple awards, including the Foreword INDIES Book of the Year Gold Winner, the International Book Award Gold Winner, the National Indie Excellence Awards Winner, the Crime Fiction/Suspense Eric Hoffer Awards Finalist, and the PenCraft Award for literary excellence.

She and her husband live in the Pacific Northwest, where she enjoys long walks, bicycling, camping, and photography—because sometimes the best word choice is a picture.

To learn more, please visit Laurie's website at
www.lauriebuchanan.com.

SELECTED TITLES FROM SPARKPRESS

SparkPress is an independent boutique publisher delivering high-quality, entertaining, and engaging content that enhances readers' lives, with a special focus on female-driven work. www.gosparkpress.com

Indelible: A Sean McPherson Novel, Book 1, Laurie Buchanan, $16.95, 9781684630714. Murder at a writing retreat in the Pacific Northwest, but this one isn't imaginary. Authors only kill with words. Or do they?

Final Table: A Novel, Dan Schorr, $16.95, 9781684631070. Written by a former New York City sex crimes prosecutor and current sexual misconduct investigator, this suspenseful political thriller brings readers along for a deep dive into a sexual assault survivor's fight to come out on top—as well as the worlds of high-stakes poker and international politics.

Absolution: A Novel, Regina Buttner, $16.95, 978-1-68463-061-5. A guilt-ridden young wife and mother struggles to keep a long-ago sexual assault and pregnancy a secret from her ambitious husband whose career aspirations depend upon her silence and unswerving loyalty to him.

Watermark: The Broken Bell Series, $16.95, 978-1-68463-036-3. When Angel Ferente—a teen with a dysfunctional home life who has been struggling to care for her sisters even as she pursues her goal of attending college on a swimming scholarship—doesn't come home after a party on New Year's Eve, her teammates, her coach's church, and her family search the city for her. The result changes their lives forever.

So Close: A Novel, Emma McLaughlin and Nicola Kraus. $17, 978-1-940716-76-3. A story about a girl from the trailer parks of Florida and the two powerful men who shape her life—one of whom will raise her up to places she never imagined, the other who will threaten to destroy her. Can a girl like her make it to the White House? When her loyalty is tested will she save the only family member she's ever known—even if it means keeping a terrible secret from the American people?

ABOUT SPARKPRESS

SparkPress is an independent, hybrid imprint focused on merging the best of the traditional publishing model with new and innovative strategies. We deliver high-quality, entertaining, and engaging content that enhances readers' lives. We are proud to bring to market a list of *New York Times* best-selling, award-winning, and debut authors who represent a wide array of genres, as well as our established, industry-wide reputation for creative, results-driven success in working with authors. SparkPress, a BookSparks imprint, is a division of SparkPoint Studio LLC.

Learn more at GoSparkPress.com